CRISIS SHOT

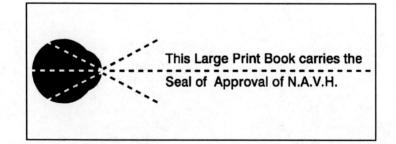

THE LINE OF DUTY, BOOK 1

CRISIS SHOT

JANICE CANTORE

THORNDIKE PRESS
A part of Gale, a Cengage Company

Farmington Hills, Mich • San Francisco • New York • Waterville, Maine
Meriden, Conn • Mason, Ohio • Chicago

Copyright © 2017 by Janice Cantore.
The Line of Duty #1.
Rogue's Hollow illustration courtesy of Katherine Dyson Lundgren. All rights reserved.
Unless otherwise indicated, all Scripture quotations are taken from *The Holy Bible*, English Standard Version® (ESV®), copyright © 2001 by Crossway, a publishing ministry of Good News Publishers. Used by permission. All rights reserved.
Scripture quotations marked TLB are taken from *The Living Bible*, copyright © 1971 by Tyndale House Foundation. Used by permission of Tyndale House Publishers, Inc., Carol Stream, Illinois 60188. All rights reserved.
Thorndike Press, a part of Gale, a Cengage Company.

Thorndike Press® Large Print Christian Mystery.
The text of this Large Print edition is unabridged.
Other aspects of the book may vary from the original edition.
Set in 16 pt. Plantin.

**LIBRARY OF CONGRESS CIP DATA ON FILE.
CATALOGUING IN PUBLICATION FOR THIS BOOK
IS AVAILABLE FROM THE LIBRARY OF CONGRESS**

ISBN-13: 978-1-4328-4454-7 (hardcover)
ISBN-10: 1-4328-4454-7 (hardcover)

Published in 2017 by arrangement with Tyndale House Publishers, Inc.

Printed in the United States of America
1 2 3 4 5 6 7 21 20 19 18 17

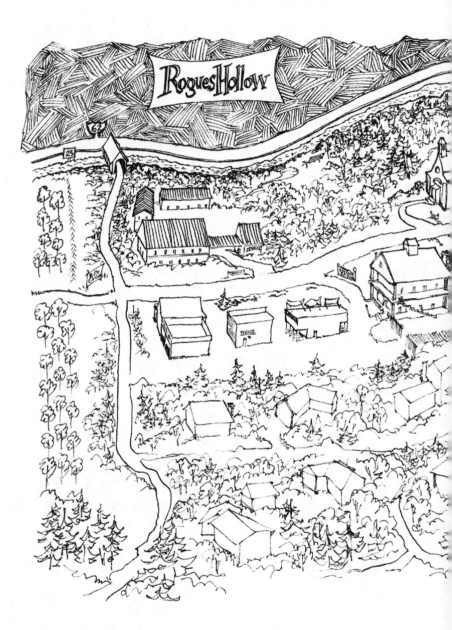

TO THE MEN AND WOMEN OF
LAW ENFORCEMENT,
KEEPING PEOPLE SAFE
REGARDLESS.

ACKNOWLEDGMENTS

So many people helped me with this book. As a newbie to Oregon, I talked to a lot of people: native Oregonians, newcomers to Oregon, and everything in between. I'd like to thank Idelle Collins, Donna Buck, Steve and Maura Lolandi, Matthew and Ila McAuliffe, Peggy Dover, John Brackett, Don Jacobson, Kristen Parr, Victor and Dianne Eccleston, Alana Fehrenbach, and so many more who have made Oregon, for me, a wonderful place to live and work.

FOR ALL GOD'S WORDS ARE RIGHT,
AND EVERYTHING HE DOES IS
WORTHY OF OUR TRUST.

PSALM 33:4 (TLB)

■ ■ ■ ■

PART ONE

■ ■ ■ ■

1

"999! 999 —" Click. The voice cut off.

Commander Tess O'Rourke was halfway to the station when the emergency call exploded from the radio. The frantic transmission punched like a physical blow. A triple 9 — officer needs help — was only used when an officer was in the direst emergency.

Adrenaline blasted all the cobwebs from Tess's brain. Dispatch identified the unit as 2-Adam-9, JT Barnes, but had no luck getting the officer back on the air.

She was early, hadn't been able to sleep. Seven months since Paul left and she still wasn't used to sleeping alone. After a fitful four-hour nap on the recliner in the living room, she'd given up, showered, and decided to head into work early in predawn darkness, at the same time all hell broke loose.

17

Tess tried to get on the radio to advise that she was practically on top of the call and would assist, but the click and static of too many units vying for airtime kept her from it. Pressing the accelerator, Tess steered toward Barnes's last known location.

A flashing police light bar illuminating the darkness just off Stearns caught her eye. She turned toward the lights onto a side street, and a jolt of fear bit hard at the sight of a black-and-white stopped in the middle of the street, driver's door open and no officer beside it. It was an area near the college, dense with apartment buildings and condos, cars lining both sides of the street.

She screeched to a stop and jammed her car into park as the dispatcher wrestled to get order back on the air.

Tess keyed her mike. Voice tight, eyes scanning. "Edward-7 is on scene, will advise" was her terse remark to the dispatcher.

She drew her service weapon and bolted from her unmarked car, cold air causing an involuntary inhale. Tess was dressed in a long-sleeved uniform but was acutely aware that she was minus a vest and a handheld radio. As commander of the East Patrol Division in Long Beach, her duties were administrative. Though in uniform, she wore only a belt holster, not a regular patrol Sam Browne. It had been six years since she worked a patrol beat as a sergeant in full uniform.

But one of her officers, a good one, was in trouble, and Tess was not wired to do nothing.

"JT?" she called out, breath hanging in the frigid air as her gaze swept first the area illuminated by yellow streetlights and then the empty car.

The only sounds she heard were the gentle rumble of the patrol car engine and the mechanical clicking of the light bar as it cycled through its flashes.

A spot of white in front of the car caught her eye and she jogged toward it. Illuminated by headlights were field interview cards scattered in front of the patrol unit as if JT had been interviewing someone and was interrupted, dropping the index cards.

Someone took off running.

She followed the line of cards between two parked cars and up on the sidewalk, where the trail ended, and then heard faint voices echoing from the alley behind an apartment building. Sprinting toward the noise across grass wet with dew, she rounded a darkened corner and saw three figures in a semicircle, a fourth kneeling on the ground next to a prone figure.

"Go on, cap him, dawg! Get the gat and cap him!"

Anger, fear, revulsion all swept through her like a gust of a hot Santa Ana wind. Tess instantly assessed what was happening: the black boots and dark wool uniform pants told her Barnes was on the ground.

"*Police!* Get away from him!" She rushed headlong toward the group, gun raised.

In a flood of cursing, the three standing figures bolted and ran, footfalls echoing in the alley. The fourth, a hoodie partially obscuring his face, looked her way but didn't stop what he was doing.

He was trying to wrench the gun from Barnes's holster.

Was Barnes dead? The question burned through Tess, hot and frightening.

"Move away! Move away now!" Tess advanced and was ignored.

Sirens sounded loud and Tess knew help was close. But the next instant changed everything. The figure gave up on the gun and threw himself across the prone officer, grabbing for something else. He turned toward Tess and pointed.

She fired.

2

"Ow," Tilly murmured through chapped lips as her knee scraped cold asphalt. Then the shivers started. She tried adjusting what she'd wrapped herself with, but that much movement brought the pounding in her head.

"Ugh." She kept her eyes closed and stuck her tongue out a few times, mouth feeling stuffed with dirty cotton. Now her head throbbed like it always did when sleep faded away and the day began. And she itched. An internal itching that demanded a chemical fix. She had a little weed left, but that wouldn't scratch the itch. She needed something stronger to face the day.

Her eyebrows scrunched together tight as an internal conversation began about where she would go, who she could count on to help her. The list of people willing to help grew shorter every day.

The voices made her focus, made her realize it must be later than she thought and she should have already been gone. Shifting position as cautiously as she could, she opened her eyes, squinting as bright vehicle lights hit like pinpricks.

Three men. Two were tall; for the third, she could only see a shadow of a short, thick body.

Could they see her? Fear slapped and then dissipated. She was safe; it was still somewhat dark, and the men talking were illuminated only by the taillights of two vehicles. They weren't just talking; they were arguing.

"... *you're all in whether you want to be or not,*" said the short man.

"*Hang on a second. This was supposed to be voluntary, free to stop at any time.*" There was something in this man's voice she recognized.

"*It's too profitable now. You can't quit. You want us to keep your secret, you keep ours and help us when we need it.*"

The two tall men had their backs to her; the shorter man stayed in the shadows. They were so focused on each other that she relaxed a tad. She was tucked in a corner behind a Dumpster, the smell of putrid decay and rotting garbage so familiar to Tilly that she was nearly oblivious to it.

Decay, dirt, and disgusting things cloaked her, kept her hidden. Invisible was good as far as Tilly was concerned. People often passed her on the street without looking her direction, without seeing her. Most of the time she liked it that way, unless she was looking for handouts. Now, something inside warned her that it was imperative these men didn't see her. The argument, the setting — they wanted to stay as concealed as she did. She would give them no reason to look behind the Dumpster.

The tall man who'd protested about things being voluntary tried to walk away, and the other tall man grabbed his arm, spun him around, and slammed him against the back of a truck. She jumped at the solid thud of the man against the vehicle, then held her breath, but no one paid her any attention. She focused on the truck for a moment. It was a business-type truck; she could see part of a logo.

The men raised their voices.

Was there going to be a fight?

"All right, all right," the man whose voice she recognized said tersely as he shoved the other man away. *"You win. Just give me what I need and I'll cooperate."*

"Keep your voices down," the short man hissed. *"There'll be no more talk of leaving.*

We need each other."

She struggled to place the tall man's voice but his name eluded her. The truck was also familiar; it belonged to him. The other two guys were speaking in harsh whispers now; she couldn't make out what was being said.

She'd been born and raised here, and even though people often thought she was stupid or crazy, there were few locals she didn't know. And she understood a lot more than she let on. She'd learned an important life lesson a long time ago: Play crazy and people will leave you alone.

"Just so we're clear." The third man stepped from the shadows and handed something to the man she'd recognized.

Tilly focused on the item. The writing on the box was familiar. She blinked hard and squinted in the low light. She recognized the design.

Drugs. The good stuff — pharmaceutical-grade drugs, the kind doctors had long since stopped giving Tilly prescriptions for. That was way more than a box of samples. Desire flared and she leaned forward as far as she dared, transfixed now by the conversation.

The man accepting the box was certainly not a doctor. She bit back a snort of derision as he put the boxes in his truck and his name popped into her head. He was a hypocrite! He was the one most likely to spit in her direction and call her a filthy drug addict. She guessed the others were no different. Upstanding citizens.

Thankful that her thoughts were generally clearer in the morning than they were at any other time of day, and that she hadn't burst out a snort that gave her away, Tilly continued to watch. She saw cash changing hands — lots of it — and lots of boxes of drugs.

The short man spoke, but she caught only a few words — *middle school,* she thought.

Tilly blinked. It was getting harder to focus as the itch grew more insistent. Part of her yearned to get her hands on the product they were obviously preparing to distribute. She was already starting to shake with the need for a dose. But inside her foggy, drug-dulled mind, she believed the men were talking about a new market for drugs. About high schools and middle schools.

"Hook 'em early, we'll always have a business."

Something sparked inside Tilly. She looked around as if seeing the dirt she lived in for the first time. She hadn't always lived this way.

Kids. Memories folded into her foggy

brain. She was clean, smelling of lilacs, and with her nieces. They called her Aunt Tilly, Silly Tilly, and together they laughed until their sides hurt. She lifted one grimy hand and studied it. She could almost feel that small little hand in hers. True, she rarely saw them and wasn't sure about how many she had now, but did she want her nieces and nephews to end up behind Dumpsters?

Tears fell and Tilly rubbed her face with the grimy hand.

The men continued to discuss their business and the amount of money they made off of stupid people. Tilly knew she fit into that category. She'd stepped off a cliff into drug use and could not see a way to ever climb out of the valley she was in. She wasn't certain if the men were still talking about kids. Tilly recognized that she was hearing bits and pieces of a complicated strategy, but already the fog was building in her mind and she was having difficulty processing everything the men were saying.

Long after they'd gone, Tilly stayed quiet, trying to remember what she could of all she'd seen and heard. Though most of her ached for a dose of something that would drown out the world and its pain, make her forget the men, part of her rebelled. She had to tell someone; she had to expose them, stop the cycle, prevent someone else from ending up in her self-made Dumpster hellhole. But would anyone believe her?

After a couple of minutes, she realized there was someone who would believe her. Glen — she had to find Glen.

3

Chaos.

Tess had watched it on TV, had trained for it in simulations, but never had she seen it, on this scale anyway, up close and personal. She couldn't be involved, could only watch because she was on administrative leave, which was normal after an officer was involved in a shooting. Three days was the standard leave, unless extended by the department shrink. Only her leave had been extended indefinitely, not by the shrink but by the chief.

Not because the shooting looked bad to trained investigators. No, because it looked bad to a crazy blogger who hated police.

"Execution by Cop — Our Kids Aren't Safe in Their Own Backyards" was the headline Tess woke up to the day after the shooting. Cable networks had grabbed the line from the blog *Pig Watch,* making the blogger famous overnight. The man who ran and wrote the blog, Hector Connor-Ruiz, was a local irritant with an ax to grind with the PD. He often penned poison anti-police letters to the editor in addition to writing the blog. Tess knew his radar had zeroed in on her in the earliest moments after the shooting. Because he listened to a scanner all the time, he'd arrived at the shooting scene before homicide investigators and the DA shooting team.

"Climbing the rank ladder wasn't enough for you, huh, Commander?" he'd taunted from outside the yellow police tape. "You had to get down and dirty with blood on your hands."

He'd agitated a crowd of onlookers, and before long rocks and bottles started to fly. Luckily, both Barnes and the subject Tess shot were transported by paramedics so the investigative teams wrapped things up as quickly as a thorough investigation would allow.

But Connor-Ruiz wasn't finished.

With half-truths and outright lies, he lit the fuse that exploded the bomb of rioting. As the hours passed, rocks and bottles gave way to trashed patrol cars, angry mobs, fires, and looting. News crews from all over the world descended on Long Beach filming everything with a kind of ghoulish glee.

Tess's mother and brother, who'd both moved to Sacramento two years ago, begged her to come stay up there, away from the madness, but Tess couldn't leave. Her department, her friends and colleagues were going through fire and brimstone because of her; she couldn't run away now.

"It'll blow over." Terry Guff, a retired cop who'd worked with her father, sat across from Tess. His craggy, lined face with puffy bags under his eyes sometimes reminded her of a bloodhound, but his gaze was hard and appraising, more like a wolf's. "It calmed down after the Watts riots, and again after Rodney King."

Tess sat huddled across from him in the corner of the restaurant booth, baseball cap pulled down, signature red hair gathered into a ponytail and sticking out the back of the cap. She and Terry were in a diner in Huntington Beach, a place Tess felt she wouldn't be recognized.

It had been five days and things seemed to be getting worse, she thought as she held her coffee mug in two hands and fought the frustrated tears that threatened.

The chaos had almost made it to her front door. She'd been called a lot of names in her lifetime because of her red hair — Ginger, Fire, Red — but now, in print,

Connor-Ruiz was calling her "the Red Menace." This morning, spray-painted on the row of mailboxes outside her condo complex was the phrase *Fry the Red Menace.*

It was disconcerting to say the least that protesters had discovered where she lived. What saved her from completely freaking out was the fact that her condo community was gated. The malcontents could hang out in front, vandalize mailboxes, but couldn't come to her front door.

She swallowed and looked her friend in the eye. "Gruff," she said, calling him by an earned nickname, "it's different now. During Watts, even with King, the brass, the politicians — they all backed the badge. That's not true any longer. Now, if they think it's politically expedient, they throw us under the bus before all the facts are in. The mayor has done that with me."

The night before, the mayor of Long Beach had given a press conference to announce that he would convene a grand jury to look into the incident, effectively saying he considered the shooting a questionable decision by Tess that could lead to criminal charges against her. And this before the homicide investigators and the DA investigative team had finished their work, before all the evidence was in, before any police

31

board of inquiry had been convened. Tess felt hung out to dry.

The Long Beach PD officer-involved shooting policy was simple and clear: for the use of deadly force to be justified, the officer had to articulate all the facts surrounding the incident and state clearly that they feared for their life or the lives of others.

Tess feared for Officer Barnes when she first arrived on scene, and when the subject beside Barnes pointed something at her, she feared for her life, believing he had a gun.

Now, because of that fraction of a second — the blink of an eye, really — when she believed she had to fire in order to save her life and Barnes's life, she was being second-guessed in the public eye, at worst being called a cold-blooded killer, and at best incompetent.

It'll blow over?

Things hadn't gone sideways with the brass immediately. The subject she'd seen bent over Barnes was trying to take his gun, she was certain. What saved her life was the fact that Barnes was wearing a retention holster; the thug never could have pulled the service weapon out the way he was yanking. But he had pointed something at Tess, and she'd fired. Her focus was on *sav-*

ing her life and the life of a fellow officer. That was an in-policy shooting in anyone's universe.

But it turned out to be Barnes's Taser he'd pointed, something that further investigation showed was nonfunctioning, either because Barnes had dropped it or someone had knocked it from his hand or belt. And when the guy Tess shot died in the hospital and it was discovered he was only fourteen years old, her universe was shoved off its axis.

Added to the crushing realization that the subject she'd shot was only a boy, he was also a star football player for Poly High. Six-one, 180-pound Cullen Jamal Hoover already held a slot on the varsity squad. And it seemed to Tess that every time a picture of Hoover was flashed on the TV screen, he looked younger and more innocent. She figured soon she'd be seeing his baby picture.

Connor-Ruiz's first headline had made her sick to her stomach. And so did worry for Barnes. He was in a coma and couldn't tell investigators anything. He'd suffered a horrific head injury, most likely from a baseball bat found on scene.

The homicide investigators tasked with the case developed the theory, a guess really, that he'd stopped someone, maybe one of the subjects who'd fled when Tess arrived, maybe Cullen. JT had followed and found himself in the middle of an ambush. He'd gotten off the 999 call just before being hit with the bat.

"Tess, you did nothing wrong," Guff said, breaking her from her brooding. "You have to have faith in the system. The mayor is in full CYA mode. He did you a favor in a way. The grand jury will clear you, and then there will be no question that you did what you had to do."

Tess sipped her coffee and hoped Guff was right. But the sick knot in the pit of her stomach wouldn't unwind.

Two days later some good news came when JT Barnes finally woke up. Tess wanted to go to the hospital, but she knew her presence there would bring the chaos from the streets. And Barnes didn't need that.

"He doesn't remember anything." Jeannie Haligan, a dispatcher and Tess's best friend, wrapped her in a hug as soon as Tess opened the front door. "I talked to his wife for a long time. He remembers going to work that night, but that's it."

Tess released Jeannie and shut the door. They walked to the kitchen, where Tess had dinner ready.

"But he's okay? No permanent damage?" Tess handed her friend a glass of iced tea.

"So far, not that they can tell. He has a traumatic brain injury, but the swelling is down and he's talking and walking — only he can't remember anything from that night."

Tess said nothing, just set about putting dinner on the table. She'd baked a chicken with potatoes and made a salad. It struck her that she couldn't remember the last time she'd gone all out on a home-cooked meal. Maybe a long time ago for Paul? But with the promotion to commander, she rarely had time to do anything other than fast food or something thrown in the microwave.

"Smells great," Jeannie said.

"Thanks. Hope it tastes good."

As they sat down to eat, Jeannie talked about life in the communications center with all the madness going on in the city. Right now they were enjoying an uneasy truce. They'd only just backed down from twelve-hour shifts, and Jeannie hadn't had a day off since this started.

She filled in many of the blanks for Tess, things that wouldn't or couldn't be aired by networks or cable, because all Tess had seen of the action in Long Beach was on the television. Things had calmed down some in the week since the shooting, but often when officers made stops or contacts, they were surrounded by angry crowds or people with cameras.

"A lot of the people we go 10-15 with don't even live in Long Beach," Jeannie said, commenting about the hundreds of arrests that had been made. "The other night, of the sixteen arrests made, only one person was local."

"Where are they coming from?"

"All over." Jeannie shrugged. "But a lot from Los Angeles and the Antelope Valley."

Tess played with her food, unable to even taste the chicken, which Jeannie said was wonderful.

"Last night a graveyard guy went to make an arrest and got jumped by supposedly 'concerned neighbors.' " Jeannie rolled her eyes. "He's okay. When backup got there and they arrested the group, we learn they're from Nevada. Big neighborhood."

Tess put her fork down. "Ah, Jeannie, I hate this. All this violence because I *had* to shoot. What if someone else gets seriously hurt because I did what I was trained to?"

Jeannie reached out and put her hand over Tess's. "And you were trained well. You did nothing wrong. The guys can handle it.

36

They all know you did what you had to do for JT. This stuff, it will all blow over. These morons must have lives to get back to."

Tess sighed, drawing her foot up onto the chair and hugging her knee. "That's what Gruff said. But it just keeps going, and the grand jury hasn't even been completely seated yet. I don't see how anything can ever return to normal. And I can't believe that kid was only fourteen."

She swiped a tear away and shook her head. "Do you know, if we'd had a kid when Paul wanted to, I'd have a fourteen-year-old running around now."

"Stop it, Tess. You know he forced your hand. What was your dad's rule? Bad people and all?"

In spite of everything, remembering her police officer dad and his rules made Tess smile. She'd eventually made her own rules, and the one Jeannie referred to had made it onto her list.

"Rule #9: 'Bad people make bad decisions — never blame yourself for that.' "

"Right. That kid made a bad decision to smack JT in the head with a baseball bat and then to point the Taser at you. Don't blame yourself."

The bat recovered at the scene had Barnes's blood on it, and the only fingerprints belonged to Cullen. Yet headline after headline repeated the meme that he was unarmed. Connor-Ruiz even speculated that the teen was trying to perform CPR on the fallen officer. Protesters began marching with posters proclaiming, *CPR Will Get You Shot!*

"That's the hardest part in all of this. I keep wishing it could have gone another way." She toyed with her now-cold chicken. "I even asked Dr. Bell if I should reach out to the mom —"

Jeannie gave an exaggerated shake of the head. "That woman wants your badge and a big payout. What did Bell say?"

"He and the city attorney both thought that was a bad idea."

"Emotions are too high, and she's surrounded herself with people who want to turn this into a payday," the city attorney had said. *"After all city liability has been adjudicated, you can try if you still want to, but not now."*

"Tess, you made the only choice you could at the time. Stop second-guessing yourself."

Tess knew Jeannie was right. And bottom line, she'd make the choice again. She'd *believed* that lives were in danger and she had no other option.

But Tess's belief held no water with a

38

media culture that seemed intent on painting her as a heartless killer and Cullen as a spotless innocent victim. The truth was lost in hyperbole and mischaracterization. Tess had to cling to the truth or she'd lose herself in what-ifs. No one could know what was going on in Cullen's mind, but he made a bad decision and had forced Tess to make the hardest one she'd ever made in her life.

Now, the place she'd grown up in, the city she'd devoted her life to, was becoming foreign and angry. *What if it doesn't stop?*

4

MARCH

"Why didn't you wait for officers who were equipped with radios and ballistic vests before confronting the subject?"

"How can you be certain he was trying to remove Officer Barnes's gun?"

"Is it protocol to enter a possibly dangerous situation so ill equipped?"

"It was dark; you couldn't clearly see what he was pointing at you — why did you fire?"

"How do you know he wasn't trying to help Officer Barnes?"

With a few of the grand jury questions still torturing her thoughts, Tess felt like she'd followed a rabbit down its hole, falling into a nightmare wonderland. Instead of the Queen of Hearts calling for Alice's head, a cacophony of angry voices was calling for Tess's. It was only rule #9 that kept her from screaming on this, the ninth day of grand jury deliberations.

She knew the truth. The officers who arrived on scene immediately after the shooting knew the truth and so did the investigators handling the incident. She'd learned the hard way that in this nightmare, backward world, the truth didn't seem to matter. People made up their own truth.

Connor-Ruiz kept writing provocative headlines while JT worked his way through rehab, only to learn that he'd never be 100 percent again. Motor skills and some cognition had been affected by the injury. He certainly couldn't ever be a cop again. And the three people who ran away the night of the incident still hadn't been identified.

Yeah, Tess clung to rule #9 like it was a life preserver. Trouble was, quoting it wouldn't work on the grand jury or the multitudes of angry people who seemed convinced she was a cold-blooded baby killer.

After a couple weeks of quiet, when the grand jury finished its work and began deliberating, the protests started to ramp up again. Downtown hotels filled with journalists, TV people, and what Tess and a lot of her friends believed were paid protesters.

A group formed at the east substation where Tess worked, but when they learned she was still on leave, they gathered at the main station downtown. Nasty signs and graffiti continued to appear outside her gated community. At one point protesters formed a human chain and blocked the 710 freeway, a major trucking artery. They wanted Tess's head.

From an administrative perspective, over the months preceding the shooting, she'd watched a frightening anti-cop sentiment ripple across the country after a few high-profile incidents back East and in the South. She never thought such a poisonous flame would catch in Long Beach, but it had. It became a raging bonfire fanned by Connor-Ruiz with the news of the boy's age and the fact that he did not have a gun. There was no video of the incident, just Tess's account, and despite physical evidence supporting her version of the incident, the mayor and the DA wouldn't take a stand, leaving everything up to the grand jury. And now Tess's fate was in their hands.

Tess had lived and breathed police work her whole life. Her father and grandfather had been cops. In her baby pictures she was posed between her dad's badge and the LBPD shoulder patch. She'd worn the uniform with pride for seventeen years, had never fired her weapon outside of the range before that night, and truly loved her job. She knew it was often popular to vilify cops for simply doing their jobs, but the personal vitriol directed her way hit like a sucker punch with brass knuckles.

The door to the DA's office, where she waited to hear if the deliberations would end today with a recommendation, opened, and Tess turned, holding her breath.

"How are you holding up, Commander?" Detective Jack O'Reilly joined her and she exhaled temporary relief. She was here and not holed up at home because rumor was they were close. It was getting toward the end of the day's session; she should know soon if a decision had been reached or if this would go on another day.

"I'm feeling powerless, but I'm okay." *Powerless* didn't begin to describe the weak, helpless, impotent feeling inside, but it was the best Tess could do.

"They can't ignore the evidence no matter how loud those protesters scream."

"I hope you're right."

"I am." He held up his fist for a bump. "Us gingers and O's got to stick together."

The comment made Tess smile, and she bumped his fist, working hard to be as optimistic as he was. She'd worked with Jack years ago when they were both new on

43

the job. That had been their nickname, the ginger and O unit. O'Rourke and O'Reilly, both redheads. Now Jack and his partner Ben Carney were the team investigating the shooting for the department. And she knew even weeks later they were still working tirelessly to locate the three unknown subjects who'd been with Cullen Hoover that night and clarify every moment that led to the shooting.

"We're on tactical alert tonight?" Tess asked. The pattern with past shootings influenced the police response now. If Tess was exonerated, it was likely the crowds would shift from peaceful to violent and the department would not want to be caught flat-footed. And Connor-Ruiz never stopped the poisonous rhetoric on his blog and over social media in anticipation of a grand jury decision he didn't agree with. She knew the department wanted to be ready no matter what the decision was. Ever since the Rodney King riots in the nineties, the city had a firm, comprehensive emergency operations plan. Tess had helped fine-tune the plan and been to many simulations over the years. Now she was watching it in action.

"Yeah, all days off canceled; everyone's been issued riot gear. And the fire department is also at the ready. We'll keep everything contained."

"I just hope no one gets hurt," Tess said as she got up to refresh her coffee, even though she felt like she could float away in a river of caffeine. When the office door opened again, this time it was Deputy Chief Ronnie Riggs, her immediate supervisor and her father's old partner. He'd never swayed from supporting her. Tess knew that behind closed doors, when the brass was meeting, Riggs was her advocate, and that buoyed her.

He looked at Tess, his smooth coffee-brown features completely unreadable. "They've made a decision. It will be made public in about an hour. They recommend against filing charges, Tess. They view the shooting as in policy and unavoidable. No criminal charges."

Jack gave a whoop and grabbed Tess in a hug. But even though she should have been elated, she couldn't help but feel as if she were still swirling down the rabbit hole, straight to the waiting axman.

5

After the decision, the madness started again immediately and got even more violent. Three cops were injured the first night, seriously. Tess was summoned to the chief's office the second morning.

As she dressed, she watched a press conference on TV happening on the front steps of the PD. The deputy chief had been tasked to give the conference. He'd updated the news outlets on the number of arrests and the conditions of the injured officers. Now he was making a statement.

"You know as well as I do that police departments never close," Ronnie Riggs said. *"We operate 24-7 and contact people at their worst, in the most emotional of situations, in the midst of and immediately after violent crimes, after tragic accidents, in the middle of difficult problems, fights, to catch bad guys.*

"Any citizen contact has the potential to go bad. Sometimes police work is ugly, brutal,

but not illegal; the grand jury just affirmed that in this case. Sometimes things blur, life-and-death decisions have to be made in a split second. Commander O'Rourke did her job. No one is more upset that a young man lost his life than the commander herself. Let's acknowledge that the grand jury has done its job and not lose sight of the fact that in this country people, even cops, are innocent until proven guilty and Commander O'Rourke has been cleared of any wrongdoing."

At that point the conference descended into chaos as protesters began to shout the DC down. Tess turned the set off, grateful for his support but lamenting the fact that there was a segment of the population who became incensed every time force was used — any kind of force — and they resisted hearing the facts. That disturbed Tess. Unfortunately, please and thank you didn't always get the job done.

The chief was the first to suggest it. After going over a few things that pertained to the East Division, he was nearly blunt.

"Tess, maybe it's time for you to move on."

She could feel her face flush as heat coursed through her body. "Sir?"

"You've had a good career — seventeen years, right? We won't fight an early retirement at this point. You're young enough to do something else with your life."

He hadn't pressed the issue, but Tess knew that would probably come. Numb when she left his office, she almost didn't check her phone when it beeped with a text. It was Ronnie Riggs, asking her to stop by his office on her way out.

Feeling as though she were sleepwalking, nodding to people who greeted her with support, Tess made it to his office in a fog.

"Come in, Tess; have a seat."

Ronnie and Tess went back a long way for a lot of reasons. He was a big man; he'd played pro football for four years, a tight end for a team in New York. When he was cut from the team, he left the game completely, relocated to a state with a warmer climate. Now, years later, he still had the thick, solid build of a professional athlete. But for the gray hair at his temples, it looked as if he could suit up and play a game any minute. Today he looked more tired than Tess ever remembered seeing him.

"Hey, Ronnie, you look beat," she said as she took a seat. Tess respected and admired Deputy Chief Riggs, but they went too far back for rank to be any kind of separation.

"Speak for yourself. I see a little more gray in that red head than I used to. This controversy is wearing on everyone. What did the chief have to say?"

"That he's behind me —" she held up her thumb and forefinger, barely a space between them — "this much."

"I figured as much. City hall has been hounding him," he said. "You know me — I'm a straight shooter."

"My dad always said you were the straightest."

He nodded and brought his hand to his chin. "Yep, and I can't sugarcoat this. They want you gone. I'll fight for you as long as I can, as much for you as for your daddy's memory, but the mayor wants to be re-elected, and that truck is going to roll over me and straight into you. See if you can get a job somewhere else; you got my recommendation for sure."

Tess took a deep breath. She'd known this, felt it, but had not wanted to acknowledge it. Now it was out, and she couldn't ignore it.

"I don't want to leave Long Beach, Ronnie. I've been a part of this force since before I could walk. Why should I be forced to leave? My dad's name is engraved on the memorial plaque downstairs . . ." Voice breaking, Tess wiped away tears with both palms.

Ronnie sighed, got up, and moved from behind his desk, placing a large, warm hand on her shoulder. "I know. I know. But your dad would be the first to say it's a waste of time to fight a losing battle. And to him, all cops, all PDs, were related, brothers — you know that."

She folded her arms and nodded, remembering her dad saying, *"We all bleed blue, Tess."*

"It's the job, not the title or the town," Ronnie continued. "Cops everywhere do the same thing. They protect and serve. You want to stay in law enforcement, there's no shame in putting on a different uniform, polishing a different badge. That's what your dad would say."

"What if no one else will have me, Ronnie? What then?"

He puffed out his cheeks, blew out a breath. "You have to try. I don't want the hammer to fall on you, couldn't bear that. Send out your résumés. I'll write the best recommendation ever."

Despite an overwhelming show of support from people she passed as she made her way out of the station, Tess left feeling defeated and deflated. She stopped at the memorial plaque, but tears clouded her eyes and she couldn't read it. So many emotions bubbled up inside at the thought of leaving. She loved Long Beach: the city, the department, all of it. It was her home. The people she'd worked with for seventeen years, had known even before that, when her dad was alive; the people she'd trained, mentored; and the great people under her command at the East Division, not a slacker in the group.

How can I leave?

But driving out of the lot, seeing the posters — *Fry the Red Menace; No Justice, No Peace;* and *Justice for Cullen* — made Ronnie's words hit home hard.

Besides the protesters who wouldn't let go of their grievance, the grand jury's decision hadn't made Connor-Ruiz go away. The blogger continued to pound her and the department in his blogs verbally and physically by organizing protests at every city council meeting demanding Tess be fired. And with an election approaching, he'd even submitted paperwork to run for mayor.

She remembered when a young officer back east shot an unarmed man, an incident that sparked destructive riots. He was exonerated of any wrongdoing but turned in his badge anyway because of the fallout. She'd thought at the time he should have fought it. But could she?

The next day, two letters to the editor brought Ronnie's words back to her thoughts as if fired by a cannon. The letters exposed something that hurt way more than the thought of leaving the area. She had to call Jeannie and meet her for coffee. Terry Guff joined them.

"The long knives are out," Gruff said, face twisted with disgust as he slammed the paper down. "Like sharks, they smell blood in the water. Those zips never respected rule #2."

"But I thought these people were my friends." Tess held the paper in her hands and fought to keep the emotion from causing her to crumble because of the knives in her back. Two officers — one a lieutenant she'd worked around for years and the other a sergeant she'd trained — had penned letters to the editor. Terry knew rule #2 because it was another rule she'd borrowed from her father: *Never let a partner in blue down.* These guys had not only done that; they'd lynched her.

Tess was headstrong and cocky, difficult to work with and prone to taking unnecessary chances, they said, an unfortunate incident waiting to happen. They stopped just short of sounding like Connor-Ruiz and calling for her arrest. They did suggest it was time for her to leave police work.

"They want your job, Tess, and both of them are bottom-feeders. How long have they tried to promote higher and gotten bupkes? They see an opportunity for promotion if you're gone."

Tess bit back frustrated tears, the betrayal hitting her almost as hard as Paul's infidelity had. The fact that it was only two men and the clear majority of her coworkers had urged her to stay and fight didn't ease the sting. True, some people avoided her altogether, but she guessed they were simply afraid, realizing that what happened to her could have happened to any one of them.

"I agree with Gruff," Jeannie said. "I hate those guys. But maybe . . ."

"Maybe what?"

"Maybe you should retire already," Jeannie said. "I don't want you to go, but you're young; you don't need the aggravation of this job. You have a lot of talent; you could do anything you wanted to."

"I want to be a cop. It's all I've ever wanted to be. Am I supposed to let Connor-Ruiz chase me out of a job I love?"

The irony wasn't lost on Tess that she'd been the focal point of the incident that started Connor-Ruiz's career of hateful cop rants. She was a patrol lieutenant four years ago when a small private plane had crashed short of the airport on the 405 freeway, killing the pilot, injuring one person in a vehicle, and causing a major traffic issue. The freeway was CHP jurisdiction, but none had arrived, and Long Beach officers on the scene had their hands full with traffic, injuries, and a dead body in public view.

Connor-Ruiz had been stuck in the traffic backup. He left his car and approached the crash site claiming to be a reporter and snapping pictures. Officers requested credentials, which he couldn't produce. He was asked to leave because he was interfering with their job and he refused. When he was threatened with arrest for obstruction, he shoved an officer out of his way saying he had a right to take pictures. He was placed under arrest and he fought. In the scuffle his camera was broken, the memory chip destroyed.

Tess approved the arrest. Connor-Ruiz was eventually fined for battery and obstruction and released. He filed an IA complaint against the officers and a lawsuit against the city. Tess stood up for her officers at every stage of the investigation. Eventually the complaint was closed "unfounded" and the lawsuit was thrown out. The next day

Connor-Ruiz started his *Pig Watch* blog, convinced that the justice system was corrupt.

It stung that someone like the blogger, with an obvious personal grudge against the police for just doing their jobs, could cause the end of her career.

"Tessa," her mother had said, *"it's a thankless job you have. I told your father that many times, but he loved it and ignored me. You are your father's daughter."*

Tess sucked in a breath and swallowed the lump in her throat. It always came back to Pop. He'd been a cop, a good one. Tess had idolized Daniel O'Rourke and had wanted to follow in his footsteps for as long as she could remember. Guff knew that better than anyone.

She looked away from Jeannie. "Gruff," she said, "what should I do? What would my dad do?"

The creases in his face deepened. "Sorry; I can't speak for your dad other than to tell you that he was a fighter. Fought hard as anyone I ever knew. But, Tess, your dad and I operated in a different universe. There were no bloggers or morons with cameras on every corner. Got the job done without making headlines." He shrugged. "Maybe you do need to be looking elsewhere for work."

Later at home, trying for sleep that wouldn't come, Tess got up, made some hot chocolate, and sat at the table. She closed her eyes and thought of her dad. *What would you say, Pop? What would be your advice? Would you tell me to move on like Ronnie and Gruff?*

"Good cops don't do this job for thanks or money," he'd told her once. *"We do it because we make a difference. We're the thin line between order and chaos."*

"I'm a good cop!" Tess slammed her hand down on the table, spilling her cocoa. Standing to get a towel and swallowing more tears because Mom always said tears were useless things, she worked to get her mind around the fact that she'd worked hard her whole life to be the best she could be, and now it was all gone simply because she'd done as she was trained.

Green boots.

A memory of a story she'd read once crossed her mind as she wiped up spilled chocolate. It was a story about mountain climbers on Mount Everest. Because of the expense and danger in recovery, when people died trying to reach the summit of Everest, their bodies were most often left where they fell, and so it was with "Green Boots." Believed to be a climber from India, he succumbed to the elements in 1996 and died just off the trail in a small cave. His distinctive green boots, highly visible on his now-frozen corpse, became a landmark; climbers knew which direction to turn at the green boots. Some people passed by the corpse, barely looking and fearing the same fate, while others filmed the sad sight, determining not to succumb in the same way.

That's me now, Tess thought. *Frozen in place. Pitied by some, feared by others, and being passed by. And that's what I'll always be if I stay here.*

Suddenly it didn't seem so difficult to look online for job openings and start sending out résumés.

6

MAY

LAX was a zoo as usual, so Tess was glad to be in her seat, on the plane. In the month and a half since the jury's decision, she'd sent out twenty-five résumés all over the country, searching the web for any law enforcement jobs that were compatible with her experience. Among the many "thanks, no thanks" letters came one request for an interview. Since the last few weeks had been fraught with ups and downs, Tess was used to the roller coaster, so this interview situation was no different. On the upside, the job was for chief of police; on the downside, the department was tiny: eight sworn officers and three civilian personnel.

The plane ride would take a little over two hours and Tess would land in Medford, Oregon. From there she'd rent a car and drive forty minutes to a small town on the Rogue River. The Rogue's Hollow city council wanted to meet her in person.

That was a good sign, wasn't it?

Tess thought about every interview she'd ever had. They were all in-house; they all pertained to LBPD. Her first application interview, later an interview to advance to detectives, the interview for sergeant, one for lieutenant, and the last one for commander. She'd aced them all.

But she was more nervous about this one than any of those. She still didn't want to leave Long Beach, but the hints she should leave had not gone away. Rather they'd gotten stronger, more pointed. She'd tried to return to work at the East Division, but Connor-Ruiz and his minions had made it impossible. She was temporarily assigned to the downtown station, to fill in for a commander out for medical reasons, but the tension there was thicker than a hard copy of the California penal code.

She only hoped she'd find another job before the city decided to force her out. And the closer the election drew, the greater the likelihood that the ax would fall. Leaving a job voluntarily was a strain, but not a stain. As a commander, she didn't enjoy civil service protection.

Tess forced herself to relax as the plane took off and eventually headed north. She reviewed all that she believed the city council in Rogue's Hollow would be concerned about. She'd risen through the ranks to commander, run a division, and — she thought sourly — dreamed of being the chief someday, but the chief of *LBPD*. Her dad would have been so proud if that had been the case.

Swallowing the emotions that bubbled up as she thought of her dad, Tess accepted a cup of coffee from the flight attendant and nibbled at the complimentary pretzels, staring out the small window as the plane sped north.

Coffee and pretzels were long gone when Tess felt the plane shift and head downward as the Fasten Seat Belt sign clicked on. She'd never taken hers off. Now the view out the window began to change, and Tess's breath caught in her throat as they dropped below the clouds. Before her lay the Rogue Valley and it was postcard gorgeous. Snow-capped hills bordered a green — so green — valley, chopped up in what she guessed were large farms and, here and there, small clusters of homes and structures.

There was no sprawling metropolis here like you saw on approach to LA, miles even before you got close to the airport. She saw what she thought had to be Medford, with a ribbon of highway running through it that must be Interstate 5. Tess felt herself calm somewhat. If this was to be her exile, at least it was a beautiful place.

The airport was simple to navigate, small, compact, and Tess was in her rental car less than thirty-five minutes after she disembarked.

Checking her watch, she realized that if she drove straight to Rogue's Hollow, and it only took forty minutes, she'd be two hours early. Despite the enchantment she'd felt viewing the valley from the air, she didn't feel like sightseeing. It was cold even though the sun was out, only puffy clouds dotting the sky now — bone-chilling cold, a shock to her Southern California constitution. Firing up the heater, she decided she had time for an early lunch and a visit to the county sheriff's department.

Rogue's Hollow was in Jackson County. She'd done a little research, curious about the organizations she'd be working with and around. It had been astonishing to her how large an area so few officers were responsible to cover. But, she had to remind herself, the population they served was so much less than LA County.

A sheriff's deputy might be able to help give her perspective.

She found a restaurant off Interstate 5 called Elmer's and picked at a salad. While she ate, several friends texted her good luck wishes. Jeannie had been sad at the thought of Tess moving so far away, but she understood.

"I know being a cop is more than just a job for you," she'd said when she dropped Tess off at the airport. *"But I'll miss you so much, it's not funny."*

"You can always come visit."

Tess tried not to think about life without her close friends a short drive away. It was hard enough to visualize life without LBPD. She found the sheriff's department easily, off Highway 62, the same highway that would take her to Rogue's Hollow.

She parked and got out of her car about the same time a tall, good-looking blond deputy stepped out of the station.

Tess caught his eye and saw confusion, then recognition, then confusion again.

He stopped his progress to his car, hooked a thumb in his belt, and said, "Uh, hello, can I help you?"

Tess stepped up onto the sidewalk. She was barely five-six and generally had to look up to everyone; it was no different with this deputy. His name badge said *S. Logan.*

"Sure, Deputy Logan." She held her hand

out. "Tess O'Rourke."

He gripped her hand in a firm, warm handshake. "I thought I recognized you. Steve Logan."

"You recognized me?" Caught off guard a bit, Tess stiffened. But she'd been all over the news for weeks; didn't it make sense that anyone who wasn't living in a cave would recognize her?

"Yeah, we've been watching everything going on down south." He shook his head. "Sorry things got so sketchy for you there. You did a great job. Should be hailed as a hero, not as . . . well, what they're saying."

"Thank you." Tess felt her face redden. Sometimes it was harder to take a compliment than a criticism.

He seemed to sense her hesitation. "What brings you up to our neck of the woods?"

She explained about the interview.

"Oh, Rogue's Hollow. That's right; they're short a chief. They actually hired a guy from Grants Pass for the job last month, but he dropped dead before he could be sworn in."

"Oh" was all Tess could manage with this info and an awkward second passed before Logan cleared his throat and continued.

"I'm sure you'd make a great chief. It's a quaint place, has its own vibe. The sheriff isn't in, if you wanted to talk to him."

"No." Tess checked her watch. "I just had a few minutes to kill and was hoping to find out the pressing issues in this county from the street level, and a little bit about mutual aid."

He smiled. "I'd be happy to answer any questions. I don't make it up to the Hollow often, as much because it's quiet there as because I'm usually assigned to White City." He motioned to a bench. "I'd take you inside, but they're painting and the fumes will knock you out."

Tess had noticed the utility truck, the ladders, and the paint. "That's okay. I only have a few minutes." She shoved cold hands into her jacket pockets and sat next to Logan, glad the bench was in the sun, the familiar creaking of his leather comforting. He was one of those men who exuded testosterone, a masculine presence, something Tess was used to and knew had its positives and negatives. They were the hard chargers, but they could also be the hotheads.

What was Deputy Logan? she wondered as he filled her in on the basics of law enforcement in the Rogue Valley.

"Thank you, Commander O'Rourke, for flying up here for this interview." Mayor

Doug Dixon welcomed Tess, and he seemed warm and sincere, which helped beat out the last remaining butterflies.

This wasn't a grand jury; this was a small city council looking for a qualified and committed police chief. Tess was certain she fit the bill.

There were four city council members, and thankfully Tess didn't have to memorize their names; they all had nameplates on the dais in front of her: Casey Reno, Adeline Getz, Cole Markarov, Forest Wild, and the mayor in the center.

First came the easy part: they asked her for an opening statement and she told them the truth — she'd wanted to be a cop all her life and eventually the chief of a department. Law enforcement was an important part of any community because quality of life was important. If people didn't feel safe where they lived, there was no quality of life.

The question and answer was the hard part. Cole Markarov in particular was antagonistic. Casey Reno was less so, but Tess didn't think the woman was on her side. Forest Wild didn't ask any questions, but he listened, and Councilwoman Getz asked about her knowledge of budgets. But Markarov made the biggest impression.

"You were just on trial for a serious crime; is that why you want to leave Long Beach?"

"Technically I was never on trial. No charges were filed —"

"You sat before a grand jury, correct?"

"The grand jury makes a recommendation as to whether an indictment is warranted. They found no wrongdoing on my part, no reason for an indictment to be issued. Additionally, I was cleared by a district attorney's shooting team."

"But they investigated this horrible shooting? This boy, what was he? Fourteen?"

Mayor Dixon interrupted, "Cole, we agreed the topic of this interview is her ability to work here in Rogue's Hollow; we're not rehashing the past."

They went back and forth for a few minutes, and Tess knew that Markarov did not want to hire her. What about the rest?

As they finished, the last question asked came from Casey Reno. "Tell us honestly, why do you want to leave Long Beach?"

Tess took a deep breath. She could only give an honest answer to that question and hope that it flew.

"Mrs. Reno, in all honesty, the reason is the shooting. While I am certain I did nothing wrong, the controversy surrounding the incident makes it impossible for me to do

66

my job effectively."

"What makes you think it will be any different here?"

"I can only hope that people here will examine the facts and not be swayed by emotional rhetoric."

Tess was in her car, driving back to the airport a few minutes later. The negatives of the interview were tap-dancing in her brain and she felt crushed by a growing pessimism about her situation.

7

Pastor Oliver Macpherson sat back and listened to the debate bouncing around him. Rogue's Hollow urgently needed a new police chief. The city had hired one several weeks ago, but he died of a massive heart attack before being sworn in. In the scramble for a qualified replacement, the city council had narrowed down the list to one name — a controversial name — and so the debate raged. He'd sat in on the city council process many a time, but this was a first for him, the process to select a police chief. Oliver wanted to hear all sides, vowing to stay quiet unless asked and to help give the highlighted application impartial consideration.

The applicant had flown in for an interview. Oliver hadn't been asked to sit in on that, but he'd been told that she'd acquitted herself quite well. According to Addie Getz, the woman answered every question thrown at her solidly, even antagonistic questions, and gave good, logical, thought-out answers. According to Mayor Douglas Dixon, it was the interview that sold him.

"Professional, thoughtful, experienced — just what we need," he'd said to open this meeting. And the debate had started there, mostly between Dixon and Councilman Markarov.

Cole Markarov, local bed-and-breakfast owner, was one who'd asked hostile questions at the interview, and he was probably the most animated member of the council at this meeting. He didn't want to hire the woman, and that didn't surprise Oliver. The council's first choice had been Cole's friend and he'd pushed hard for his hire. Oliver didn't think any replacement would satisfy Cole and especially not a woman. Cole didn't think any woman was up for the position of police chief, an opinion he'd voiced often.

"A woman doesn't have the judgment to lead," he'd said.

"She killed a fourteen-year-old, for heaven's sake," he said now, throwing his hands up dramatically.

"A fourteen-year-old who looked thirty and was trying to take another officer's gun." Mayor Dixon continued to lobby for the applicant and stand up for her, which surprised Oliver a bit. Doug generally had an aversion to controversy, and controversy was written all over this woman. He wondered if there was an ulterior motive and then stopped himself. Doug needed to be given the benefit of the doubt. He'd said the woman would be an asset to the town; Oliver should take him at his word.

"So she says," Cole huffed. "There's no video of the incident; she could say anything."

"Doug," Casey Reno, owner of Rogue's Hollow Bookstore and Notions, spoke up.

Oliver leaned forward; he respected Casey as a thoughtful person and valued her opinion.

"I know this woman is qualified. She'd probably have no trouble running our small department. But as much as it pains me to admit it, I'll have to agree with Cole. She could have snowed us in the interview, told us what we want to hear. All the press she's gotten, none of it is good. According to the local paper in Long Beach, even before the shooting, she had a reputation for cockiness, for bending the rules."

Oliver didn't miss the look of triumph Cole shot the mayor. Raising an eyebrow, he sat back. It wasn't looking good. Rogue's

Hollow had simple — some said outdated — bylaws. Between the mayor and the four council members, the applicant needed a simple majority vote to be hired, but if two were solidly against, and so far only the mayor was solidly for, the math was tight. As Casey noted, she was more qualified than their first pick had been, overqualified, really. She'd run a police division in a large department, supervising around 150 officers plus another ten civilian employees. Here in Rogue's Hollow, she'd be supervising eight officers plus three civilians.

"If she really was a problem before the shooting, why wasn't she fired?" Dixon asked. "How could she rise to such a high rank?"

Oliver thought that was an interesting point. With all the bad press she'd gotten, if this woman were a proven problem employee, any city would have been justified in her firing. She hadn't been fired, but according to Addie, during the interview, when asked why she wanted to leave, she seemed honest in stating, *"The controversy surrounding the incident makes it impossible for me to do my job effectively."*

While Dixon pleaded his case to Casey, highlighting another truth that the woman never had an officially documented negative performance review, Oliver turned his attention to the last two council members: Addie Getz, co-owner of Rogue's Hollow Inn and Suites, and Forest Wild, owner of the gas station and auto repair shop that bore his name, Wild Automotive. They were studying her résumé and hadn't said much.

"Everyone deserves a second chance," Oliver's wife, Anna, had said that morning over breakfast. *"I have a feeling about the woman. I believe she'll be a good fit here."* Anna's prayer group had been praying for a new chief ever since the old one retired nearly a year ago.

"Perhaps," Oliver had said with a nod, happy Anna was engaged and smiling after the last round of chemo. *"But she might need some divine intervention. You'd have to have been in a coma to not hear or read about how bad this shooting looks."*

Anna reached across and patted his hand. *"Now, Ollie, we both know things can get distorted when politics are involved. She was never charged with a crime. My heart tells me she's okay. A little grace is called for now. Pray for the council, that they give her a fair chance. She deserves at least that."*

He smiled and put his hand over hers. *"I will. I do trust your feelings more than I would ever trust a news article."*

Oliver was not a member of the council. He attended meetings only to offer the opening prayer and guidance if requested. Because the council sought to be transparent, this was a public debate. The other non–council members in the room were some people with business interests in the area: the mayor's brother, Roger, the manager of the market in town, and his wife, Helen; Bart Dover, manager of a local organic farm; Beto Acosta, CEO of a large, valley-wide home security company called Platinum Security Systems, or PSS; Pete Horning, owner of the Hollow Grind, a local coffee shop; Gwen Owens, the city treasurer; Arthur Goding, a local gadfly who sat in on every meeting; and a group of people Oliver knew were interested in changing Rogue's Hollow's policy on cannabis sales. Oliver couldn't tell what their thoughts were. Arthur was playing on his phone, and the others were simply listening.

There was also an off-duty Jackson County sheriff's deputy in attendance, Steve Logan. He didn't live in Rogue's Hollow but in Shady Cove. Oliver had spoken to him earlier, and he'd said he was simply interested in seeing how the process worked.

Earlier, when the debate started, a couple

of Rogue's Hollow officers had been in the back of the room, listening. But they were forced to leave when Tilly Dover, a local homeless woman and Bart's sister — Oliver noted how Bart ignored her completely — had disrupted the meeting.

Tilly was a tortured soul Anna and Oliver had tried often to help. She'd been in and out of jail for the last few months, only recently returning to town. Instead of being happy about her release, she'd been uncharacteristically angry about something and profane, but Oliver couldn't understand what she was going on about. When she'd started throwing things, Cole jumped in before Mayor Dixon did and asked the officers to escort her out. Since they hadn't returned, Oliver guessed the poor girl had been arrested again. Tilly battled mental illness as well as drug addiction, and at times, like this morning, she seemed beyond help.

While Oliver considered everyone in attendance, he noted that so far, no one had inquired about their opinions concerning the applicant. What would Oliver say if they asked him?

Keeping Anna's remarks in his mind, he prayed quietly for guidance. Was this California cop worth a shot?

"It's time to put this to a vote," Dixon

said, crossing his arms. "We've been without a police chief for eight months; that's too long. This woman has miles more experience than the next applicant on the list. She can start right away."

"That's another thing." Cole ground his teeth, faced scrunched in disbelief. "What makes you think that if she does come, she'll even stay? She'll be bored out of her mind in two weeks."

"We know where you stand, Cole." Dixon shot him a look of pure impatience. "That's one nay." With an exaggerated turn of the head, he looked at Casey. "Casey?"

She rubbed her forehead and Oliver saw the struggle in her face.

"I can't get past 'fourteen-year-old boy.' My daughter is fourteen, for heaven's sake. Afraid I'm a nay as well."

Dixon looked disappointed but he moved on. "Forest?"

Forest tugged on his beard, the perpetual twinkle in his eye making Oliver smile. He'd never known Forest to be down or unhappy about anything.

"I say give her a chance. Aye."

Cole grunted.

"Addie? You're the tiebreaker."

"That I am." She drew in a deep breath and looked at Oliver. "Pastor Mac, do you have a feeling one way or another?"

"He's not a voting member," Cole groused.

"I just want to know what he thinks. You've had your say, Cole."

Oliver stifled a smile; sometimes Cole was more transparent than a four-year-old. "I'm inclined to offer a little grace here," he said, injecting Anna's sentiment. "I think she deserves a shot."

Addie considered him for a moment. They went way back. She'd been on the church committee that hired Oliver eighteen years ago. Her nephew was the newest hire on the Rogue's Hollow police force. But she had a mind of her own, and he knew she'd only agree with him if she were partway there already.

Addie nodded. "Okay. Well, I liked her at the interview. Struck me as sharp as a tack. I'm an aye."

Dixon beamed. "The ayes have it. We have a new police chief."

Oliver noted that the decision made Beto Acosta happy. His business was home security. He'd been tight with the last chief and was pro law enforcement.

The cannabis people huddled for a discussion. Oliver wondered if they thought maybe a top cop from California would be more

76

tolerant of the idea of pot shops in town. Just about everyone prepared to leave.

"If she takes the job," Cole sneered as he stood, sour grapes obvious.

Dixon ignored him and motioned to Gwen, who also doubled as their scribe, to enter everything into the record. "The letter offering her the position will go out in the morning."

As they closed out the council meeting and stood to leave, Oliver wrote down the woman's name, Tess O'Rourke, in his journal and promised to pray for her. If the divided council was any indication, if she did take the job, she was going to need a lot of prayer.

8

One week after her interview, Tess found out exactly how the Rogue's Hollow city council was leaning. She read the offer of employment over again. Nearly two months since the grand jury decision and the associated fallout — including several conferences with the mayor, who bluntly suggested she retire but stopped just short of firing her — she had a place to go if she accepted.

Finally someone wanted her to work for them, to start right away. They gave her time to tie up loose ends, which for Tess included selling her condo — if she was leaving she wanted the break complete — and putting most of her belongings in storage. She sipped coffee and opened Google Earth. She'd spent only a day in the town when she'd flown up for the interview and hadn't seen much, but then there wasn't much to see of the small town. She typed in *Rogue's*

Hollow, Oregon, and watched the program zoom in to a tiny forested dot on the Rogue River, in the southern part of the state, population 5,083. The closest metropolitan area was Medford, with a population not quite reaching eighty thousand. In comparison, Long Beach was the seventh-largest city in California, population over four hundred thousand. Her salary would shrink as much as the population she served.

She picked up the letter again. They wanted her as police chief. In a backhanded way Tess would be getting her promotion to the top spot. But she'd be chief of a department of twelve, counting herself, in a backwater town in Oregon, a far cry from leading a department of over eight hundred officers in a large metropolitan city.

But I don't want to be frozen out of law enforcement. Maybe this small town will be free of mistrust and bloggers who distort the truth. At least the council was unbiased enough to offer me the job. She remembered Steve Logan, the deputy she'd met. If he was any indication, the sheriff's department would be supportive.

She turned to her computer to compose an acceptance letter. *I'll be the best chief I can be and make a difference. That should shut up people like Connor-Ruiz.*

■ ■ ■ ■

PART TWO

■ ■ ■ ■

9

ROGUE'S HOLLOW, OREGON
AUGUST

Oliver ran a hand through his hair and yawned. He'd gotten a late start on his sermon notes and now, Friday night, the clock was ticking toward midnight and he wasn't yet done. He knew a lot of it had to do with Anna. They'd had some bad news: the results from her last round of tests showed that the chemo wasn't working. Anna was depressed and angry, and it was so unlike her that he was at a loss as to how to help.

Earlier, they'd had the new police chief, Tess O'Rourke, over for dinner and things seemed good. It had been a warm, companionable evening. But right after the chief left, Anna's mood went from calm and amiable to angry, hurt.

"God is just not listening. He's turned a deaf ear," she'd cried in frustration.

He kept hearing those words echoing in his thoughts and he hated that part of him believed them. This trial with cancer had been with them for fifteen years and it had taken so much. It had taken Anna's ability to have children, removed the sparkle from her eyes more times than Oliver could count, and now if the doctor was correct, it would take her life.

God hadn't been silent all this time or distant. Oliver and Anna had reveled in the feeling of closeness to God they'd felt at times. At each of the four rounds of chemo, and the four times doctors had declared the cancer beaten back, they'd felt complete and safe in the hand of God.

But this last round of chemo had no effect. The doctor had mentioned other possible alternative treatments, but he was not at all hopeful. He came close to squashing all hope.

But with God there is still hope when there seems to be none. That was what Oliver preached often to his congregation. He'd tried to preach it to Anna but had only succeeded in raising her ire, not her hope. Her words had pierced Oliver deeper than he'd ever thought possible. He felt the fear of losing her so deeply it anchored him. In one sentence his own weak faith was thrown back at him with the force of a 100 mph fastball.

"God has turned a deaf ear, and you need to think about life without me."

Those few words acted like gasoline thrown on the smoldering flames of his doubts, and now he had a scorching fire of unbelief raging in his soul.

Where are you, Lord? We really need you now. I need a touch.

Oliver believed the hope of heaven was real, but the truth was that the thought of life now without Anna was unbearable. He stood to pace his small office, mindful that it was well past the time he should be home in bed, home with Anna. Oliver paused at his blank page. He couldn't think straight enough to write anything for Sunday.

He dropped his hands to his sides and looked heavenward, the years of tears and disappointments flashing through his mind's eye. They'd had hope fifteen years ago when the chemo helped. Anna was sick and lost weight, but they'd beaten the disease — so they'd thought. Four years later it was back. The treatment took a greater toll that time but still, when they made it through, they'd won another battle. But the cancer kept coming back. And now the treatment was doing nothing.

Deaf ear.

They'd always prayed the tough things through together, always trusted God. Why the doubt and anger now?

Taking a deep breath, then letting it out slowly, Oliver didn't even have the words to pray now. He rubbed his tired eyes, turned off the desk light, and prepared to lock up for the night. His office was above the fellowship hall. He had a short walk downstairs and across the parking lot to the small house behind the church that he and Anna called home. But before he could lock the door to the church office, he heard a knock.

A spark inside flared. Maybe it was Anna, come to apologize and walk him home.

The door opened, and his heart leapt — it was Anna.

"Oliver?" She held a large paper bag in her arms, full from what he could see. But it was her expression that froze him.

"Yes?" He stepped toward her. "What's wrong?"

"Glen . . . Glen was here."

Oliver frowned. "Your cousin? This time of night?"

She nodded. "He gave me this." She pushed the bag toward him.

He took the bag from his wife and set it on his desk, flicking the light on again. The pungent, stale odor of cigarette and marijuana smoke wafted toward him. Was it pot? he wondered. Growing pot for recreational use was now legal in this state, but its sale was not yet legal in Rogue's Hollow. But why would Glen give something like that to Anna?

Peering inside the bag, Oliver didn't see drugs. He saw money, lots of it. Fist-sized rolls of twenties and tens secured with rubber bands filled the bag. It was more cash than Oliver had ever seen in one place in his whole life.

"What . . . ?" He looked at Anna, astonished.

When she saw the contents, she whispered, "What in the world?"

Her bewildered expression matched his.

"All Glen said was 'Only God can make this clean.' Then he left. What's he done, Oliver? What on earth has my lost cousin done?"

10

"It's always too soon to quit."

Dad's favorite rule blared in Tess's mind like a siren. His favorite rule had not made it onto her list. She'd compiled her list with a mind toward successful leadership, while her dad's list had a more military flavor to it, the *never quit* applying primarily to combat or competition. Tess had never seen her job as combat. But recent events had her reconsidering.

While she wrestled with demons who told her to do just that — quit — her father's voice echoed in her thoughts, a lecture he'd given her one day, though she couldn't remember why.

"Always follow through, Tess; always follow through. The world is full of lazy people who quit when things get tough. It's only the ones who stick it out and finish the job who get anywhere in life."

For the first time she could remember,

Tess so wanted to quit.

Like stepping out of a hot Jacuzzi and falling headfirst into a pool of ice water — that was the level of shock she'd felt during her first weeks on the job in Rogue's Hollow. It was not the job that overwhelmed her. Police work was police work. But the transition from crowded, diverse asphalt jungle to small, semirural enclave . . . well, it was quite a change. It was like being a rookie all over again but without the camaraderie of her academy classmates. Even though her badge said Chief, taking charge of this small-town department was more like diving back into patrol. She was sworn in early in June and now, two months later, still felt as though her feet hadn't hit the ground.

"You won't have anything to do but put your feet up on the desk. You could stay in California and do that working security somewhere."

The voice of her ex-husband, Paul, a sergeant in personnel, reverberated in Tess's thoughts, mocking her choice to leave. As soon as he'd heard her decision, he'd shown up at her condo as she was packing, making sure she knew what a stupid decision he thought she was making.

"I guess if you want to hide out, then you picked a good place for it. Are you going to be like Barney Fife and only carry one bullet in

your shirt pocket? I predict you'll want to slink back to Long Beach with your tail between your legs before long. I know you too well."

Tess didn't toss anything back, didn't want to give him any ammo. It was because of Paul she'd sold her condo instead of renting it out. She didn't want anything remaining in LB that could pull her back, give her an excuse. This was her last chance as far as she was concerned. And the idea that he thought she couldn't do it or wouldn't like it was added impetus for her to try all the harder to make it work.

Now, sixty days into her job, Tess hated to consider that maybe Paul was right about one thing: she yearned to run back to Long Beach. Tess felt like there was barely a thin thread holding her here in this river town. While it was a strong thread, the last thing Tess wanted to do was something that proved her ex-husband right. She'd kept in touch with Jack O'Reilly in his search for the three shadowy figures who ran away that night, fantasizing that the missing guys, once found, would tell some fantastic truth that would clear all the controversy from Tess, right the universe, and enable her to get her job and position back.

Tess knew in her head that the door to return to LB was solidly closed, politics being politics. But in her heart, she couldn't accept it. Long Beach was *home.* Here, she felt like a square peg in a round hole. The officers who worked for her were standoffish. Few people in town seemed happy to have her there: *"How's someone who doesn't know the difference between a ranch and a farm gonna serve this community?"* And the majority of stuff she dealt with were annoying nuisance crimes.

That in itself was a problem. How much should she step in? In Long Beach there was plenty of patrol coverage, no reason for her to step out of her administration shoes and do police work. As commander, most of her work was done behind a computer or speaking in front of community groups. But here, with one officer per shift and some overlap by her only sergeant . . . well, Tess couldn't sit still and watch officers handle calls alone when she felt backup was needed. It just so happened that she often ended up being the backup.

And this strange conundrum was about the only positive in her life at the moment. Because she was always helping, she rarely had time to sit with her feet up on the desk. It was good for her to stay busy, but was she being a micromanager?

When she did have free time, the small

town became a claustrophobic prison and she didn't hang around. Thursdays had become her favorite down day. There was a growers' market in Medford, forty minutes away. It had become a habit for Tess to head down there early in the morning. She'd wander around, buy a cup of coffee, then order breakfast from one of the vendors. The Thai food truck was her favorite. There was a small table in front of the wagon where she could sit, eat her breakfast, drink her coffee, and watch people.

The people here in southern Oregon were different than in Long Beach, or at least the people she watched at the growers' market were. There was less rush in their steps, less impatience in their movements. They smiled a lot. They smelled flowers, examined fruits and vegetables, placed purchases in bags they brought with them, and chatted with growers. Often she saw women buy whole flats of berries. Anna Macpherson had shown her the market, brought her the first time.

"She's probably going to make jam or preserves with all of that," Anna said after Tess asked about a woman weighed down with three flats of blueberries and raspberries.

"Really? Isn't that a lot of work?"

"Canning and preserving are big pastimes

92

here. I do a little myself. Strawberry freezer jam is Oliver's favorite."

"I love strawberry jam."

"I'd be happy to show you how to make it."

Tess remembered the conversation fondly. She'd never been on the organic, home-grown food bandwagon in Long Beach, but she used to like to cook, make things from scratch. When she and Paul were first married, she cooked all the time, loved surprising him with a new meal and seeing the pleasure in his eyes when he took his first bite. It was only when her career began to take off that she had no time for cooking. But by then they were both busy. The last few years of their marriage, it seemed as though they never had time for one another.

An odd, random thought wove through her mind: *Does a woman who makes freezer jam hang on to her husband?*

Watching people and avoiding thinking about what had happened to her life and career kept her slightly sane. But today her normal Thursday routine had been rudely interrupted.

As was her habit before leaving town, to make sure her presence wasn't required for anything, she'd walked across the street to the station. This morning, with her mind a million miles away, the whine of a revved motorcycle engine barely penetrated her thoughts in time. She nearly got run over by a local teenage delinquent on a dirt bike. Leaping to get to the curb safely, she estimated Duncan Peabody raced through the middle of town at sixty-five in a twenty-five-mile-per-hour zone.

Faced flushed with anger and a bit of chagrin that she'd not heard the cycle's motor sooner, Tess stormed into the station, vowing to climb into her car and — sirens blazing — head to Peabody's house, cite him, and explain to his parents what a danger he was. It wasn't her first run-in with the boy.

But before she could deal with him, her attention was demanded by a red-faced roofing contractor with a tiny pink scratch on his face.

"That idiot almost killed me!" He pointed to the mark on his face. "He's shooting at me! Bullets are flying everywhere."

11

Tilly didn't know what to do. The gunfire had scared her more than she'd ever been scared in her life. It had scared her sober, and she wasn't even the one who'd been shot at. She'd almost run with the first boom of the gun, but the scene across Midas Creek froze her in place momentarily. Tilly stayed hidden in the bushes on one side while the man with the gun was killing her friends on the other side.

The shooter stood over her friend and fired again. There was another person there — a woman who tried to grab the gunman's arm. They struggled but the man was too strong. He flung the woman off his arm and into the creek, the roar of the water smothering her scream.

Horrified, Tilly jerked in her hiding place of scrub brush, fighting the urge to scream. Then the man looked up, across the creek. She was certain their eyes met. He fired in her direction and finally Tilly did move. She stumbled back, fell on her bottom, then struggled to her feet.

The terrain was hilly, thick with trees and brush. The natural trail took her downstream along the creek, even as the gun boomed again. But she kept running downhill, putting the scene behind her.

Midas Creek dropped steeply here, which created the waterfalls it was known for. There was no natural crossing at the point where the shooting occurred, so Tilly realized he could not have followed her.

Breathing hard, Tilly wasn't certain how much time had passed when she had to stop. Now the ground was level, the crashing waterfalls spraying the trail with moisture. And the fear evened out as the terrain did and no bullets struck.

Catching her breath, Tilly tried to process the fact that Glen was dead and there was nothing she could do for him. Then she remembered the woman, the horrific sound of a scream muffled by tumbling water. Could she help the woman who went into the creek?

Glancing back the way she'd come, the spray of water from the falls wetting her face, Tilly felt her fear flee and purpose fill its place.

Help the woman in the creek. As Tilly stumbled over wet rocks to the very edge of a large pool the creek dumped into, she squinted in the low light, searching for the woman. She could hear only the roar of the water and for a second feared the gunman was across the creek doing the same thing she was.

I have to hurry. She continued searching the churning water. Amazingly, there was the woman, her friend, struggling in the frigid swirl. Clarity flashed and Tilly knew what to do.

She looked back, but no more shots rang out; no monster was after her.

She turned to the creek and jumped in. The cold water caused an intake of breath and kept her thoughts lucid. The rocks cut into her skin, and she very nearly didn't make it to the woman before the current took them both farther downstream.

But Tilly was driven. She'd failed Glen; she couldn't fail this woman. Mostly by instinct and a sense of self-preservation, she grabbed hold of an arm and fought to pull them both from the water.

And then the angel appeared.

Tilly firmly believed in angels; she used to pray to them. He appeared at her side and helped her to keep a grip on her friend. This heavenly creature was more than help; he was an inspiration. She and her friend were free of the water, and then the angel helped them both into the shelter.

She warned the angel about the monster. Monsters were as real as angels and extremely deadly. Then, as quickly as the angel appeared, he disappeared. But the assistance he provided was pivotal. She never would have gotten her friend to a safe place without the angel.

Tilly could think now; her thought process became untangled as she looked after her friend. There was no response, no movement, but there was breath. Tilly struggled with addled thoughts to do the right thing. She didn't want her friend to die. A thought niggled: *Go to the police.*

But Tilly couldn't obey the idea of going to the police. The police would only take her to jail.

No, Tilly was on her own now. Glen was gone, the angel was gone, and she would do the best she could with what she had.

12

Terrorist? Mass shooter? Domestic dispute? What was she dealing with?

Alert and focused, Tess shelved the issue with Peabody and concentrated on the man in front of her.

"Who's shooting and where is he?" Tess noted the man's injury and was poised, ready to jump into her uniform and head toward the danger.

"He's on his porch, firing off a handgun like it was a cap gun. I'm just trying to do my job."

Now that he had her attention, the man calmed somewhat and Tess got the whole story, even as she heard gunshots echoing in the distance.

She decided quickly that the situation, while thankfully not a mass shooting, did need her attention. She took a few minutes to change into her uniform and notify Officer Bender about the situation and her intentions. As the on-duty day officer he joined her on a rural piece of property on the south side of Rogue's Hollow.

Now, Peabody forgotten, here she was, helping to try to defuse a situation that would have been funny if it weren't so dangerous.

"Yee-haw!"

Bang. Bang. Bang.

Tess sighed. Her presence at the standoff with Bubba Magee was going on twenty minutes. She'd laughed when she first heard his name — was somebody really named Bubba? — but she wasn't laughing now.

The shooter was a local boy prone to getting liquored up and acting crazy. Officer Bender told her that officers had been called out to the house before and that all of Bubba's guns had been taken away without incident by the last chief, insinuating that Tess herself was not good enough to handle the matter diplomatically like Chief Bailey had.

But obviously the prior chief had missed at least one gun.

Tess ducked even though the shots were going into the air and she was behind cover. They had a clear view of Bubba and his porch. He sat between a cooler, from which he'd grabbed a beer, and a footlocker, from which he'd taken the gun.

Beside her, Gabe Bender cursed, then shook his head. Tess heard him mutter, "Maybe we'll make a move this century," before he said out loud, "That fool drunk is going to kill someone."

Beside him, Jackson County sheriff's deputy Steve Logan raised an eyebrow in agreement with the last statement. Tess let the muttering slide.

It was no secret that Bender didn't like her. She wasn't certain about Logan and had mixed feelings about him.

When she'd met him the day of her interview, he'd been pleasant and encouraging. And in these last two months, that hadn't changed; he'd been an invaluable support, helping whenever he could make his way to the Hollow. Today, he'd responded in mutual aid so quickly she wondered if he'd already been on the way. Every time she saw him, it was getting harder and harder to deny that she was attracted to him.

Logan had been promoted to sergeant since she'd first met him, so he had a lot more freedom about where he patrolled, and Tess wasn't about to turn down the offer of extra help. In Long Beach there was strength in numbers, and everyone who could would show up to shots calls, so his presence was not out of line. But he was too good-looking for her own good. And he was not at all standoffish, not like Bender, a man who made no secret of the fact that he was not happy Tess was the new chief.

"I expect you'll waltz in here and change everything that makes this a great place to work," he'd groused the first day she'd met him. *"If I'd wanted to work in California, I'd've moved there."*

It had gone downhill from there. Bender practically broadcast the fact he'd applied to every department in the state that was hiring lateral police applicants. And job offering bulletins from all over the state had been tacked up on the station bulletin board with regularity.

It was a bit refreshing that Logan was helpful without being obnoxious.

He caught Tess's eye. They'd all tried to talk Bubba into dropping the gun to no avail. He seemed to have an unending supply of bullets. Logan had a Taser, but he'd have to get close to deploy it, and there was no guarantee it would have any effect. Fact was, a drunk with a gun was just too volatile.

And she didn't want this to end in a fatal police shooting, not if she could help it. She'd survived here so far without losing her cool or ending up in a controversy. As unhappy as she was, she knew only a major issue would make her quit, while she doubted it would take as much for the small city council to fire her. And, Paul notwithstanding, she had too much respect for her father's legacy; she did not want to be fired. As far as hating her new job, she would suck up her angst. The Hoover shooting in LB had taken everything from her but the knowledge that she'd stayed true to her pop's memory.

Today was the two-month anniversary of her appointment as Rogue's Hollow chief of police, and while her career hopes and dreams might have been dying a slow death, she didn't want any people to die.

Though she knew it hadn't changed any, Tess looked around at the personnel she had with her on this call. Logan and Bender. There was an Oregon State Police officer en route, but she wasn't sure when he'd get here or how he could help when everything they'd already tried had failed.

She'd thought about calling in an off-duty officer to help but didn't because she knew how tight the small budget was. That was a tightrope she'd walked in Long Beach, knowing the difference between essential overtime and nonessential overtime. Rogue's Hollow just didn't have the resources for nonessential.

And Bubba wasn't shooting at people; he was just shooting. Even the red-faced roofer had eventually conceded that Bubba wasn't shooting *at* him.

Bubba's manufactured home sat on a rural wooded lot. From what Tess already knew of the area, at one time he probably could have sat on his porch and shot up trees all day long. But three lots next to him had sold, and the new owner of one of them was trying to build a home. Tess heard rumors that all three properties would be growing cannabis, but that wasn't her problem now.

This was where the roofing contractor came into the picture. One of Bubba's bullets had shot out a chunk of wood from a roof truss, sending a small splinter into the roofer's face. The guy was understandably hopping mad and wanted to file charges.

"He's reckless! He could have killed me without even realizing it." The contractor wanted him stopped and thrown in jail.

Tess agreed that he had a point and was trying to do just that. But Bubba was not complying in any way, shape, or form, validating a universal formula: for instant idiot, just add alcohol. It was impossible to reason with a drunk. That he was so drunk this early in the morning certainly signified some kind of issue. To walk straight up to him, even Bender conceded, would be dangerous and crazy because he was uninhibited and unpredictable.

Though it would have been comforting to have a few more bodies, Tess would make do. Not for the first time since she'd signed her contract, she found herself missing the large Southern California police department she'd grown up in. In Long Beach, she would have had any number of resources at her beck and call to deal with someone like Bubba.

A MET unit, or mental evaluation team, a crisis negotiator, a SWAT team — heavens, at this point Tess would be happy with a beanbag-shooting shotgun. That would have a better range than a Taser.

Her gaze caught that of Officer Bender. The mocking impatience in his eyes didn't go over her head.

She'd been surprised that the eight police officers she now supervised were not more supportive of her position. She'd expected a little attitude from Sergeant Pounder, only because he'd been acting chief for eight months. But not cold shoulders from the majority of her employees.

Even in Long Beach most of the men and

women on the PD knew that the press and public opinion were wrongly persecuting Tess. She'd saved JT Barnes's life. Many of them had begged her to stay and fight for her job. But her presence in Long Beach had made it hard for the PD as a whole to operate. The last thing Tess would ever want was to be responsible for another cop being hurt. She did know that since she'd left, the protests had stopped and Connor-Ruiz was not getting the attention he wanted.

Now she owed Rogue's Hollow the best she had to offer for Pop's sake, cold shoulders or not, despite the impulse to run away.

Sergeant Logan gave her every respect, even a little deference, but Tess knew that a wrong move here on her part could destroy her image in everyone's eyes, maybe make it impossible to recover any modicum of respect.

Bubba fired off a few more rounds skyward.

"Problem solving, decision making," Tess muttered a phrase under her breath from her field training eighteen years ago.

"What?" Logan asked.

"Nothing." She handed him the bullhorn. "I'm going to try and get behind him. Keep him occupied."

Logan started to say something, then

106

stopped. He nodded. "Your call," he said and went back to watching Bubba.

In spite of everything, a shiver went through her; his eyes were so blue and the statement of his confidence in her bolstered her own. It made Tess realize how much she missed and wanted closeness with someone, anyone.

Rule #12 applied: "Keep work professional, and personal life, personal."

Forcing her thoughts to the problem at hand, Tess struggled to develop a strategy. She'd tried earlier to talk to the drunk guy but he had not responded. He simply drank his beer and fired his handgun.

She made her way back around her patrol car, then Logan's, just as Bubba started shooting again. Tess jumped and turned. The guy had a semiautomatic rifle now and was shooting that into the air.

Make that two guns the last chief had missed.

This had to stop.

Bender caught her eye as she crossed to the other side of the narrow driveway.

"Going for a walk?" he sneered.

Tess ignored him. "Hold your position."

She continued through the thick copse of trees to the left of Bubba's home. The trees would give her cover only so long. Then there was the car garden, four or five aging and broken-down vehicles of assorted makes, in various stages of decay, that dotted the lot. She thought she heard Bender mutter something, but she wasn't going to play his game. Now wasn't the time.

She pushed her way through the thick bunch of trees, hands and face getting scratched here and there. When her cover ended, Tess paused and Logan began talking to Bubba.

"Come on, Bubba, why don't you put the gun down? I don't want to see anyone get hurt and we all have other things to do today."

Bubba answered him by hooting and shooting some more.

Tess eyed the sprint she'd have to make. A good seventy-five-yard dash with two jogs to avoid cars. Tess had been a middle distance runner in college; this was a bona fide sprint in full police gear. Bubba would have plenty of time to turn and shoot her in her tracks. A quick end to a short, unhappy job as chief of police.

Bubba's back was to her, so Tess took a deep breath, counted to ten, and broke from cover, legs pumping, arms moving.

Twenty-five yards, fifty, seventy, almost to the porch. Tess leaped as Bubba turned toward her, silly grin on his face. She hit the top of the porch and launched herself into the big drunk man's broad shoulder.

The impact took her breath away. They crashed down onto the rough surface of planks that made up his porch, and Tess grabbed for his gun, but it went flying. She then reached for a fat wrist with one hand and her handcuffs with the other.

For his part Bubba didn't seem to know what hit him. The smell of body odor, stale beer, and cigarettes was pungent and thick. Tess got one fat wrist cuffed by the time Logan appeared at her side and helped her secure the other.

Shoulder aching, breath coming hard, Tess stood and brushed off and straightened her uniform while Logan, then Bender, finished securing Bubba. The big man was now crying.

Hands on hips, Tess watched as they pulled him to his feet.

"Okay now. We can book him." She looked at Logan, who regarded her approvingly.

"Nice work, Chief."

Bender only grunted an acknowledgment and took hold of the drunk's forearm.

While Tess was taking down Bubba, the OSP car had pulled in beside all the other police vehicles. The state trooper stood at the front of his car, hands on hips, watching. Tess raised a hand with four fingers to indicate the situation was code 4, under control, then ignored him. He'd been a spectator anyway.

Logan stepped close when she turned her attention back to the mobile home. "Chief, it might make more sense for me to book this guy. It will take your day officer out of service for a long time. If I go, you and Gabe can confiscate the guns. All the guns."

Bender had paused his progress to the car, his expression hopeful. Tess knew immediately what a generous offer this was. For Logan to offer to ride forty minutes to Medford to book a stinky drunk was huge.

Though it was a nice gesture for Bender, Tess could see in Logan's eyes that he was trying to help her out.

She sucked in a breath, working to stay formal, professional. "That's nice of you, Sergeant Logan. I'd appreciate that."

"No problem," he said. "I've got this." He walked to where Bender stood with Bubba, took one arm, and Bender took the other. Together they ushered the drunk to the sergeant's car. The drunk kept mumbling that he was sorry.

When Bender returned, Tess said, "Let's you and me confiscate his guns and ammo and make sure we get all of it this time."

He nodded, and as he moved to help her, Tess noted, with not a little satisfaction, that Bender wouldn't meet her gaze this time.

13

Tess tried not to pat herself on the back after the Bubba incident. Besides the fact that she was sore and achy from tackling the big oaf, she could not ignore the voice in her head that said she'd acted like a raw rookie. Yeah, she'd gotten her man, but at great personal risk.

In Long Beach, a move like that, rushing an armed man, would have been called reckless, poor officer safety, and she'd have been sent to remedial training.

But she'd so wanted to prove, especially to Gabriel Bender, that she was up for this job, that she could be a solid, fearless chief of police who could solve problems without shooting. After two months she still didn't feel connected to anyone who worked for her. True, they weren't all like Bender. Her one sergeant, Curtis Pounder, was always the consummate professional; likewise Del Jeffers, the oldest cop on the payroll, was respectful. Martin Getz, one of the younger guys, even seemed to think she had a lot to teach him. The only woman on the force, Becky Jonkey, worked swing shift and Tess had had little contact with her. Tess lamented that the camaraderie, the inclusion she'd always felt in Long Beach, was not here.

She was more hands-on here than any chief in Long Beach would be. In Long Beach the chief of police didn't even answer his own e-mail. It was all screened by a secretary first. He had a lieutenant and two sergeants working in his office to delegate to. But Tess learned right away there'd be no one screening her e-mail, and sitting behind a desk all day wasn't going to happen. It was important, given the light staffing, that she have a public presence. She'd taken to wearing the full uniform — ballistic vest, Sam Browne, the whole nine yards — while in the office, and she paid close attention to the radio.

When she wasn't hating her life, she could admit that she'd actually stepped into a well-run department. Seven patrol officers and one sergeant was tight for a population of just over five thousand, but things ran smoothly. She'd left the staffing alone. Some of it was unconventional, but it seemed to work. Officers worked three twelve-hour shifts with an eight-hour shift every other week. Sergeant Pounder worked a flexible five eight-hour-day workweek. He'd flex his hours if he thought more coverage was needed or if for some reason he was called out on overtime when he was off. The only bumps were the shortages that occurred with normal absences: vacations, training, sick days.

All the officers lived within the city limits and took their patrol cars home with them just in case they were needed and called in on their off hours. Tess had found that something similar to her sergeant's unconventional flexible schedule worked for her. Except since she'd started here, she'd logged well over forty hours every week. She would always check in before she left town and return if or when the radio indicated things were busy.

Though these two months had been filled with minor stuff, she'd stepped up wherever she could to help and support her people. Was she doing too much or not enough? It didn't seem to make a dent in attitudes. A still small voice in her head kept telling her she didn't need to take risks; all she had to do was relax and be herself and it would all work out.

But why don't I see any improvement with the confidence of my people? Why won't they let me into their inner circle?

Since Logan had offered to book Bubba, leaving Bender free to stay in town and help catalog the guns and file the report, Tess wondered if she'd be able to make any headway with the man.

As she made the turn to the station lot, Tess remembered the encounter with Duncan earlier, a little miffed that she hadn't been able to address his troublemaking sooner. If she'd been able to, she would have given his parents an earful.

Duncan Peabody was the only son of Delia and Ellis Peabody. Tess had met the Peabodys at her swearing in. The parents were cordial people. Ellis Peabody was a bigwig in Silicon Valley, Google or Yahoo! or something. He flew to work Monday morning and was back Thursday night, only actually at home for the weekends. His wife, Delia, was a horsewoman; she owned several beautiful horses and gave lessons. From what Tess had heard, she was highly regarded and very pleasant. On the other hand, Duncan was a sulky, spoiled kid who, she'd been told, had tested the PD on more than one occasion with typical teenage stunts.

She'd seen enough to classify the boy as a smart mouth with a penchant for traveling too fast everywhere. Plus, he acted as if he owned the town. He was seventeen and thought he was untouchable, most likely because of his father.

Tess had already had one run-in with the son over his riding a skateboard in town where it was dangerous and forbidden, and she knew he was going to give her headaches because of how that contact had gone.

"You need to respect the sign: no skateboards allowed here," Tess admonished, her tone light and amiable. *"It's a blind corner; you might knock someone down."*

Duncan had stared at her in mock panic, holding his skateboard up over his head in both hands. *"Oh no, what are you going to do, shoot me?"*

His friends broke into guffaws and the group jogged away, but the remark cut Tess like a straight razor.

She remembered that encounter as she looked at the clock. It was after noon and she had paperwork regarding Bubba to write and review, no time to confront Duncan and his folks over the early morning drive-by. Tess continued to her parking spot behind the station. She made a mental note to contact the Peabodys as soon as she had

116

time to spare.

Sighing, putting the teenager out of her mind, Tess lamented the fact that the growers' market was over, no recharging until next week. Bubba was on his way to Jackson County Jail with Logan, and for that she was grateful. If Bender had taken the guy, he would have been tied up for the rest of the shift and she would have had to ask Sergeant Pounder to come in early. Now, Bender would be staying in town and filing the report for the roofer who'd interrupted Tess's day.

Thoughts returned to Bubba as she climbed the steps to the station, AK-47 in hand. She'd already seen Bender enter with his arms full of confiscated weaponry. They'd recovered two handguns, the AK-47, a hunting rifle, and a bunch of reloads from Bubba's house, and all would be placed into evidence/found property. In Long Beach evidence was a huge secure storage facility. Here, since most evidence went to the state crime lab in Salem, or to the county, the only storage at RHPD was a small back room with a couple of lockers. She dropped the AK off at the table where Bender was checking serial numbers.

At first Tess had cringed at the lack of resources. Only one small holding cell. Even

Mayberry had a couple. But once it settled in her mind that there wasn't the volume of crime here she was used to contending with, a back room with lockers made sense. Her whole thought process was still undergoing a period of adjustment. Four hundred thousand people created a need for a lot more stuff than five thousand did.

Technical and procedural adaptation was so much easier than the personal adaptation. People issues were the hardest for Tess to navigate. Not everyone was as blatantly hostile as Gabe Bender. But except for the local pastor, Oliver Macpherson, and his wife, Anna, who'd become good friends; the local auto mechanic; and the couple who owned the hotel where she currently lived, Tess had not felt overwhelmingly welcomed. Even the mayor, who told her she had his full support, was not really *friendly.*

Anna Macpherson was one woman Tess counted firmly as a friend. They'd had lunch a couple of times and Tess had even been to the Macpherson house for dinner. Though grateful for her friendship, Tess had not taken up the woman's invitation to attend church. She wanted to fit into her department and to feel like she was a part of the community she served, and she hoped it wouldn't take going to church to do that.

Her phone beeped with a message and she saw it was Mayor Dixon; obviously he'd been listening to his scanner. He wanted an update on Bubba.

Tess pinched the bridge of her nose. She served at the discretion of the city council — she knew that. Mayor Dixon had bent her ear with the tale of how hard he'd fought for her hire. But he was an annoying man who treated her like a brand-new rookie. It might have been okay with Tess if he were retired law enforcement — after all, she had a whole new set of state laws and regulations to learn — but Dixon was the furthest thing from a former cop. His suggestions were never practical and his criticisms were beyond picky. She was supposed to notify him every time she responded to a call.

Dixon hailed from New Hampshire originally, though he'd been in Oregon around twenty years. Tess had been surprised by the number of people she'd met here who were from somewhere else. She wondered if his pickiness was because of his East Coast upbringing.

Procrastinating, Tess brewed a fresh pot of coffee and sat at her desk, composing her thoughts for the report she needed to file and formulating a response to Dixon. She'd only gotten the first paragraph down when she was interrupted by Sheila Cannan, her secretary, who also doubled as a records clerk.

"Chief." Sheila tapped on the doorframe. Tess made it a point to keep her office door open. She wanted people to feel comfortable enough to stop by and say hello. Though that hadn't happened yet, Tess kept the door open.

"Yeah, Sheila?"

"Pastor Macpherson is here. He'd like a minute."

Tess peered around Sheila and saw the pastor behind her, looking anxious. Anna wasn't with him.

She leaned back, frowning. "Did you make inquiries about that bag of money?"

"I did. I couldn't find any thefts, no burglaries, no losses, nothing listing that amount of money or anything close."

Macpherson had come in on Saturday with a big bag of money — $50,465 to be exact. Said his wife's cousin just handed it to them the night before. Tess bet it was drug money and that no one would ever come for it or report it stolen. She'd asked her people to keep an eye out for the cousin, a guy named Glen Elders, but so far he'd not surfaced.

Macpherson didn't want to do anything with the cash until he was certain Glen hadn't ripped someone off. Tess had it locked up in an evidence locker. She was the only one with a key. At first she wondered if that was such a great idea, but in Long Beach the money would have been locked up as found property. It would stay in found property for a period of time and if no one claimed it, the finder could. The law was a little different here in Oregon, Tess had found when she looked it up.

ORS 98.005 essentially provided that when someone found money, valued at $250 or more, they had to notify the county clerk in writing. Within twenty days the finder had to publish a note in the paper, describing the find and the final date when the money could be claimed. The note would have to run for two weeks. If no one stepped forward and proved ownership of the money within three months, the finder got to keep it. In this case, Pastor Oliver Macpherson would see his church roughly $50,000 richer.

The newspaper ad would begin its run next week, if Tess remembered right. She knew no one would pop in to say they lost a

121

bag of drug money, and felt the money was safe in their small, but adequate, evidence room.

"Did you tell him that?"

"I did. He wants to talk to you about something else, I think."

Tess nodded and turned away from her computer, feeling a juvenile delight that this was a great excuse to delay the call to the mayor.

"Send him in."

Sheila stepped aside and waved Macpherson into the office.

Of all the people Tess had met since she became chief of police, Oliver Macpherson was the most intriguing. In her mind, he looked anything but a pastor. Tess hadn't been to church since she was a teen and the image of *pastor* in her mind was that of an old man with a perpetual frown on his face. That wasn't Macpherson. He was about her age and handsome in a rugged way, looking more like a rough-hewn cowboy than a preacher. Tess, at five-six, had to look up quite a bit to meet his eyes, which were a stormy green-gray, reminding her of the powerful, smooth Rogue River, very steady and calming. He smiled easily and sincerely. He wore a beard, neatly trimmed close to his chin, the same salt-and-pepper color as the hair on his head. And he kept his hair longer than Tess was used to. In Long Beach all the guys she knew had buzz cuts or bald heads. Her ex had started shaving his head years ago.

Pastor Mac, as he was called, was well built, solid, and she knew that he worked part-time as a finish carpenter. The third finger on his right hand was missing at the knuckle, probably a result of learning the trade.

But the most interesting thing about Oliver Macpherson was his accent. He'd told Tess the story, how he'd been born here in Rogue's Hollow, but when he was small, his parents moved to Scotland to care for his paternal grandparents. Grandma died after a year, but Grandpa lasted ten and by then his parents had decided to stay. But Oliver always wanted to return to Oregon.

"We'd vacationed here a couple of summers when I was growing up and I fell in love with the forests."

When an opportunity arose for him to intern at a local church, he returned. He completed college here and worked as an assistant pastor until the spot opened up at Rogue's Hollow Community Church. By then he and Anna were newlyweds and both leaped at the opportunity. His voice still sang with a bit of Scotland. It was deep and resonant, a musical sound, and Tess understood why people came from far away to hear him preach.

Macpherson entered her office, looking to Tess a little lost without Anna.

She stood. "Hello, Pastor Macpherson. What can I do for you?"

"Please, it's Oliver. I see you've already been busy and it's still early. I saw Officer Bender on the way in and he mentioned a tackle? How's your shoulder? Not too sore, I hope?"

Tess resisted being miffed that Bender was already talking about the Bubba call. She should have expected it. One thing cops loved as much as catching bad guys was gossip and storytelling.

She rolled her shoulders and tried not to wince. He'd asked her to call him Oliver when she'd come to dinner, but for some reason she felt funny doing that.

"A little stiff. I'll be fine." She motioned to the chair in front of her desk. "Have a seat. Are you still worried about that money? I can guarantee you that no one is going to come looking for it."

He shook his head and Tess saw conflicting emotions cross his features. As he sat, she noticed how tired he looked. Was this over the money? she wondered. It wasn't as if he'd stolen it. There was something else going on.

"No, it's not the money. It's . . ." He rubbed the back of his left hand with his right hand.

"Wait a minute." Tess got up and shut her door. She came back to her desk but didn't go behind it. She leaned against the corner. "What is it, Pa — Oliver? You look as if someone died."

"You read people well, Chief. I imagine that's why you're good at your job. But it's not a death; it's . . ." He took a deep breath and seemed to gather himself before he met her gaze. "It's, uh . . . it's, well . . . Anna didn't come home last night."

"Anna?" Tess stiffened. "What do you mean, she's missing?" Was there something she'd missed in Anna, some private pain? Or were pastors just like everyone else, right down to marital troubles?

"Yesterday she was late for supper. I tried to phone her, and I got a text instead of an answer." He pulled a phone out of his pocket, tapped on it, and showed the phone to Tess.

I need space. I'll call you when I'm ready.

She read it and frowned. "Sounds as if she needs a break."

He hiked one shoulder, a pained expression crossing his face. "This just isn't like her. She doesn't often text, doesn't like it, thinks it's too impersonal, and, uh . . . well, it's odd. I've not heard a thing since this wee note."

Tess noted that stress was bringing out the accent. Her mother was the same way. Svetlana Babkin O'Rourke was of Russian descent, and the accent became thicker and peppered with Russian words and phrases when she was upset. Tess moved back behind her desk.

"When did you see her last?"

"Yesterday at breakfast. I had a meeting in Medford with some other pastors for most of the day. When I got home last evening, there was no sign of her."

"It's been a day and a little more; is it possible she does just need time?"

He rubbed his brow. "Maybe. I mean, initially I did want to give her time. But to go this long without calling me?" He shook his head. "We are at a tough spot right now, but Anna is not one to give me the silent treatment."

Something clicked with Tess. "Is this about the cancer?"

The pain was obvious as it rippled across his features. "I wasn't sure how much she'd told you."

"Just that things didn't look too good right now." Tess remembered Anna sharing her struggle with cancer but looking so content and peaceful as she talked about it that she'd wondered if it was that serious.

"The doctor is not optimistic, and Anna's last conversation with him made her angry. I thought we'd sorted out the issue. She has, on occasion in the past, spent time alone in prayer, but this is something we should be dealing with together."

Tess had to think about that for a minute. She'd had one cancer scare in her past, but the mass on her ovary turned out to be benign. Her husband, Paul, wasn't the one she leaned on. Her girlfriends were more supportive than he was. Paul was a pro at avoidance. It was never a topic of conversation between them. If it had been cancer, would he have been more involved? It surprised her the pain she felt when she thought probably not. Paul was never a shoulder to lean on. Was Oliver Macpherson?

She leaned forward. "Was she angry with you for some reason? Is it possible she's just with friends?"

He met her gaze and hesitated a minute. "Her closest friends are here in the Hollow.

She was angrier with God than she was with me."

Tess considered this. She understood "angry at God" — been there, done that. But it always helped to have someone real to vent to. She might come back to this topic, dig deeper, but for now she'd leave it. "I know you don't have kids. Does she have any relatives in the area she might be with?"

Tess thought she saw a wince as he shook his head again. "I've called her parents, been discreet. But now the worry is growing. The church does own a cabin in Union Creek. It's possible she's there . . ." His voice trailed off.

Tess had been to Union Creek, about thirty minutes away. The cabins there had quite a history, built during the Depression by the conservation corps, rustic and cozy. But the area was a dead zone, no cell service. Would Anna go there for just that reason?

She rubbed her chin and sat back, thinking. Rule #2: "Be fair, not emotional." She'd spent more time with Anna than she had with anyone in this town, but did she really know her? Would she leave by herself overnight to *pray?* For that matter, Tess didn't really know the pastor at all. Should he have been worried about his wife way before now?

Bottom line, pastor or no, he could have chopped Anna up into little pieces and tossed her in the Rogue River for all she knew. But he seemed genuinely worried. None of her internal garbage detectors were going off. And really, what would she have told him if he'd come to her late last night or earlier this morning? *No foul play. Give her time.*

"Do you have any of the find-a-phone apps on your phone?" She asked the question knowing that such an app wouldn't matter in a dead zone.

He sighed. "Afraid I'm not that gadget savvy."

"She have any enemies? Do you have any reason to think she'd be in danger?"

"I don't know a soul who ever had a cross word to say about Anna. She's a gentle, well-liked person."

Tess considered that. Anna was probably the nicest person she'd ever met in Rogue's Hollow — or Long Beach, for that matter. "Did she leave on foot?"

"No, she took her car."

"What about belongings?"

"What?"

"Belongings — did she take her purse, pack a bag? Are her clothes still home?"

129

He looked befuddled for a moment. "Her purse is gone, but I didn't think to look in the closet."

Tess stood. "Why don't we go back to your house. I'll take a look around and —"

She paused when she heard a commotion in the outer office, voices raised, and then there was a rapid knock on the door. It flung open. It was Sheila, with a man behind her, a man Tess recognized but couldn't place. He reminded her a bit of Deputy Chief Riggs, only older, and he was agitated, sweat glistening on his face.

Sheila said, "Chief, sorry to interrupt, but we have a situation."

"What?"

She glanced at Macpherson. Tess felt dread pierce her gut. What if Anna had been found and it wasn't good?

"Pastor, can you excuse us for a minute?"

"Sure." He nodded and got up and left the room.

"Either I'll send someone or I'll be by your house as soon as I can," Tess called after him as he left. She turned back to Sheila as she and the man stepped in.

"Chief, I'm Arthur Goding. Not sure if you remember me from your swearing in, but I was fishing with Del Jeffers this morning." He took a deep breath. Del was Tess's senior patrol officer; he'd been a cop here the longest, twenty-five years.

"Don't tell me you've found his wife." Tess feared the worst regarding Anna.

Goding frowned. "What? No, I wasn't looking for her. We were flagged down by some distraught hikers. They stumbled on a body. A dead body. Del is trying to keep the scene secure and the guys there for you to talk to. He sent me here to tell you. A murder, Chief, the first one ever around here from what I can remember. Some guy's been shot."

14

Tess grabbed the keys that she'd just hung on the peg in her office. The department-issued vehicle, a four-wheel-drive blue-and-white SUV, was getting a workout today. A lot of her territory was rural; in fact, most of the residential streets in Rogue's Hollow were gravel, and she'd already been thankful for the four-wheel-drive capability. Her personal vehicle was a convertible sports car, a splurge she'd indulged in after her divorce became final. Shopping to ease the pain. The little red number had been fun in California, but it was out of place here, at least as far as her job went.

Bender stood up from his desk when she walked into the outer office. "I heard a lot of what Art had to say. My report's done. Do we need the SO?"

"We'll wait on notifying the sheriff until I know exactly what we have."

Tess considered the officer, her thorn in

the flesh. Pounder would be in soon; she'd rather work with him. No, she decided. Rule #2 applied here for sure: "Be fair, not emotional." She wasn't going to solve her problem with Bender by avoiding him.

"Join us," Tess said. Then she turned to Arthur, asking as they walked out of the office, "Do we know who the dead guy is?"

"We didn't poke too close. Del didn't want to mess up the scene. From what I saw, though, he didn't look familiar. Pastor Mac might recognize him. He knows a lot of people. If the guy is from the area, he's likely to know him. Maybe we should bring him with us."

Tess could see the pastor preparing to cross the street and return to the church. For a second she hesitated; after all, he had his own problems. And he needed a report filed about his wife.

But Arthur called out, "Pastor Mac, think maybe you can give us a hand?"

Macpherson turned.

Before he could speak, Tess said, "Pastor, you have your own situation to deal with. I'll send someone —"

He waved her quiet. "If I can help you, I will. I'm not certain about my problem. It may be nothing. I don't want to overreact. What is it that's happened?"

Arthur filled him in.

Macpherson's eyebrows rose. "A murder? Here?"

Tess could tell the thought appalled him.

As well it should, Tess thought. She'd dealt with a lot of stuff here that in Long Beach would be considered minor. Sure there were drugs, drunks, and wild tourists, but there weren't shootings and stabbings and murders every other night. The place was peaceful and, except for occasional outbursts by Bubba Magee, too many tourists in the summer, and noise complaints from the local trailer park, relatively quiet. It was disturbing how that calm had now most likely been shattered by a heinous crime.

"Ride with me, Pastor. We'll all follow Arthur back to the scene."

Macpherson nodded and stepped over to the passenger side of Tess's cruiser. She started the car as he hopped in.

Tess pulled in behind Arthur, while Bender followed her. Arthur led them east on River Drive, then turned right on Midas Drive, the road that ran parallel to Midas Creek, which was the natural eastern boundary of Rogue's Hollow. A quiet residential section of town spread out to her right. Once they were on the road, she turned to Macpherson.

"You sure you're okay with this?"

He sighed. "I'm really not sure about Anna. What if I'm wrong and she just needs some space? Would filing a missing person report be a sign that I don't trust her?"

"That all depends. Does she have a reason for wanting to get away from you? Is your marriage in trouble?"

For a second their eyes locked. Then Tess looked away to keep her eyes on the road. But in that second she saw only care and concern in the pastor's stormy eyes. She trusted her instincts and doubted Oliver Macpherson was the problem here.

"I'd have said we had an almost-perfect marriage."

"Almost?"

"It's the cancer. It's clouded our lives for fifteen years."

"That long?" This surprised Tess. The impression she'd gotten from Anna was that this was recent.

"She was first diagnosed three years after we were married. It's been a part of our lives ever since." He shook his head as if shaking away bad memories. "Anyway, this last round of chemo was not effective." His voice broke and he paused. "The doctor was worse than not optimistic about her prognosis. Anna . . . well, she said she needed to think about that, consider all the ramifications by herself before discussing everything with me."

Pained, Tess bit her tongue. Her knuckles turned white on the wheel, and she couldn't speak. Her thoughts were selfish at first. *Anna is my only friend here, and she's going to die.* And then she had to address the obvious question.

"She's not suicidal, is she?"

"No." His answer was quick and firm. "If I thought that for a second, I'd have come to you immediately. She just wants to sort things out."

Tess swallowed as pavement gave way to gravel and they began to climb. Arthur continued up the road that paralleled the creek. Midas Creek ran down from the mountains year-round, fed by a spring, and eventually joined the Rogue River at Rogue's Hollow. This road led to trailheads and dry campgrounds.

"If that is what this is about, maybe you should give her time. But it wouldn't hurt to have someone check out the cabin in Union Creek. If you want, I can send an officer."

"No, that's not necessary. I can call and ask a friend who lives out that way to check and see if Anna is there."

They passed a partially filled parking lot for a viewing platform and bridge that spanned the creek. Midas Creek tumbled down a beautiful tree- and rock-lined path and was known for two spectacular waterfalls, the Stairsteps. The two steep drops resembled hand-fashioned stairs. After the Stairsteps, the terrain leveled so that eventually, at the confluence of the river and the creek, it was a gentle joining.

Arthur continued climbing before turning onto a smaller, less-used road that headed directly toward the creek. He drove for about a hundred yards before coming to a stop in a small, dusty parking lot where the road ended. They were at least half a mile upstream from the Stairsteps, and the forest was thick here, the terrain rugged. There was a truck parked in the lot with three men sitting on the tailgate. She recognized her officer Del Jeffers as one of the men. Tess parked next to Arthur and Bender pulled next to her.

She turned to Macpherson. "I'll take a look first. I can't guarantee it won't be gruesome, so you don't have to look if you don't want to."

"I've helped pull unfortunate bodies out of the river when people have drowned, and visited many a deathbed. I'll be fine." He moved to get out of the car with her.

"Suit yourself, but listen to me. I don't want the crime scene contaminated."

Tess didn't wait for a response. She got out, opened the back, and pulled her brand-new crime scene kit out. This would be the first time she would put it to use. She strode to where Del was. He stood up to greet her.

"Afternoon, Chief."

"Del, what do you have?"

He pointed. "The body is near the creek's edge. Arthur and I were on our way to a fishing spot when these guys —" he pointed to the hikers — "flagged us down. I tried to make sure nothing was contaminated and sat them down here to wait for someone on duty. It's definitely not self-inflicted."

Del was her only black officer. He was an older, experienced cop, and it sounded as if he'd made a lot of good decisions. He worked days, the other side of the week from Gabe Bender. He was one officer who seemed okay with Tess being in town. While not overly friendly, he was never cold like Bender.

"Good job," Tess said. She looked at the hikers. "Did you guys see anyone else around the body?"

One shook his head. "We saw no one until

138

Del and Art showed up here."

"Okay, I'm going to check out the body before I talk to you. I need to know exactly what I'm dealing with."

They both nodded.

She turned to Bender, handing him a roll of yellow police tape. Pointing to a tree, she said, "Tape this area off as best you can. We might get looky-loos, and I don't want anyone tramping in by accident."

He nodded and began unrolling tape. Del stepped up to help him.

She started to move forward, but Del grabbed her arm.

"There's also a dog there, next to the body. It's a pit bull. It let us get close enough to verify that the guy was dead by unnatural means, but . . ." He hiked a shoulder. "I didn't want to force it to move."

"What's it doing?"

"Nothing. Just sitting there with the body. Probably the dead guy's dog."

Tess paused to process this information. In Long Beach pit bulls were the dogs of choice for gang members. They were trained to fight and usually mean and protective of their owners. She remembered a call she assisted on where an officer had to shoot a pit bull. The 9mm bullet he fired basically bounced off the dog's head and he kept coming. Two other officers fired before the dog was stopped.

A shudder rippled through her. Tess loved dogs. But she would have shot that snarling eighty-pound missile of teeth if the guys around her hadn't. It had made her all the angrier with the stupid gang member who'd trained the poor animal to be a weapon.

Was that what she had here? She hoped not, but she unsnapped her holster just to be on the safe side. She continued on in the direction Del indicated, calling for Bender to follow when he finished with the tape. Arthur and Del stayed with the hikers. Tess would speak to Del later at length about his observations.

She noted that she'd been directed a way that was off the main trail, but the path taken was obvious. The dry grass was smashed down by many footfalls. Tess pondered this. One dead guy, two hikers, then one of her officers and a local man she'd seen around town often. There was more destruction to the grass than she imagined five people would account for. She stopped and turned.

"Is this a popular spot for any reason?" she called out to Del.

"Nah. Too close to Stairsteps."

Tess could hear the water rushing down

140

the channel. The steep drop at this portion of the creek was what made the Stairsteps so spectacular. The creek came down from the mountains along a rocky path, wide in some spots but narrow here, which worked almost like a kinked hose to shoot the water toward the falls.

"The hikers were headed farther up the creek," Del continued. "They were going to try and reach the headwaters."

She nodded and kept going. There was a campground farther up, Tess knew, a backpackers' campground, rough and dry, with only a couple of pit toilets and a trail that took people up to the headwaters of Midas Creek.

The main section of Rogue's Hollow and all the businesses sat on the Rogue River, near where Midas Creek joined the river. There, fishing was good, and swimming was even possible. Since she'd stepped into the chief's shoes the first day of summer, she'd already been through two of the busiest tourist months in Rogue's Hollow. Camping, fishing, boating — you name it, people came here to the Hollow for great outdoor adventures.

Tess made her way toward the creek's edge, paying attention, looking for anything that might be evidence. She could see there was a steep bank here as the creek rushed toward the falls. People didn't raft down Midas Creek.

The creek itself was a natural boundary; on the east side was Bureau of Land Management land. Tess hadn't explored much yet, but she had read bulletins from the BLM that complained about bike riders destroying habitat. She'd not had the time or the inclination to check out their complaint.

If this was indeed a gunshot victim and he was killed here, it was doubtful anyone had heard the shot over the roar of the water. Even people on the viewing bridge below were not likely to have heard or seen anything. The Stairsteps were loud, and the view downstream less obstructed than the view upstream. Del had confirmed this was not a locals' fishing spot. One thing she'd learned in the last two months was where most of those were.

She smelled the body before she saw it, death's signature aroma, but since it was a warm afternoon, the smell would be a lot stronger in a couple of hours. Tess had viewed many homicide scenes in her career. She'd worked homicide for two years before promoting to sergeant. Her first month in homicide had the distinction of being the busiest month in the history of LBPD homicide, with thirty bodies in thirty days. Tess was baptized by fire. So nothing surprised her, and she took in the scene with a practiced, jaundiced eye.

The victim was still stiff with rigor; he hadn't been here more than twelve hours. She looked at her watch; it was close to 1 p.m. He'd been shot earlier in the day, maybe while she was dealing with Bubba. There had been a struggle. There was a circle of smashed grass, broken branches, turned-up dirt. The dead man lay on his left side, right arm flung out as if he were pointing to the river. She could see two holes in the flannel shirt on his back, and when she got closer, she saw what was probably the coup de grâce, the bullet hole in the back of his head. A row of thorny blackberry bushes likely kept him from going over the side into the rushing Midas Creek.

The dog was half-sitting, half-lying on the man's right thigh, his snout resting on the hip. Definitely a pit bull. The distinct broad forehead, powerful jaws, and dark eyes gave him away. His ears weren't cropped, though. Gang members in Long Beach often cropped their dogs' ears off with scissors or knives, leaving a jagged mess. This dog, at least, hadn't been butchered in that way.

It raised its muzzle as she approached. Tess chose to ignore it for the moment while she concentrated on the man. She kept her hand on the butt of her .45, comforted to know that caliber was not likely to bounce off the dog's head. The man looked to be in his thirties, wearing jeans and a dark flannel shirt that was torn, in addition to the bullet holes. Was that from the struggle? She could see a dark T-shirt under it.

He'd been killed here. Blood had pooled beneath him. As Tess waved away flies and looked around at the trampled grass, she wondered if this was a chance encounter or if he knew his attacker. She also wondered if she was seeing crime scene contamination courtesy of the hikers.

"Oh, my," Macpherson said and it startled Tess. The water was so loud and he'd been so quiet she'd forgotten he was with her. He'd walked up on her left and peered down at the man.

"Sorry. That's why I wanted to check things out before I brought you out here."

"It's not that. It's just . . . well, I know him. That's Glen, my wife's cousin."

15

"I like her. I think she'll do a good job."

Anna's comment shortly after Chief O'Rourke had been sworn in came back to Oliver as he watched the woman work.

"I want to make sure she feels welcome and supported here."

He'd agreed with Anna that day. The chief needed support, a fair chance to do well. So far, Oliver hadn't been disappointed. She was conscientious, careful, and smart. Her attitude with this horrible crime was confident, composed. There was no straining; she wasn't trying too hard. He saw her simply as a consummate professional in her element. She observed the entire scene, and he doubted she would miss anything.

Anna would be happy that her intuition was spot-on. He sighed as he remembered the day of O'Rourke's swearing in as a good day; they'd not yet heard the doctor's bad news. He'd not yet heard Anna doubt God and question something they'd both be-lieved in for as long as he'd known her.

Was Anna now somewhere private just sorting things out? She'd done that once before, during the first battle with cancer they fought, the one that made it impossible to ever have children. Two days passed before she let him in. Was that going on now? He prayed it was and that she'd be home when he got there.

Oliver tried to shift his thoughts to the scene at hand. He folded his arms and watched Chief O'Rourke, wondering how to help here. He knew nothing about a murder investigation, but if the chief needed something from him, he'd be ready.

Chief O'Rourke gave orders in a way that instilled confidence. Watching her delegate and organize this murder investigation, Ol-iver was even more certain that they had a winner. He wanted to share all of this with Anna. He also wanted to be the one to break the news about Glen to Anna and hoped she didn't hear it from the radio or newspaper.

After the shock of realizing that the dead man was Glen, he'd forgotten the area was a dead zone and tried calling Anna's cell. It didn't go through, and now he was frus-trated that he couldn't even leave a message that her cousin was dead. He was torn between not wanting her to hear the news on the radio and wanting her to, because maybe that would bring her home.

Then he considered the money. He knew the only way Glen could have gotten that kind of money was illegally. As he stared out at the rushing creek, he wondered, was that why he was lying here dead?

"Are you okay, Pastor?"

Oliver looked away from the creek to the concerned face of Chief O'Rourke.

"Yes. Well, as okay as possible under the circumstances." He held up his phone. "I tried to call Anna, forgot there's no signal here. It's frustrating."

She nodded, and as he observed Chief O'Rourke assessing the situation, he realized she had even more layers. Professional and she had a heart, Oliver thought, knowing that she was concerned about the dog.

"You know him — what about his dog? Is it friendly or not?" she asked.

"Glen rarely if ever came here to Rogue's Hollow to visit us. I've never met the dog, only heard about her." Oliver searched his memory. What was it Anna had told him about the dog?

"It's a female?" Chief O'Rourke asked.

"Yes, I think so. He's had her about two

years. Glen may not have had the common sense God gave a goose, but he was never cruel to animals. I think I remember Anna saying the dog was well behaved. But for the dumb name he'd given her, she was a good dog."

"Dumb name?"

"Yes, he called her Killer."

The chief placed her hands on her hips and stared at him.

"I don't recall Anna saying anything about the dog being a problem or vicious," he added lamely.

"I have rules for things, and my rule #7 applies. I think this situation requires a 'trust but verify' attitude, Pastor."

She left Oliver and he watched as she cautiously approached the dog.

After a few minutes she backed away. "The dog is hurt. She's wet and bleeding. Whoever shot the master also shot the dog," she muttered.

She was silent as she studied the dog. "Didn't I read somewhere that we have an animal advocate in this town? Someone who might be able to help with this dog? I know animal control is too far away."

"Yes, we do. Casey Reno is involved with an animal sanctuary. She might be able to help."

"Do you have her number? Can you give her a call?"

"I'll have to walk out to the road a ways for a signal."

"Would you mind?"

"Not at all." Oliver was happy to put distance between himself and Anna's dead cousin. "I'll be back in a few minutes."

He called Casey Reno, who arrived quickly. The two women huddled together and assessed the situation. He watched as they coaxed the injured dog away from his owner. It was a serious injury; Oliver could see that. The poor animal's right front leg hung uselessly and there was a lot of blood. Casey carefully led the dog to her truck and got her inside on a pile of towels. She left with the dog to take it to the vet. O'Rourke said she'd pay for the care.

The last chief wouldn't have been so kind-hearted.

While Oliver watched O'Rourke's cool competence and tried to keep his mind from anxiousness about Anna, he couldn't quell the dread building in his gut about his missing wife.

First Anna leaves, and now her cousin is found murdered.

If Oliver believed in bad omens, this would be a doozy. He also wished he'd listened closer to Anna when she'd said she needed time. Did he miss something in her tone? Her choice of words?

His thoughts snapped back to the here and now as Tess strode toward him, peeling off her latex gloves as she did.

"Okay, Pastor, I can't search his pockets until the coroner gets here, but if that is your cousin-in-law, does he live here in the Hollow?"

"His last real address was in Shady Cove. Lately, I believe he was mostly living on the streets, out of his Jeep. He had a drug problem. Anna tried to help him many a time. Nothing ever took."

Her probing gaze held his. Oliver wondered if she was full Irish. Had to be with that wild red hair and those green, green eyes. He felt as though she could see down into his soul and not miss a speck.

"He said nothing the night he gave Anna the money? Not about where he'd been or where he was going?"

"No. According to Anna, all he said was 'Only God can make this clean.' Then he fled into the darkness."

She considered this. "This makes me more concerned about Anna. We've been looking for Glen since you turned in the money. Any idea where he might have been?"

Oliver sighed, crossing his arms. "Not really. Some months ago, Anna did visit him from time to time in Shady Cove, at the last place he was living. She speaks about praying for him often, that he was wasting his life with drugs. His parents are divorced. His mother lives in Washington State but his father is still in Shady Cove."

"Would he have been with his father?"

"I doubt it. His father is not a forgiving or compassionate man."

Tess said nothing for a minute and Oliver went on.

"I think her being gone and him being here is just a coincidence."

Tess shook her head. "Sorry, I just don't believe in coincidences. Not like this. Not at all."

16

Wanting to finish everything before it got dark, Tess methodically began photographing and processing her crime scene as soon as the dog was gone. She got lucky and found a shell casing a short distance from the body. She only found one when there should have been at least three more, so it was probable the killer policed his brass. Tess was certain that someone firing a 9mm automatic handgun had shot the dog and killed Elders here, right beside the creek. With luck they'd pull a print off the casing and solve this quick. There was also a possibility that the coroner would pull a spent slug from the body that would further help them evidence-wise.

The scene wasn't giving her much. Back home she would have set up a line of officers to search the grassy area inch by inch, but here she didn't have the resources. She and Bender did the best they could. The sheriff was sending someone to pick up the body, but right now they couldn't spare any other personnel.

Bender had provided a second ID, besides Macpherson; he recognized Elders as well. Bothering Tess was the nagging indication that there had been at least two other people here with Glen. Begging the question: Were there two killers, or was there another victim to be located?

The hikers who found the body were adamant that they hadn't tramped down all the grass, likewise Arthur and Del. Del had tiptoed in to be certain the men saw what they thought they saw. The reason Arthur had driven to the station to deliver the news was because they hadn't brought phones with them, due to the area being a dead zone. Tess knew a lot of guys liked that about the creek. While they fished, they didn't want to be disturbed by phone calls.

But Tess could make out two sets of large footprints and one smaller set of tennis shoe impressions. One set of impressions matched Glen's shoes and the smaller set of tennis shoe impressions was always next to his. Most of the impressions disappeared in a mess of disturbed grass and dirt, and to Tess, that indicated a scuffle.

As she considered the body, she wondered

about Glen — homeless with a drug problem, not a good combination. Was he a loner? Did it make more sense that he'd be here alone rather than with someone? She needed to find out more about her victim.

She stepped as close to the edge of the creek as the brush would allow and watched the rushing, swirling water. In California there would be a railing here. Tess was surprised that only the Stairstep Falls were fenced off, not this rough section of the creek. But locals had told her that besides the fact this was a wilderness area — and who would be crazy enough to try to fence off all the wild? — most everyone respected the power of the creek.

Bending over the ravine, hearing and watching the rushing water gave Tess pause. Did another victim fall over the side into that crashing gully? There was an opening here in the thick brush — narrow, but there nonetheless. Her eye caught a flutter of fabric snared in the blackberry thorns. She knelt down and stretched as far as she could, the creek roaring in her ears. At nearly the very end of her reach, she grasped the fabric and pulled it free. A couple of inches long, it was a shred of flowered flannel. Definitely not from Glen's clothing.

She frowned, looking down at the churning water. Did someone fall in here? If they did, was there any possibility they survived?

Rule #4: "Never assume." They had to find out, and fast.

"Find something?" Bender yelled to be heard over the water and startled her as he appeared at her side.

She jerked toward him. He'd been respectful and helpful so far, and Tess hoped she was making headway with the man.

"I found this." She stood and held the fabric up for him to see. "There's a possibility someone went over, into the creek here and on to the Stairsteps. Anyone ever survive that?"

His eyes narrowed. "Once or twice, but they get all banged up. I've lived here all my life, and mostly, you go over the falls, you die. If someone fell in here, odds are that if their body hasn't already been seen, it will be soon. It would hit the Rogue, head downriver, where there are tons of fishermen and rafters. Someone will see it."

"We need to check. I heard Pounder log on, didn't I?"

He nodded, then anticipated her next question. "You want him to check out the viewing platform?"

"Yes. Ask him to take a look. I don't think anyone could get out of the creek until after the Stairsteps; the banks are too steep."

"That's about right."

"Okay, then notify the sheriff, tell him we think someone went in. They can check farther downstream or let us know if the body has already been seen and we just haven't heard yet."

"Right away." He stepped away and she heard him relay her instructions.

This was the most time Tess had spent with Bender on a serious call. She realized that when he cooperated and did the job, he was good at it.

"Curtis is on his way to the viewing platform, and the sheriff copied our request. They'll put the word out, check downriver. If someone did fall in here, we should know soon."

Tess nodded. If there was a second victim/ witness to this mess, she or he was most likely dead like Glen. She continued to peruse the ground around the body and saw a glint of something. She knelt down, hoping for another casing, but what she found was a bit of metal, burnished bronze in color, maybe a broken key chain. She held it up, turned it over in her hands. It looked like three letters, part of an *o*, then *SS*.

She looked at Bender and held up the bit. "You recognize this?"

He stepped forward. "Platinum Security Systems." He pulled a matching key chain out of his pocket. "I've got one. Beto Acosta gives them out like candy."

With the whole thing intact, she could see that it was a *PSS*. What she held had broken off from the *P*.

"Hand me an evidence bag. Maybe it belonged to our killer."

He opened a bag for her to drop the broken key chain inside.

"Coroner is en route." Bender repeated what she'd heard the radio say.

She acknowledged his statement with a nod, knowing that her small department would be the lead investigators on this homicide, according to what she'd read in the procedures manual. But Jackson County had deputies and a detective ready to help smaller agencies with all major crimes.

"Are we going to handle this or give it over to the SO?" he asked, hands on his Sam Browne, appraising her, a little of his snootiness back.

Bender was basically in the middle when it came to seniority on her police force. Del had twenty-five years; Pounder, her sergeant, had twelve; the newest officer, Martin Getz, had two years on. Bender was at seven. Of all the people she'd want to work a homicide with, it wasn't Bender. But he was here, and he was working hard, and his plans to leave notwithstanding, Tess wasn't going to be petty and push him aside for someone she got along with better. She was going to work with Bender.

The fact that no one could remember when the small town had had a homicide meant all the officers would be green.

Sure, there were always deaths to deal with. Tess had, in her short tenure, handled two accidental river drownings and one fatal car accident.

As for Bender, aside from his obvious resentment over her appointment, Tess had been impressed by the quality of his work, his reports, and his overall hard-charging attitude. Trim and wiry, Bender would have fit in on LBPD. With his close-cropped dark hair and a neatly trimmed mustache with a small hint of gray, he could be on any recruiting poster.

She shrugged. "We may need some assistance, but I worked homicide in Long Beach for a couple of years. I think I can handle this. What about you? You up to doing some detective work?"

His features and body language changed almost imperceptibly. "You mean me being a backwoods hick and all?"

"That's not what I meant." Anger flared and Tess fought to keep her composure. She'd never insinuated any such thing, had she? "But if that's what you think of your abilities, maybe I should call in Sergeant Pounder."

"I'm a cop, a good one. I can handle this."

"That's what I thought," Tess said in a measured tone. "And I may know how to run a homicide investigation, but you know the area and the procedures much better —" She was interrupted by a commotion behind her.

"I demand to know why I wasn't notified about this sooner!"

"Sir, you can't go in there. This is a crime scene." Del had his hands full, but he was properly forceful. Tess saw why. Douglas Dixon, the chicken-chested mayor of Rogue's Hollow, was trying to force his way into the crime scene.

Tess sighed and counted to ten. She should have known she couldn't put this off for long. She'd worked with her share of micromanagers while in Long Beach, but she was learning that Dixon was a micro-manager on steroids. He was a Dr. Jekyll and Mr. Hyde. Supportive but hands-off one minute and a hovering nanny the next. Tess tried to cut him slack. She knew his wife was disabled and he was the primary caregiver. You can't be all bad and take care of an ailing wife.

Funny, no one warned her about him. Addie Getz, the woman who ran the inn where Tess was currently living until she found something more permanent, had told her of the narrow margin by which she had been hired, and that one of the dissenting voters might try to undermine her. But it wasn't Dixon Addie was worried about; it was Cole Markarov.

"Watch out for Markarov," she'd said. *"He's a horrible chauvinist. He even calls his wife 'the little woman.' "*

Tess remembered Markarov from her interview. A jerk, pure and simple. But she'd seen little of the man since her hire, while Dixon seemed to always be listening to the scanner. He'd appeared at just about every major scene. She'd been surprised he hadn't popped up at Bubba's. He had a funny way of showing his support.

"Chief O'Rourke, Chief O'Rourke! Why was I not notified about this crime? Why did I have to hear about it on the scanner? And is this officer here on overtime? We can't afford that. Why didn't you call Jackson County for assistance?"

Dixon was in his sixties with a potbelly

and a mostly bald head. Thankfully he didn't employ a comb-over, but what he did do struck Tess as just as odd. He wore what hair he did have long, in a braid that went halfway down his back.

Tess had deferred to him at every incident before this. But something snapped now. This was a homicide; she was not going to let him muck up the investigation. If it got her fired, so be it.

"Mr. Dixon, I'm in the middle of a murder investigation. That requires my concentration and attention. It makes no sense to stop in the middle of what I'm doing to phone you. Now please step back behind the yellow tape before you contaminate my crime scene."

"Wh-what did you say?" Dixon turned crimson. For a second he reminded Tess of a cartoon character about to blow his stack. She didn't have time to coddle him. In Long Beach even the mayor knew better than to invade a homicide scene.

Pastor Macpherson stepped forward. "Doug, the chief knows her job. There is no need for you to interfere."

She'd forgotten the pastor was there. He'd been conversing with the hikers.

"Why is Pastor Macpherson here?"

Tess swallowed a chuckle at the whiny,

petulant tone in the man's voice.

She brought a hand to her mouth to compose herself, then said, "Pastor Macpherson came along in the hopes of helping us ID the victim. He has since proven a big help in calming down the hikers who found the body."

"Who is the victim?" The mayor's voice took an anxious tone. Tess wondered at that. It was almost as if he feared her answer.

"We believe he's a homeless man. Glen Elders. Do you know him?"

Dixon relaxed somewhat but frowned. "I've heard the name. He's a druggie, isn't he?"

Tess nodded. "So I've been told. Please don't share that information with anyone. I don't want the next of kin to hear about this on the news."

"Of course, of course."

"Del was off duty when he was flagged down about the body by a civilian. It made sense to keep him here to secure the scene. The sheriff is stretched thin today but someone will be here as soon as they can to collect the body. Until then I want the crime scene closed, so I need my people. Is there a reason you want to walk into my scene and disturb the dead body?"

He huffed. "I don't want to disturb anything. But I am the mayor. You are required to keep me up to date on what is happening in my town!"

"I would have called you when I got back to the station."

Bender waved at Tess. He'd heard the chatter on the radio while Tess had missed it. "Chief, the coroner is here. Can't get in because the mayor's car is blocking the way."

Tess turned to Dixon and arched an eyebrow. "Mr. Mayor?"

Flustered, he said, "I'll move my car. But I want a full accounting of this incident as soon as you return to your office." He wagged his finger at her before turning on his heel and stomping away.

"He bother you at every crime scene?" Oliver Macpherson asked.

"Goes with the territory, I think."

Sergeant Pounder down at the viewing platform asked for Tess on the radio. "Chief, I don't see anything here, but the light is getting bad. It's shady here. If you're sure someone went into the creek, we'll need to walk the banks."

"You think someone went in the water?" Oliver asked.

"It's a possibility."

"Chief." Del stepped up. "I'll walk the east

bank. Been fishing this creek nearly twenty years. Don't mind taking a look."

"Thanks, Del. I'll submit overtime for you. Meet Sergeant Pounder at the viewing platform; he should walk the west bank."

He nodded and left for his truck.

Tess turned to Oliver. "How are the hikers doing?" When she'd conducted her interviews with the men, she'd noted that one of them was having a hard time dealing with the fact he'd found a murder victim.

"Still quite a bit shocked, but they've settled down."

Tess nodded. "Thank you. They can go now. I'll tell them. As soon as the body is removed, I can ask Arthur or Gabe to take you home."

"I appreciate that."

"Have you thought any more about filing that report on your wife?" Tess hoped her thoughts on coincidences had sunk in. She was already nursing a bad feeling about Anna.

He gave her a thoughtful look, then a resigned sigh. "Let me wait a bit. As soon as I get home, if she's not there, I'll ask a friend to check into the cabin at Union Creek. And I'll pray. If she just needs time, I'd hate to step on that."

Tess had to be satisfied with that. As the

sheriff's van backed in, she left the pastor to his thoughts and went back to her homicide. She frowned when she realized that someone had died on her anniversary after all.

17

Del and Curtis spent two hours, until it was dark, below the Stairsteps and found nothing. Dixon was furious.

"Waste of money! No one would survive going over the Stairsteps. And if someone had fallen in and died, the body would have been seen by now. You're not even certain someone did fall in. You wasted their time and our money." He continued on, repeating his lecture about public service overtime budgeting and spending.

Tess barely listened and let him rant. In her way of thinking, money or no, it was more prudent to be safe, not sorry. *Never assume.*

After he left, she and Bender went to work on the homicide. She'd given him a brief in-service on running a homicide investigation, careful with her tone and manner now that she knew at least part of what bothered him, and then left him to make sure all the evidence was sent to the state crime lab in Salem. Since she'd trusted him with that task, would he thaw?

Sheriff's personnel notified Glen Elders's father in person about the death, but Tess had spoken with him by phone, as well as several other family members. She pulled a rolling whiteboard into her office to begin a murder board and started a timeline, but by 2 a.m. she was too spent to do much more and she called it a night.

Before leaving the office, she checked her phone for text messages she'd had to ignore earlier. She and her friend Jeannie tried to text one another at least once a day and there was a Hello, how you doing? text from her. There were also a couple from Jack O'Reilly. He sent her regular updates about the search for the three individuals who'd run away the night of the shooting. He finally had at least one name, and he and Ben were confident this lead would go somewhere.

Tess sighed after she read that, not wanting to get her hopes up. In any event, she was due to return to Long Beach in the near future. Word was that a wrongful death civil lawsuit from Cullen Hoover's family was coming anytime now. And Tess's lawyer had advised her to be prepared to come back and give a deposition.

It wasn't the deposition that worried Tess. Most nights, it was the part of her that was afraid if she did go back to Long Beach, even for a painful deposition, she'd never return to Rogue's Hollow. She'd find some hole to crawl into and hide.

But right now, exhausted, mind spinning with the homicide investigation, when considering a trip to Long Beach, Tess couldn't help but think to herself, *I have to solve this murder first.*

Yawning, Tess couldn't wait to get to bed and close her eyes — when she returned to her room at the Rogue's Hollow Inn. She hadn't yet found a home to rent or purchase, though she hadn't even really looked. Adeline and Klaus Getz, the couple who owned and ran the inn, had graciously offered her their best room at a reduced rate until she did find a place. They were the only other couple besides the Macphersons who'd worked to make Tess feel at home. Addie had mentioned that the old chief had been rather lazy by the end of his career.

Klaus had muttered, "The man made donuts and police more of a truism."

Addie had shot her husband a glare and said, "The force will probably run a whole lot smoother now."

Their welcome and kindness toward Tess did take the sting out of Dixon's pushiness and the cold shoulder she got from some of the cops who now worked for her, notably Gabe. Since the burst of anger when for some reason he'd thought she assumed him to be a backwoods hick, he'd been all cop, and for that Tess was grateful.

She was dead on her feet when she unlocked the door to her room and switched on the light. And at the moment she was talked out and glad for the quiet, solitary room.

All that was on her mind was a shower and bed. But an out-of-place item caught her eye right away.

There on her nightstand sat a card with her name on it propped in front of a cupcake — her favorite, she bet, carrot cake. She dropped her bag on the floor and stepped to the bed. Picking up the cupcake, she smelled it and smiled. Addie baked the best carrot cake Tess had ever tasted, and she had told her so. She opened the card.

Happy two-month anniversary! So glad to have you here!

Tess had to sit down and read all the names on the card. Some of them she

169

couldn't put a face to, had only heard the name before. A quilting club met in the inn restaurant every Monday morning and they'd all signed it. A couple of people in the city council signed it, and a couple of cops, notably Martin Getz and Becky Jonkey. So had Oliver and Anna Macpherson. She was touched and a lump rose in her throat. At least a few people trusted her; they believed in her. The last thing Tess wanted to do was let them down. But as always when she got back to her room at night and sat by herself, the specter of the shooting would rise up and bite her in the throat. It still scorched that she'd been run out of town.

You can't do this job. What if it happens again?

You were only a commander. What makes you think you can be chief?

Something will happen; you'll blow it eventually.

You're only running away.

Tess sniffled and wiped her nose. She rose from the bed and began to shed her clothes to take a shower. *I did nothing wrong,* she insisted to herself while she let the water warm up, trying to ignore how that fact hadn't helped her case. She stepped under the stream of warm water, letting it run over her tired and aching shoulder. She even noticed a few bruises from tackling Bubba.

"You won't last two weeks in that hick town," Paul had said. She could still hear his taunting voice in her head. *"You'll be begging for a spot parking cars somewhere back here before long. I know you."*

"You don't know me as well as you think you do," she muttered out loud, though the argument was months ago and Paul was miles away.

Now, even as she fought the desire to run back home and never return to this Rogue River town, she thought, *I'd tell him. I'd show him. I've been here two months and at least some people like me, support me. I'm not going to beg for anything.*

18

When he got home and had a strong signal, Oliver left a voice mail message for Anna, asking her to call, saying it was urgent and it concerned Glen. Then he barely slept. Friday morning, after tossing and turning, he finally gave up and got out of bed in predawn darkness, memories of Anna, and of her unfortunate cousin, shredding his thoughts. He would call the chief, make a report. This was too unlike his wife. Then he finally got a text from Anna.

Will call you soon was all it said, but it did Oliver's heart good.

He texted back, Please hurry, I miss you, and stared at the phone, hoping for more from her, but nothing else came.

Keeping the phone near, he spent the next hour in prayer. But by the time the early morning sun was bright in the sky, he'd heard no more from Anna. He had a men's Bible study to lead that morning, so he couldn't stay in prayer by the phone for the whole day, which was what he wanted to do. It was a relief that she'd finally contacted him and he understood Anna's need for private prayer on one hand, but on the other hand, wasn't this a point in their lives where they needed to pray together? He pleaded with God for an answer. Where was his wife?

"God has turned a deaf ear."

Why was God so silent lately? The answer to that question was not forthcoming.

At least it was Friday and he wouldn't be headed into the church office right away and have to answer questions about where Anna was. On Fridays his day started with a men's breakfast and study that was held in the fellowship hall. Klaus Getz cooked for the thirty-five or so regulars who attended, and Oliver already had a message written. If Anna called, he'd answer, even if it meant stopping his message in the middle.

As he showered and dressed, checking the phone over and over, he began to wonder at the text. Anna would know that he had the breakfast to lead. Why send a cryptic message like that? It wasn't like her to text instead of call in the first place. By the time he was ready to leave, the text gave him more anxiety than peace. She'd not acknowledge the message he left about Glen.

True, he hadn't told her about the murder, but why not respond concerning her cousin?

Oliver decided that if he could make it through this breakfast, he would call Chief O'Rourke and talk to her about the text — if Anna hadn't called by then.

His chest was tight with emotion as he crossed a path he'd walked so many times over the years. The river, the church, the town — all played a part in the life they'd built here. He and Anna had shepherded this church their whole married life. It was more than home, more than just work. It was a large, diverse extended family. He prayed as he walked through the property he loved, flashes of events over the years that he and Anna had been part of. They'd grown up here. Happy events, weddings, baby showers; and sad events, funerals, memorial services. He laid his fears out in his prayers, asking for clarity for whatever actually came.

Oliver had never found it easy to let go, usually struggled to lay his petitions before God and move on, but still he tried. Letting his worry for Anna go and trusting the Lord was like cutting off his own arm with a dull knife.

As he stopped at a point next to the river, before he'd turn away onto the path for the fellowship hall, he gazed out at the powerful, rolling river. The sight calmed him, strengthened him. He could always trust the river to do that. And he knew he could always trust God to order his life. It all came down to simple trust. His whole life would be a lie if he couldn't trust God at this most painful and personal part of it.

Rogue's Hollow Community Church had a storied history. The main sanctuary was one of the oldest buildings in town, and it occupied the town center on a choice piece of land with river frontage. The church maintained a beautiful park on its section of the mighty Rogue River. This portion of the river, thick with the confluence of Midas Creek, was calm and steady. People came from all over Oregon in the summer to hold weddings and other outdoor events in the park.

Originally a sawmill, the main structure had been turned into a church in the late 1960s, several years after a big flood had washed away a good portion of the mill and damaged the rest, effectively putting it out of business. The fellowship hall was a newer structure, something Oliver added during his tenure as head pastor. The church offices were all above the hall. The small house Oliver and Anna shared was originally the mill office and had been spared by the flood because it sat on higher ground. It was protected by a retaining wall, but since the dam went in at Lost Creek in 1977, the flood threat had been lessened, if not solved completely. Only twice since the dam was built had there been high waters, but they'd done no damage.

The office was renovated into a parsonage in the seventies. Oliver and Anna had extensively remodeled the home when they first arrived at the church to make it more comfortable and homey for the children that never came.

Feeling stronger, Oliver continued on. As he reached the fellowship hall, he could see by the number of vehicles in the parking lot that many men had already arrived. It was a good group. A few came all the way from Medford for this Friday breakfast and study. He loved the mixture of people and personalities in his congregation. From a wealthy business owner to a disabled Vietnam veteran and everything in between attended on Sundays, and it was Oliver's passion to deliver the full counsel of God and truly shepherd his flock.

The smell of bacon tickled his nostrils as he opened the back door of the hall to enter through the kitchen. There bacon was sizzling, eggs cooking, and hash browns frying, a regular artery-clogging, wonderfully tasting old-fashioned breakfast.

"Morning, Klaus. It smells delicious."

The big German turned and flashed a grin, waving his spatula. "Good morning, Pastor Mac! I hope you brought a good appetite today."

"You bet." He clapped Klaus on the shoulder and continued into the hall, where tables were filling up. All the regulars were here and one or two who weren't so regular. Mayor Dixon walked in with a stride that told Oliver he was going to get an earful.

"Oliver, can I have a word with you, please?"

Not knowing how to avoid the man, Oliver nodded. "Only have a minute before Klaus puts breakfast on the table."

Dixon pulled him out the side door. "I don't think it's fitting for you to undermine my authority in front of the new police chief." He pursed his lips like he always did when he was upset.

"I don't believe that I did undermine your authority. I simply pointed out that we hired the woman to do a job and we have to let her do it." Dismayed, Oliver shoved his hands in his pockets. Cocking his head, he said, "You pushed for her hire, telling us

177

she was the most qualified candidate. Have you changed your mind?"

"No, I haven't. But there is a learning curve to the way we do things here — you know that. She needs to follow the procedures outlined by the council." He punctuated almost every word by pointing his index finger. "That includes notifying me of major incidents."

"I'm not a cop or a mayor, but it seems to me the first thing you'd want her to do is her job, which is to handle law enforcement issues. That's what she was doing. I'm sure she would have notified you in due course."

"Due course? What if she misses something or makes a bad decision? That reflects on the entire council — why, on the whole town, for heaven's sake. I stuck my neck out. Besides, maybe if they'd watched her more closely in Long Beach, what happened there would not have happened."

The clanging bell that signaled breakfast was ready rang out loud and clear, and Oliver praised God silently. Placing a hand on Dixon's shoulder, he said, "Now, we hired the woman because she was qualified. We owe her the chance to show her stuff, do her job. Why don't we let her? Breakfast is ready. You joining us?"

The mayor's expression went petulant.

"I've business to attend to this morning."

Dixon turned on his heel and left Oliver standing by the side door, scratching his head over one of Dixon's comments. *"If they'd watched her more closely"?*

He realized that Tess had better be good because the mayor would not allow any room for error. But when he considered how she had handled herself yesterday, he decided Dixon was the one who needed to watch his step.

19

Tess tried to slip out of the inn quietly, without breakfast, but she wasn't quick enough. Addie caught her. The feminine half of the innkeeping team was a large, big-boned woman, gray-blonde hair always pulled back neatly into a bun and covered with a net or a scarf. She smiled easily and often, not at all concerned about the large gap between her front teeth. Her eyes were a pale, washed-out blue but nonetheless sharp. Tess got the impression that nothing got past Addie.

"Make you an omelet this morning?"

Hand on the doorknob, Tess turned. "Aw, Addie, I hate to put you to any trouble."

"It's no trouble. This is a restaurant, for heaven's sake. Now come find a table and I'll get you some coffee. You're too thin to be skipping breakfast."

Tess sighed and did as she was told. Though physically very different, Addie reminded her of her own mother, and Mom never took no for an answer. Tess headed toward a table on the waterside so she could watch the river. The one place she could look when the desire to run back to Long Beach hit. Something about watching the strong current, the smooth and continuously rolling river, calmed Tess, mesmerized her. The view from her room at the inn was spectacular. It was no small thing to her that Addie and Klaus gave her their best room during the height of tourist season.

If Addie and Klaus were special, so was the inn itself. Built in the late 1960s, it was a rustic structure, part log and part plank with big picture windows in the dining room overlooking the water. There were a few tourists and several regulars already seated in the dining room. Victor Camus was one face she recognized right away. He was an outdoor guide specializing in hunting and probably the only man she'd met so far who intimidated her. He wasn't a tall man, but he was broad and rough edged like an old-fashioned mountain man. A deep scar on the left side of his chin gave him a dangerous air. His steel-gray hair was kept short and neat. It wasn't that he'd ever been mean or rude; it was just obvious he was a no-nonsense, don't-mess-with-me kind of guy.

He reminded her of a sergeant she'd had in the academy, a Vietnam vet, a man who had pushed her to her absolute limit, and someone she would always respect. Victor certainly had a sterling reputation as a hunter's hunter. Groups he led always came back with a deer or an elk or whatever it was they were seeking.

At least that's what Tess had been told. Hunting was a new aspect to consider here, something just not talked about in California, but very popular in southern Oregon. Tess got a little queasy when she considered killing deer or elk and then cutting them up to bring home. And she'd already responded to several vehicle versus deer or elk or cow calls, which were always bloody messes. No, she might fit in eventually, but not by becoming a hunter.

She nodded Victor's way as she sat down and got an almost-imperceptible solemn nod in return.

At the other occupied table was the group of regulars Tess knew made up the quilting club. She gave them a smile and worked to remember their names. *Gladys, Alana, Linda, Helen, and Ruby.* She couldn't clearly remember who was who, but she was sure those were the names because they'd been on her card, so her smile was heartfelt.

Addie soon arrived at her table with coffee. "You got in late last night. I hear we had a murder. Glen Elders."

Tess sipped her coffee, working to get used to the light-speed fashion in which news traveled around this small town. What was it Anna had called it? The Rogue telegraph? But then her youngest officer, Martin Getz, was Addie's nephew, so it was no secret where Addie had heard the news.

"Word sure travels fast around here. Yes, we did. Poor guy. I contacted next of kin, and you know what his dad said?"

Addie cocked an eyebrow and harrumphed. "I can imagine. I knew the Elders family; they used to live up on Broken Wheel. I remember Glen when he was just a bit." She held her hand out flat to indicate the height of a child.

This got Tess's attention. She'd learned that Broken Wheel was the high-rent district in Rogue's Hollow with the most expensive houses. The Peabodys' home was at the end of the street. It was the biggest house, a mansion really, with acreage that backed up to forest. Thinking of the Peabodys made Tess remember Duncan racing through town yesterday. She really needed to speak to the Peabodys about their son, but at the moment, the murder took precedence.

She wondered what Addie knew about Glen Elders.

"The Elders family has money?" Tess asked, holding her coffee mug in two hands as Addie answered.

"They did. But then came divorce, and it was nasty. He tried to hide assets; she tried to take every penny she could. In the end they divided the proceeds from the sale of the house and he quit his job, saying he wouldn't work to pay half of it to her as alimony. He bought a place in a shabby trailer park and filed for food stamps. She tried to do right by the kids and got married again, but she sure had poor taste in men." Addie tsked. "Probably why Glen turned out the way that he did. What did Pa have to say?"

"Just that he was sorry but he really couldn't be bothered; then he hung up."

Addie arched an eyebrow. "It was always amazing to me that they were any relation at all to Anna Macpherson. That woman and her parents are good people, kind people."

Tess grunted. "Yeah, I heard he was a cousin. Had you seen him around here lately?"

"No, but you should talk to Forest. Glen had an old Jeep that always needed work.

Forest was his go-to guy for repairs. That Forest is a softie. Sometimes I'm amazed he stays in business because he falls for every hard-luck story there is. Now, what kind of omelet?"

"Thanks for the tip, and how about just a bowl of oatmeal?"

"With walnuts, raisins, and a glass of milk?"

"Yeah." Tess nodded, not wanting to argue. Both Addie and Klaus thought she needed to put on some pounds. She hated to admit she liked the fussing. She hadn't been fussed over in longer than she could remember. Her mother wasn't a fusser; that had been more her father. And Paul only ever fussed over himself.

Pulling out her notebook, she wrote down Forest's name. He was almost as interesting as Victor but not nearly as intimidating. On her first day in uniform he'd seen her at the coffee shop and commented on her car. He'd been very pleasant, really liked Tess's convertible.

"Wow, nice open-top coupe. SLC Roadster, right? Brand-new?"

"Yep, six months old."

"Sweet. You ever want to part with it, let me know."

Forest reminded Tess of a hippie. Even his

full name said free spirit — Forest Wild. Not his given name, no; she'd been told he legally changed his name the day he turned eighteen. He wore his hair long and was given to donning tie-dye shirts. She'd heard that he could fix anything, but he specialized in motorcycles. There was even a rumor floating around that in his youth he rode with the Hells Angels motorcycle gang. He did have a lot of tattoos, but they were mostly faded and unreadable and she'd never asked him if that tale was true. But he was a colorful guy and she made a note to talk to him about Glen Elders.

One intriguing aspect of moving to a small town like Rogue's Hollow was the information highway and the few degrees of separation. Almost everybody knew one another and there were a lot of relations, brothers, cousins, and grandparents. Though she'd met several transplants like herself, most folks were tied to the area by history. She'd met two families who resided on property their distant relatives had homesteaded after traveling across the country in covered wagons.

All of this made for a less transient attitude in people than she'd found in Long Beach. People here were a part of their community, connected. Tess envied that feeling.

"Chief O'Rourke, can I have a word with you?"

Tess looked up, and there stood Casey Reno, the animal advocate. She was also the owner of Rogue's Hollow Bookstore and Notions. Tess loved to read and had stopped at the bookstore once or twice, though she had scant little time to read any of the books she picked up. And Reno had given her a decidedly cold shoulder. Tess tried not to be paranoid, but she was certain Reno's standoffishness was because of the shooting in Long Beach. One of these days she planned on asking the woman just what the problem was, but not today. Today, seeing Reno reminded Tess of the dog.

"Oh, uh, sure. I was going to call you when I got to the office. How's the dog?"

"She lost her right front leg," Reno said, holding a sixteen-ounce cup of coffee from the Hollow Grind, a coffee shop across the street, and looking uncomfortable. "But she'll live."

Tess saw a pretty girl, a younger version of Reno, maybe in her early teens, standing near the door to the restaurant. She looked familiar and Tess figured that she'd probably seen her at the local market. She'd learned since her hire that the market was a summertime hangout for teens.

Reno noticed her gaze. "My daughter, Kayla."

Tess cleared her throat. "Why don't you have a seat. I see you already have coffee." There was a bit of an awkward silence.

Reno cast a glance back at Kayla and gave the girl a slight nod before sitting. "I have a busy day planned, but I wanted to talk to you first." She hesitated, stiffly, on the edge of a chair.

She was probably a couple of years older than Tess. Her long hair was grayer than any other color and she wore no makeup to cover her wrinkles. But the wrinkles said this was a woman who laughed a lot and enjoyed life. Tess remembered that when Casey got the dog into her truck, she flashed a smile, and laugh lines and dimples made the years fall away. She bet that Casey was a fun person to be around.

Reno looked away and then looked back at Tess. "She really is a sweet dog. Dr. Fox couldn't believe how well behaved she was when she had to be in such pain."

Tess had that feeling when they approached the dog. Pit bulls could look so scary. And a dog named Killer? She was thickly muscled, certainly powerful, and with pain obvious in her eyes. She hated to admit to Reno she'd been ready to shoot the dog. But the bookstore owner had managed to lead the dog away from Elders without causing so much as a whimper.

"I'm glad to hear it." Tess wondered what made Reno so uncomfortable and if there was anything she could do to alleviate her discomfort.

"You probably won't be when you get the bill." Reno shook her head. "I still don't understand why you don't just bill the city. It's all work related."

"Mayor Dixon explained the budget to me. I'm pretty sure a vet bill for saving a dog isn't in there."

This seemed to relax her a bit and Reno gave a wry smile. "As a council member, I know you're right, but when it comes to animals, well . . ." Her voice trailed off and she cleared her throat. "Thank you for calling me. And don't take this personally — I just need to get this out there, clear the air as it were. I was a no vote when it came to hiring you."

Tess leaned back, not sure what to say. She remembered Casey being somewhat hostile at the interview — not as bad as Markarov, but not friendly either. And she knew the vote for her hire was close but hadn't really thought much about it. The overwhelming nature of the reason she'd ever left Long Beach dominated her thinking. Besides, she'd been hired. It was up to her now to do a good job.

"As a mother, it's hard for me to get past the fact that you shot a fourteen-year-old. I'm trying to — I mean, I want to get past it, but . . ."

Tess had no response. But after a few seconds, Reno continued.

"When I step into my city council shoes, I can now say I was wrong to vote no. You've done a great job for the two months you've been here. And yesterday . . . well, as an animal lover, I truly appreciate you saving Killer's life when you would not have been faulted for killing her. I know Chief Bailey would have shot her without a second thought. I hope that someday I'll be able to look at things differently from my role as a mom." She met Tess's gaze. "I'm behind you from the city council side. I just wanted you to know that."

Tess fought the emotion that welled up inside. Addie, Klaus, and the Macphersons had all extended the hand of friendship, but no one else came close. Now, for this woman, who admitted voting against her, to say that she regretted it made a permanent place here seem possible.

"Mrs. Reno, I —"

"Please, it's Casey."

"Casey, I don't fault you for not voting for me. After all the press, well . . ." She stopped short of saying she'd been afraid she would never find a job in law enforcement. "I hope to be able to prove I'm not the monster the cable news networks tried to make me."

"I can see that now, and I guess Long Beach's loss is our gain. Oh, and I nearly forgot." She reached into her purse and pulled out a baggie with a note attached. "Dr. Fox plucked this out of the dog's mangled leg. He actually dropped it off at my house late last night. Kind of amazing it was still there."

Tess considered that. When she'd arrived on scene, she'd thought the dog looked wet, that she'd been in the creek. Was it really possible she did fall in, and not only did the bullet stay with her, but she wasn't drowned?

"God was watching out for that little one," Casey said with a look of awe in her eyes.

Tess took the baggie and her spirits soared. Not about the God talk, but about the fact that the vet had the presence of mind to write down where he'd gotten the slug, what day and what time, and that it was him and him alone who handled the

191

slug and sealed it into the baggie. Talk about preserving the chain of evidence. He'd even noted the time he'd given the baggie to Casey.

"I don't know about miracles or God, but this is awesome. Let me write down the time and date you gave it to me and have you sign it as well."

They did that and Tess put it in her bag, making a mental note to send it to the crime lab in Salem as soon as possible.

Casey smiled. "As much as I'm gratified to have come to the conclusion that you'll be an asset to Rogue's Hollow, I really don't want to be a part of any more of your interesting days. I think I can go the whole rest of my life without seeing any more dead bodies. I didn't know Glen that well, but I had stopped him to pet that dog once or twice. I had nightmares about his body."

Tess nodded knowingly. "I understand. I'm sorry you had to be involved at all. It was Pastor Macpherson who told me you were the animal person."

Casey held her hand up. "Don't apologize for that. I'm glad to have helped. I'm involved with an animal sanctuary out in Ruch, and I'd probably come to another crime scene if it meant saving an animal, but that was disturbing."

She made a face and Tess smiled. She liked Casey Reno.

"That's why I own a bookstore," Casey continued. "My murder and mayhem is all fictional."

"I can understand that sentiment. I like the fictional stuff as well."

"I noticed that, and I have to say, a lot of the books you've shown an interest in are books I've read or I want to read — crime, mystery, and craziness. In print, just not in person."

Tess gave her a thumbs-up. "I've always loved to read. First horse books, then some science fiction, now action, thrillers, and mysteries."

"Is that why you became a cop?"

"Not really. My granddad and my dad were both cops. I like to think it's in my blood. It's always been the only job I've wanted. To me it's interesting, rewarding work."

Casey's gaze went somber. "Even after what happened in Long Beach?"

Tess sucked in a breath and batted her coffee cup from one hand to the other. She fought to keep her face from showing she felt gut-punched. It wasn't that she thought the subject would never come up — Casey herself had just referenced it — but in two months, this was the first direct inquiry and she'd not been prepared.

Casey must have sensed her discomfort and started to backtrack.

Tess raised a hand. "It's okay. I expect people are curious about that mess. But I did my job. I won't apologize for that." *Or get defensive,* she thought. "I deeply regret I had to take a life, but he gave me no other choice. I hashed it out with the department shrink, and I know in my heart there was nothing else I could have done that night." Her eyes met Casey's, and Tess saw no judgment or pity there.

Casey looked away. "I will admit, after all the press — at least what I saw and read — I imagined you were a trigger-happy, cold-hearted monster, but I know now you're not that person. I hope it hasn't been difficult. I mean . . . well, I really hope *I* haven't made it difficult for you to fit in here."

Tess ignored the pinch of self-pity as Casey's words hit home. It had been hard, but she'd tried to ignore the snubs, the side glances. But she wasn't going to whine about it.

"I've been busy learning a whole new system," she said with a shrug. "That's all I can do, my job. I can't worry about what people think of me."

"Fair enough."

Addie interrupted by returning to refill Tess's coffee cup and to ask if Casey wanted to order breakfast.

"I can't stay. Kayla is waiting," Casey said as she stood. "My daughter and I are on a field trip today, on our way to Crater Lake."

"Thank you for giving me the update on the dog, and the evidence. I appreciate it."

"I'm glad I could help. If you need to find a home for the dog, let me know."

"I will, after I'm certain none of the family wants her. I've notified the next of kin. And I'll be asking people about Glen, trying to find anyone who can tell me what he was doing here. Besides the dog, did you say that you didn't know Glen well?"

"I've only seen him around, said hello; that's about it. And I heard Anna talk about him, asking for prayer, mostly. I spoke to him a couple of times only because I liked the dog. I never met a dog I couldn't say hello to. But he wasn't a reader, so he never came into the shop." Casey slapped her forehead. "Wait a second. I did see him a few days ago, last week maybe. Thursday."

Tess sat up straight as Addie set her breakfast down. "You did? Where?"

"He must have been coming from Forest's. The bookstore is next door to Wild Automotive."

"Right." Tess knew that. "Did you speak to him?"

"No, he was on his cell phone. He stopped for a minute in front of the shop. I could see he was having an animated conversation with someone."

"If you saw him, then someone else must have as well." Tess thought about the layout of the town, trying to visualize where Glen might have gone next. She was still in the process of learning the ebb and flow of the place. "Do you have any idea where he might have gone? Somewhere in town maybe?"

Casey shrugged. "Could have gone to the church, to see Anna."

Tess shook her head. "I've spoken to the pastor. No luck there."

"That's right. Pastor Mac was there with you when you found Glen. Well, Glen was friends with Cole Markarov. Maybe he got a room at Charlie's."

"Markarov?" Tess wondered if he'd be a help or a hindrance.

"Yeah." Casey let out a heavy sigh. "Ashamed to say I voted with him. He's childish at times. And a chauvinist. Beware."

"I've heard that from Addie as well, and

I've met my share of those."

"I bet that you have." Casey said good-bye and left the inn.

Casey had given her a good lead. Charlie's was Charlie's Place, a bed-and-breakfast at the farthest edge of the town, the only private business on the east side of Midas Creek. There was a state-run concession and a couple of campgrounds past Charlie's Place, but that area was state owned, not Tess's responsibility.

Right after her swearing in, Tess had read a book about Rogue's Hollow written by a local historian. The beautiful Victorian mansion that was now Charlie's Place had a large role in that history. The home had a storied past and it was built practically on top of what had given the town its name.

Perched on a rise overlooking the confluence of the Rogue River and Midas Creek, Charlie's Place sat just below the hollows, a series of tubes, or caves, left over from long-ago volcanic activity that extended from Midas Creek and ran along the river. The caves were not as extensive as the Oregon Caves, an attraction a couple of hours northwest of Rogue's Hollow, but their story was more colorful.

Rogue's Hollow was initially called Midasville because it was founded during the southern Oregon gold rush. After the gold vein near the headwaters of Midas Creek petered out, the town faded as gold hunters moved on to Jacksonville, Prospect, and other more promising towns.

In the late 1800s and early 1900s the hollows served as hideouts for bad guys, robbers, rustlers, and during Prohibition, for moonshiners. One industrious moonshiner built a shack over the hollows. In fact, at one time during Prohibition, after a particularly bloody raid, the federal government almost filled them in with cement to prevent their use as hidey-holes. But locals saw a sightseeing opportunity. After all, Crater Lake was attracting people to the area — why not give tourists something else to see on the way? Midasville was only fifty miles away from the beautiful volcanic lake. Drawing people to their portion of the Rogue River to see mysterious caves shouldn't be that difficult. The caves were saved from concrete but not officially developed into a scenic stop until the late 1930s.

What eventually resurrected and saved the town was logging. The hills in the area were flush with wooden gold. A large mill was built, and business and labor flooded back into town. By then a lumber tycoon replaced the moonshiner's shack with a big Victorian mansion to oversee the sawmill, and he set up a concession to give visitors tours of the caves. He got the town to vote at that time to officially change the name of the town from Midasville to Rogue's Hollow.

The mill owner and his descendants operated the "Tour through the Hollows" for years, until the big flood of the 1960s, when a portion of the mill, the bridge to the Victorian, and part of the main street were washed away. Houses and neighborhoods on high ground survived. It was questionable whether or not Rogue's Hollow would make it, but it did, and it slowly rebuilt.

The town hung on even with business gone and the Victorian deserted. The caves were almost forgotten until the 1970s, when the state realized their value and rebuilt the bridge to the area. They took over the caves and renovated the historic gift shop just north of the Victorian. Tess had toured the caves the first month she'd been in town, been fascinated from a law enforcement standpoint at how intricate the cubbyholes and hiding places were, formed by nature but utilized by devious minds.

The downtown area was resurrected at that time, and as logging faded out, the demographics of the town changed again. Small businesses brought tourist trade in, and the neighborhoods filled with retirees, outdoorsmen, families, and people who enjoyed the quirky nature of the town.

The Victorian remained boarded up for years, threatened with demolition now and again, until Cole and his wife, Charlotte, bought it and renovated it into a bed-and-breakfast.

Tess loved the inn where she was staying, but she had to admit the bed-and-breakfast was special. The Markarovs had built a beautiful and cozy place. Tess guessed that it was all Charlotte, really. The touches were too feminine and homey to be from the guy Tess had met at her interview. She'd heard Cole had little to do with the running of the B and B; Charlotte did it all and wonderfully.

Tess's mother and brother had stayed there when they came to Rogue's Hollow for Tess's swearing in. They only came for the weekend, but both said the bed-and-breakfast was wonderful, worth the price, and a place they'd stay again. And from what she could see, it was an inviting place. Tess had met Charlotte briefly. The woman was a whirling dervish of activity and the perfect hostess. Cole had been out of town that weekend.

Jeannie had already purchased plane

tickets to fly up in November, and she would stay there. Tess looked forward to the visit. She missed her friends being a short drive away for spontaneous lunches or movies or just goofing off.

Thoughts of Long Beach brought with them the realization that she hadn't heard from Jeannie yet. Usually she got a text every morning, a kind of security to send and receive a message from a friend.

Tess sent off a text to Jeannie as the sting of Casey's admission that she hadn't voted for Tess's hire faded. Instead she felt a sort of relief that even though two months ago she hadn't wanted Tess to be here, now the woman was extending her hand in friendship.

Her phone pinged with a return text. Tess laughed. Jeannie had sent the results of an election poll. Connor-Ruiz was polling dead last in the three-way race for mayor of LB.

Will I ever find a friend as good as Jeannie here? she wondered. Then she thought of Anna and put a reminder on her phone to check in with Pastor Macpherson.

Breakfast was tasty, and she was glad Addie had forced the issue. As she ate her oatmeal, her thoughts latched back on to the homicide. Busyness was what she wanted. Serious police work would help her lose herself in a puzzle and ease the pain of missing people back home. She had just been getting used to life without Paul when the shooting happened.

Once she finished her breakfast, she gathered her things up to leave the dining room and looked around at the place filling with patrons. As nice as it was here, and as good as Addie and Klaus had been to her, this wasn't a home; it was a temporary place to stay. Did that have something to do with the reason she felt so unsettled? She'd not felt motivated at all to look for a place to buy or rent. Most of her belongings were still in storage in Long Beach.

When she had time on her hands, she wondered if she hadn't looked that hard for a home because she didn't truly feel she could keep this job. She served at the whim of a city council that had barely hired her.

In her strong moments, she didn't mind the slim margin of her hire. After all, the city council was only four citizens and a mayor, all part-time. She had the job and the knowledge to be good at it. But in her weak moments she felt so inadequate. She'd been confident and proactive in Long Beach, and had just been doing her job when the shooting happened. What if she was involved in a shooting here? Was it possible this whole town would rise up and kick her out? Where would she go then?

She pushed those thoughts from her mind and left the inn. She'd stop at the station, log in the bullet, and then head for Wild Automotive.

This August morning was as pleasant a late summer day as she'd ever seen. The tourist trade was still active, rafters were preparing to be shuttled to launch sites, fishermen dotted the river, shoppers walked River Drive, outside seating at the coffee shop was full, and the days were warm while the nights and mornings were cool. Tess realized, with some chagrin, that she had a fleeting thought about what winter would look like here. Was it a good thing she considered the future here, or was it scary?

20

Standing in front of the inn, Tess looked across the main street, River Drive, at Wild Automotive. This was essentially where downtown Rogue's Hollow began. The business district had a simple layout. The Hollow bridge was the turn-off from Highway 62, and once over the bridge and Rogue River, past the town's only stoplight, River Drive began. On the riverside was the Rogue's Hollow Inn and Suites. The church grounds took up the rest of the river frontage, extending all the way to Midas Creek. Wild Automotive began the business district on the other side of River Drive.

She crossed the street to the station and spent a few minutes logging the bullet Casey Reno had given her into evidence. She placed herself on duty and told Sheila that she'd be out talking to people in town about Glen.

From the station, Tess decided she'd walk

this morning, not take her car. It would be easier, she thought, to get a feel for where Glen went last Thursday when he arrived in the Hollow. River Drive ran east-west on the south side of the Rogue River through downtown. Heading east from the highway turnoff, the drive was only about four blocks long and eventually made a right turn to run along Midas Creek. To reach rural Rogue's Hollow one had to drive west on River Drive.

Tess headed to the auto repair yard first. Besides a repair shop, Forest also owned a mini-mart and a gas station, the only one between Trail and Prospect. Forest was in a tie-dye T-shirt and Tess could see him in the garage before she stepped onto the lot. Forest employed a lot of people: pump attendants, a couple of clerks for his small convenience store, and around five mechanics. Tess never remembered seeing any of them idle. She'd heard that Forest was the guy to see for any auto or motorcycle repair job in Rogue's Hollow — and most of the Upper Rogue, for that matter. He had the city contract to service the police cars. Forest had a solid rep as a man who did good work at a fair price.

Tess had quickly discovered that here, in this southern Oregon valley, word-of-mouth reputation was as good as gold. Unlike Southern California, where services proliferated and so did consumers, and businesses could get by with shoddy work or poor customer service, here word got around quickly. If someone couldn't be counted on, people would take their business to a more reliable place.

"Hiya, Chief." Forest saw her and stopped what he was doing as she walked toward him. He pulled a rag from his back pocket and wiped his hands as he greeted her. He was smiling; in fact, every time she saw Forest, he was smiling.

"Hi, Forest. You sound as if you expected me."

"I did. I heard about Glen. That's his Jeep over there." He pointed to a battered two-door Jeep off to the right. "He dropped it off a week ago, Thursday to be exact, and asked me to do a little work on it, which I did. He never came back and he owes me $200."

Tess strode to the Jeep, noted that there was a messenger bag on the passenger seat. Glen had nothing on him but an empty wallet and some change in his pocket. What was in the bag?

"Was that the only reason he was in Rogue's Hollow — to get his Jeep repaired?

Did he mention being here for any other reason?"

Forest shook his head. "All we talked about was the Jeep. Something was wrong with the four-wheel drive. Said he was planning to take a trip on some rough old logging roads and needed the four-wheel drive to be working properly. I had to order the part, so I told him it would take a couple of days. He didn't seem bothered, just told me to call his cell when it was done. I called and left a message, never heard back."

Cell. Casey had seen him talking on a phone. But Glen hadn't had a phone on him or near him. She should have known that he would have a phone. It was amazingly easy for homeless people to get cell phones these days.

"Can you give me the cell number you had for him?"

"Sure thing." Forest rattled off a number and Tess entered it into her phone. Phone records needed to be obtained. This could be a good lead.

"How did he seem to you?"

"What do you mean?"

"Was he nervous, angry, uneasy, jumpy — anything like that?"

Forest rubbed his hands together and thought a moment. "No, he actually just looked mellow and at peace." He shrugged. "I mean, I've seen him tweaking and stoned in the past, but come to think of it, that day he wasn't stoned, just happy. He had his dog with him, as usual. Killer is a sweetheart. I'm an animal lover. I heard you were able to save her."

"Yeah, I guess she's a tough animal. Did Glen have any close friends that you know of?"

"Tilly."

"Tilly?" Tess had heard that name before.

"She's an unbalanced girl, homeless mostly. Glen tends to look after her."

"But she wasn't here that day?"

"Not with him. He might have been trying to find her. When she's in town, she hangs out near food places, looking for handouts, digging in the trash. I was letting her sleep behind my place." He hiked a shoulder. "I just wanted her to be safe. But my insurance guy thought it was a liability, so I had to tell her no more."

"Have you seen her lately?"

He stroked his beard. "I can't think of when I last saw Tilly here. I think I heard that she was staying in Shady Cove. In fact, Glen generally spends more time in Shady Cove. I've seen them both in Aunt Caroline's Park, across from Shady Kate's —

you know, the antique store? But I can ask my guys. The mini-mart is open 24-7; they might have seen her."

"Thanks. I'll talk to them." Tess walked into the mini-mart and quickly got the attention of the two clerks. One was a woman Tess guessed was well past sixty-five and probably supplementing Social Security with the job, and the other was a twenty-something guy with a safety pin through his lower lip. Neither had seen Tilly lately, but they did see Glen when he dropped his car off. They promised to call if they did see Tilly.

Walking back to Glen's Jeep, Tess asked herself some questions. Was Tilly with Glen when he was killed? If she was, had she fallen into the creek and just not surfaced yet, or did she survive and was now hiding somewhere? She didn't know Glen and worked to form a picture of the guy in her mind's eye. In her prior experience, homeless drug addicts were an unpredictable lot. The men usually stole to support their habits, and unfortunately the women often sold themselves to do the same. Thinking of the hopeless lifestyle sent a shiver up Tess's spine.

The vast majority of murder victims knew their killers. Unless Glen was hiking early in the morning and stumbled on someone who decided to shoot him, it was a good bet he'd met his killer there for some reason. A bracing thought struck her: in this small town where everyone knew everyone, his killer could be hiding in plain sight.

That led her to motive. On the surface, it appeared that the person with the strongest motive for murder was the one whose money Glen brought to Anna. But maybe after she learned more about Glen, a stronger motive would surface. She needed to keep an open mind and learn as much as she could about her victim.

There were a lot of things to consider, and the timing still bugged her. Glen dropped his Jeep off on Thursday, then gave the money to Anna Friday night and showed up dead a week later. Where was he in the interim?

"If they haven't seen her lately," Forest said when Tess returned, "it's not unusual for the daytime. You might come back and ask the night shift."

"Thank you. I see there's a bag on the front seat. Did he have anything else? Did he take something with him?"

"Just a small backpack. I saw him put dog food in it. He also bought some bottled water from the store." Forest pointed toward

210

his small convenience store. "That's about it."

If Glen didn't come here with the money he handed to Anna Macpherson, Tess wondered, where did he get it? And when? More questions.

"You say he owes you two hundred dollars. Does he usually pay you? I mean, I've heard him described as a homeless drug addict. How did he keep his Jeep gassed up and running, and pay you?"

"Glen makes money under the table doing odd jobs and grunt work. Yeah, he was homeless, but he did earn enough to take care of what was important to him. His dog, his car, Tilly — not necessarily in that order. I would sometimes give him work to pay his bill." He pointed to the area behind his station. "I was planning on having him clear the brush back there if he didn't have the cash this time."

Tess considered this for a moment; then her attention went back to the vehicle.

"Is the Jeep open? I'll need to take the bag and anything else in the vehicle and place it into evidence."

He nodded. "Have at it."

Tess grabbed the door handle. "If you need a receipt, come by the office later and I'll have one for you."

"No problem."

She slid into the front seat and turned back to Forest. "Would you mind keeping the Jeep secure for me?"

"Not at all. I'm still out two hundred bucks."

She went through the car carefully but found it was mostly full of trash, dog hair, candy bar wrappers, and fast-food bags. But being that she'd been told Glen lived out of his car, it was surprisingly clean. Taking the messenger bag and then locking the Jeep, she thanked Forest before continuing her search for information about Glen Elders.

After Forest's yard ended, the business walk on River Drive began, starting with Casey's bookstore. She walked past the bookstore, a woman she'd not met yet behind the counter. Next was Hotshot Fishing, a sandwich shop on one side and a fishing/outdoor shop on the other side. Tess had had a sandwich or two at the place, but since she didn't fish, she'd only glanced at the other half. They also rented bikes and did raft trips, one day and multiday. She wanted to take a raft trip but decided she'd probably wait until Jeannie made a summertime visit. It would be a great lure to convince her to make a second trip.

The woman behind the counter remembered that Glen had bought a sandwich to go and then continued on down the street. Next door to Hotshot was the police station/ city hall and a small post office. Glen hadn't stopped there. Tess stopped inside to drop off the bag she'd retrieved from Glen's Jeep. She'd go through it later.

Across the street from the station, on the river side of Hollow Drive was the church property.

Tess paused, still bothered by the co-incidence of Glen's death and his cousin Anna's disappearance. After a minute she continued to the next business, the Hollow Grind, where Casey had gotten her coffee and a place Tess visited often. Beans were roasted on-site and the smell was heavenly. Oregonians loved their coffee, something Tess truly appreciated. If it wasn't a quaint coffee shop like this, there were numerous drive-through coffee huts all over the valley where a person could get a coffee fix.

"Hey, Chief, the usual?" Pete, the owner-operator, greeted her, though the place was busy.

"No coffee today, but I had a couple of questions to ask. Do you know Glen Elders?"

His face fell. "I did. My morning custom-ers were already talking about that, that —"

he frowned — "well, his death."

"Had you seen him lately?"

"He was in here last weekend. He actually paid me back some money he owed, and he started a tab for a friend of his."

"A tab?"

"Yeah, he has a homeless friend. I've complained to the cops before about her. She begs in front of the store and once or twice got aggressive with tourists. Anyway, he put forty dollars down in her name. So when she shows up, I'll give her coffee and food until the money runs out. He didn't steal the money, did he?"

"Not that I'm aware. I'm just trying to retrace his steps. This homeless woman, is it someone named Tilly?"

He nodded. "Tilly Dover."

Tess had thought about this name since Forest said it, and she knew she had heard it before. Or read it. Then it came to her. In her studying up on local laws and problems, Tilly was listed and described as an unpredictable bipolar homeless woman. She'd been arrested numerous times and then kicked out of jail because of overcrowding. Tess had never seen her, had only heard stories.

"Was Tilly with him?"

Pete shook his head. "She did come in on

Monday, by herself, clean and half-normal. Got coffee and a couple of breakfast bagels. Haven't seen her since."

"Thanks. If you do see her, could you give me a call? She's not in trouble. I just want to talk to her about Glen."

"Will do."

On the other side of the Hollow Grind was a vacant storefront. At one time it had been a thrift store, but now a big For Lease sign graced the window. Rumor was, it would soon be a real estate office.

PSS, Platinum Security Systems, occupied the next slot. There was a sign on the door with a clock, the hands showing that someone would be back at noon. Tess had met Beto Acosta a couple of times. He'd tried to talk her into upgrading the security system at the PD, but that was something he needed to talk to Mayor Dixon about. He was nice enough, but to Tess it was as if he tried too hard. And he was a close talker; he liked to encroach on personal space, and Tess hated that.

She paused, not because she thought Glen would have stopped here, but because of the broken key chain. If they were handed out like candy, like Gabe said, it might not be much of a clue. But right now, it was on the short list of what they did have.

She kept walking, mentally making a note to stop back at some point. A craft store came next, quilts, yarn, threads. Tess went inside to ask, but the two old women working had not seen Glen.

The following business was the second biggest in town next to Wild Automotive: RR Bakery and Confections. The aroma here rivaled the coffee shop's. They mostly sold commercially and supplied restaurants all over the valley with fresh, organic baked goods. Pete got his bagels and pastries from RR. Tess had eaten a few tasty things and had to admit that before RR she'd always thought organic baked goods equaled cardboard. The stuff RR sold was great.

The retail portion sold a lot of day-old stuff, some fresh, but Tess had learned you had to be an early bird because they ran out of fresh-baked items fast. She had no luck in the bakery; no one remembered seeing Glen. This side of the street ended with a large parking lot for bakery trucks, and then Hollow Drive jogged to the right and became Midas Drive as it ran along the creek for a bit.

Across the street from the bakery, on the corner of Midas and Hollow, was Rogue's Grocery, a small market, and next door, what would have been only a food truck in

California. But this place, Max's Grill, was stationary; the wheels were gone. Max, the owner, barbecued and grilled ribs, chicken, and occasionally fish. People walked up to the window to order and ate at outside tables that faced Midas Creek. There was an area that could be shielded from the elements between the truck and the market, but Tess knew people generally preferred eating outside when weather permitted. She crossed the street and started with the food truck.

"Chief, you here to eat?" Max asked, peering at her from the order window.

Tess had eaten there once or twice. Everything was good. Because of her light breakfast her stomach growled as the smell of grilling food assaulted her nostrils, but she wasn't ready to stop her progress through town.

"Not right now, Max. I had a couple of questions for you."

Max was no help. Tourist traffic had kept him busy lately and he'd not seen Glen. He did know Glen, though.

"He looks after Tilly," Max said. "I like that. I knew Tilly's dad. It would break his heart to see her like she is now." He shook his head. "But it would also comfort him to know that she had someone like Glen to look after her. I sometimes give them free burgers if they show up at closing. I was sorry to hear about him being killed. Hope you find the guy who did it."

"Thanks, and I will."

Tess continued into the market. She knew the manager was related to the mayor; they'd been introduced at her swearing in. Roger Dixon didn't look anything like his brother. He was tall and lean, reminding Tess of an officer she used to work with who was crazy for marathons, had competed all over the world, and had the gaunt build of a long-distance runner. That was Roger Dixon, only the store manager had a little more panache.

Rico Suave came to mind, a term often used by officers she worked with to peg a guy who thought he was too good, too cool, for the cops to mess with. Roger Dixon dressed like a male model, expensive-looking clothes, tidy and perfectly pressed. His light-brown hair well groomed.

His wife, a member of the quilting club that met at the inn, likewise was always dressed impeccably. That was a little out of the ordinary. Tess had found Oregon to be a lot more casual than California, something she didn't mind. She was more comfortable in jeans than a skirt or a suit. Most of Tess's formal clothes, usually only donned for court, were still in storage. Even Mayor Dixon, an accountant besides being mayor, was never as dressed up as his brother, the dapper grocery store manager. The disparity between the two men made Tess wonder if one or both of them were adopted.

It was loud when you first walked into the store. The front corner was dedicated to video games and housed a mini arcade. Tess remembered that at her swearing in, Roger Dixon's wife, Helen, who was quite a bit older than he was, had bragged to her about the arcade supported by the market.

"We want to keep children from mischief, don't we?" she'd said. *"Roger and I provide a safe place for them to interact."*

Tess had thought that arcades and video games were passé, what with cell phones and PlayStations, but you'd never know that by the crowds of kids usually packed in here. Today was no different; there certainly were a lot of kids playing games in the arcade. Briefly Tess realized that while she might have seen Kayla Reno here, she didn't recall ever seeing Duncan Peabody. That kid definitely needed a different hobby.

She looked around the small market and saw Roger Dixon immediately. Pressed slacks and a button-down shirt covered by a

219

vest, hair neat and held that way with a light gel, chiseled facial features, this Dixon could be on a magazine cover. He was talking to a couple of giggling girls who looked to be high school age. She caught his eye.

"Chief, are you looking for me?" Dixon said good-bye to the girls, who disappeared down an aisle. Then he smiled and walked her way, hard soles clicking on the linoleum.

He was so different from his brother.

"Mr. Dixon, I was wondering if I could ask you a couple of questions."

"It's Roger, and what can I help you with?"

"We had an incident yesterday — a man was murdered."

"Glen Elders, I heard."

"Did you know Elders?"

He nodded. "Oh yes, I knew him. I threw him out of here for shoplifting a while ago. I didn't file a police report." He hiked one shoulder. "I figured he got the message."

"Had you seen him lately?"

"A few days ago, I think. He was walking toward Charlie's. I didn't see him go in; I just noticed him walking that direction."

"Do you remember exactly what day that was?"

"Sorry, no." He gave her a sympathetic look. "Days run together when you're working, you know?"

"Yeah, I do. Thanks." She turned to go.

"A horrible thing, this murder. Do you have any leads? Any idea who would do such a thing? Or is it difficult because you're not from around here?"

She held his gaze for a moment while an unpleasant feeling rippled through her. Even though there was nothing in his demeanor that said it, he was mocking her.

"Murder is a horrible thing, and yes, I have every confidence we'll solve it."

"Good. I'm just concerned it will be difficult to solve because you're an outsider — a qualified one, but still an outsider."

"I'll manage fine, Mr. Dixon. Thanks again for your help."

Tess left the market frowning, wondering at the strange vibe she'd gotten from Dixon. He'd been nothing but cordial to her, and his wife was very nice. Maybe it was just the fact he was the mayor's brother that gave her the bad feeling.

The local hair salon didn't look like a place Glen would stop. It wasn't. The women inside, though they cut men's hair as well as women's, hadn't seen Glen lately.

She stopped at each remaining business and asked about Glen. Two other people saw him, but one wasn't certain what day, and the other said the same thing Casey and Dixon had said: maybe he was heading to Charlie's.

At the end of the paved portion of Midas Drive was Rogue's Hollow's only bar, The Stump. It was closed and was likely that way when Glen had walked by. It didn't open until two in the afternoon.

She had to backtrack to cross Midas Creek and visit Charlie's. Before she turned around, she realized Glen could have taken a hiking path from just above The Stump here that would have eventually led to the area along the creek where he'd been found. The drive she'd taken to the spot the day his body was found was quicker than the hike, but Glen was without his Jeep.

Did he take the path before he got to Charlie's or after visiting there? The time gap bugged her. No one so far had remembered seeing him after the weekend when he dropped money off for Tilly at the Hollow Grind.

Tess paused for a moment, writing some notes before she continued down the road, then up and over the bridge to the B and B. She noticed a thin, dirty man off to the left of the Victorian's front steps. He was smoking a cigarette and eyeballing her in a way that made her Spidey sense tingle.

She'd seen him before, at the trailer park, she thought. He did landscaping and handyman work if she remembered correctly. Tess looked at him out of habit, prepared to say hello, but he turned away to walk down the steps toward the river. Odd, but not unheard of. She knew the police uniform made people nervous, often for no reason at all, but she filed a reminder to herself to find out who the man was and verify what he did for a living.

She climbed the stairs and noticed the charmingly decorated porch. There was a swinging bench that faced the confluence of the Rogue River and Midas Creek, and beautiful needlepoint pillows. The vases were empty, though, and Tess wondered about that. She'd seen Charlotte more than once at the growers' market buying flowers.

She opened the front door to the B and B, thinking she'd see Charlotte, but instead, behind the counter was Cole. He was conversing with a man Tess recognized as Beto Acosta, owner of PSS. The conversation stopped and both men turned toward her when she walked inside.

"Chief." Markarov held his hands up in mock surprise. "You found the bodies, and I hid them so well." Markarov was a tall man with a head of thick dark hair that Tess was certain he dyed. He had the build of a onetime athlete — maybe baseball, possibly basketball — who'd quit playing and let himself go soft.

Acosta laughed too hard at the unfunny joke. Tess managed a smile, thinking maybe the phrase was from a movie but she couldn't recall the name. Her contact with Cole had been limited. He hadn't shown up at her swearing in, and the sting from the interview had dulled, so she tried not to proceed expecting him to be unpleasant.

"Mr. Markarov, Mr. Acosta, good morning."

They both said good morning and then Acosta slapped both hands down on the counter.

"Chief, have you given any thought to that security upgrade I was telling you about?" Acosta asked. Originally from New York, his accent was thick. He reminded Tess of an uncle she had who still lived in New York. He looked more like he could be Roger Dixon's brother than Doug Dixon. Though he had a darker complexion, he was tall and lean, always dressed professionally, with a strong jaw and dark eyes. The only glaring difference between him and Rico Suave was that his hairline was receding and most of it was graying.

"Sorry; you'll really have to bring that up with Mayor Dixon."

He gave a half nod. "Of course. But it would help me if you put in a good word." His lips curled into an oily smile.

"I'll look into the system you suggested."

"That's all I ask. Well, I've got to get back to my business. Cole, see you later." He nodded at Tess and started to leave, then stopped. "Unless of course you need to speak to me?" He pointed at his chest with his thumb.

Tess might, at one point, talk to him about the key chain, but she didn't want to talk to them both at the same time.

"Not right this minute. I came to speak to Mr. Markarov. You'll be at your office later?"

"All day. See you then. Ciao." With that he left the B and B.

"And how can I help the young lady today?" Markarov asked as the front door closed.

Ignoring the odd comment, Tess determined not to be thrown off her game. "I have a couple questions for you. I'm trying to figure out where someone was last week, Thursday specifically. Were you behind the desk then?"

"Thursday? I have to say I was. That was the day the little woman left for Portland.

She'll be back tomorrow. Until then I'm the chief cook and bottle washer."

"Did Glen Elders come in here that day? Has he registered for a room?"

He scrunched his brows together. "Why no, I haven't seen Glen in quite some time. He wouldn't come here for a room. Our rates are far above his pay grade. What's he gotten himself into this time?"

Tess frowned. The way Casey had talked . . . "I was under the impression Glen was your friend."

"I don't know what gave you that impression. Yes, I hire him from time to time for grunt work. That's it."

She considered this for a moment, then said, "He was murdered yesterday."

That seemed to shock him. But something ruffled Tess. His response appeared almost practiced, as if he was waiting for someone to give him this news so he could act surprised.

"A murder? Here in Rogue's Hollow?" He shook his head. "I hate to say it, but I thought this would happen."

"What, you thought Glen would be murdered?"

"Not him specifically, but I saw this crime spree coming. No disrespect, Chief, but I feared the appointment of a woman as chief

226

of police would embolden the criminal element in the valley. They just aren't inclined to fear that you will be a force to be reckoned with." His weak smile was insincere, and Tess felt the hair stand up on the back of her neck as she fought to keep her expression blank.

"Well, if that's true, they're mistaken. They'll find I'm as serious about law enforcement as any man." She turned to leave.

"Maybe so, but that'd be too late for poor Glen, wouldn't it?"

21

Rule # 5: "Don't step on anyone's macho."

Tess didn't believe she'd done anything to step on Markarov's macho, yet he was quite the jerk. Checking her temper, grateful she had a walk to cool off, she left the B and B and started back to her office to view the contents of Glen's saddlebag.

Cole Markarov was everything she'd been told he was, she thought as she walked. He'd so thrown her off her game she'd forgotten to ask about the thin man she'd seen on his property. As far as police work went, Tess felt fortunate that such blatant chauvinism was relatively rare. Women older than she was had worked a lot of the kinks out of law enforcement before her time. True, there'd been bumps along the way she'd had to deal with, being a woman in uniform — guys who would ignore her and talk only to the male partner, female servers in restaurants who were so intent on flirting with the male officer, they'd never get her order right.

The only blatant episode she'd ever dealt with had happened when she was a rookie. She and her training partner stopped a man who turned out to have several warrants totaling bail of over a hundred thousand dollars. The man had been acting macho, ignoring Tess, and being generally disrespectful. When the dispatcher gave them the information that their subject was 10-29 Frank — that he had felony warrants — her training officer gave her the nod to make the arrest.

Tess was confident in her weaponless defense skills, and there was no little satisfaction when the man resisted and she took him to the ground with a picture-perfect takedown move. Seconds later he was in cuffs and barely knew what had hit him. Her training officer beamed, and Tess got perfect marks that day. And the incident led to her to pen rule #5. If it was possible to avoid a confrontation, she was all for it. She'd have to find a way to get the same satisfaction from that jerk Markarov.

Once back in her office, she'd cooled off considerably. Tess tried to push Cole out of her head. She smiled and said hello to Sheila, the PD's civilian clerk, and Gwen, clerk for the city of Rogue's Hollow. They were cross-trained and each did both jobs well. The third civilian Tess supervised was Martha, a code enforcement officer. Her duty shift was twenty hours a week with Fridays off.

On the board outside her office were the names of the officers on duty. There was also a new BOLO for a runaway teenage girl from Ashland. And she noticed another job bulletin, this one from Grants Pass, advertising the need for lateral applicants for the PD. She left it, vowing not to let that get under her skin.

Day shift today was Bender. Curtis Pounder was also on duty, but it was a short day for the sergeant. She saw that Bender was on a disturbing-the-peace call in the trailer park, and Curtis was on a break.

She logged on to the computer and read an e-mail from Bender. It documented everything he'd sent to Salem for analysis. Tess considered it for a moment and wondered if she'd made any headway with the man after his little outburst. He'd been extremely professional yesterday and she was pleased with that. She didn't need her people to be her friends, but she did need them to do their jobs. If that was all she got out of Bender, she'd be satisfied. He was a good cop; she'd hate to see him go if he did get offered a job elsewhere.

He noted in the e-mail that he wasn't sure when they would hear back on anything.

Once the rest of her e-mails were read, she emptied the contents of the bag from Glen's car onto her desk. She listened to the police radio as she multitasked, hearing Curtis finish his break and go back into service. A short time later both he and Bender responded to a dispute between fishermen. Just a normal day in Rogue's Hollow.

She concentrated on the contents of the messenger bag. There wasn't much: a set of keys, some pennies, a bag of chips, a bag of M&M'S, and pieces of what she decided was a note, ripped up and crumpled. Nothing legible.

She pulled the evidence envelope that held all the items recovered from Elders's person and added these new items.

No great leads here. No indication of where he got the money, or who else might have been with him when he was killed. Tilly was at the top of the list, but suppose it was someone else?

Tess's stomach rolled unpleasantly when another name came to mind: *Anna.*

She felt in her bones that Anna's disappearance was somehow tied to Glen's murder, but the *why* escaped her.

Tess stepped to the murder board she'd started the night before and filled in her timeline with what she had so far. There were still a lot of blank spots and questions. And suspects? She put a big question mark. Same with the questions "Where did Glen get the money?" and "Where is Tilly?" As she considered the board, she realized that she'd have to end her open-door policy. There was no need for the whole town to know what progress had been made on the investigation.

Progress? The most promising tidbit from today was the slug recovered from the dog. It would be useful to match with a gun. If she ever uncovered the murder weapon.

22

"Get help. Get help." The voice in Tilly's head kept repeating, but fear muffled it and it grew fainter and fainter.

Tilly wrestled with herself. She knew that her friend needed more help than she could provide, but if the police didn't believe her and she was taken to jail in Medford, even if they let her right back out, it would take her forever to get back to the Hollow. That would not help her friend.

The angel was gone, and no matter what she said or did, she couldn't bring it back. After doing everything she could — tending wounds, changing clothes — Tilly ventured out. She scored some meth and it calmed her jitters and made her bold enough to believe she could handle everything on her plate by herself.

She tried to think of what Glen would have done if he were still alive. Glen didn't trust many people. Tilly had been hurt enough in her life to believe that "trust no one" was a good overall philosophy. She was positive he wouldn't have gone to the police. He might have gone to Pastor Mac. But Tilly was in a place where she couldn't even trust a man who'd only been kind to her. Glen was the only person she could trust, and he was dead.

But her friend needed her and she had to help.

She returned and checked on her friend. There was no change. She made sure she drank some water, then pulled on Glen's hoodie and left her hiding place one more time.

Maybe she couldn't go to the police or Pastor Mac, but she would do something.

After breakfast Oliver walked back to his house, debating whether he should call Chief O'Rourke or work on his Sunday sermon notes. The text from Anna still troubled him and he was deep in thought. But the minute he reached the porch, he knew something was wrong. His door was half-open and he clearly remembered closing it. He rarely if ever locked the door, but he had closed it.

Through the opening he saw chaos. Anger flared as he shoved the door wide and stepped into the house.

He heard a crash and realized the burglar was still in the house. Without thinking, he rushed toward the noise coming from Anna's sewing room.

"Who's there?" He burst into the room and saw a blur of movement and blue color on his left.

As he turned, he had a brief view of the person, a woman, but before he could react, she lowered her head and charged, ramming into his midsection.

Oliver's breath fled and he fell backward, stumbling over a pile of something on the floor, even as he tried to grab the woman. A split second before she was in his grasp, she raised her head and gave him a solid head butt, catching him under the chin. The impact made him bite his tongue, and as he fell onto his backside, he saw stars.

When his mind cleared, he found himself on the floor, entangled in a pile of Anna's fabrics. Rubbing his chin, tasting blood in his mouth, and sucking in air, Oliver sat up to get his bearings. After a second he pushed himself up to his feet and found his legs a little wobbly. He'd not been sucker punched in ages. The last time had been when he was a new pastor and an abusive man had gotten angry that Oliver had counseled his wife to leave him.

This woman's ram to his midsection had caught him totally by surprise. He hurried to the front door in time to see a flash of blue disappear into the bushes at the far end of the property. He did not feel up to giving chase. He steadied himself in the doorway before turning to take total stock of his messed-up house.

It was trashed. He moved back into the living room and saw that books and papers littered the floor, along with the contents of a chest Anna used to store fabric and small blankets. As he walked around, he could see the vicious ransacking extended through the living room and Anna's sewing room. His thoughts cleared and the identity of the woman who attacked him popped into his mind. He had to stop, the shock of recognition almost as sharp as the head butt. But in that brief instant when he'd seen her, he knew who it was. Tilly Dover. And Oliver knew she was Glen's friend.

Glen is dead. Does she know that? Did she know Glen had given Anna a bag of money? Even though it was a week ago, that had to be what she was looking for. He and Anna didn't have expensive possessions. There was no reason for anyone to break in here.

His balance returned and he made a quick

survey of the downstairs before rushing upstairs. There was damage there as well, but mostly to Anna's stuff. All their drawers were open, but it was Anna's clothing that was strewn about. This gave Oliver pause. Was Tilly looking for something to wear? Fuming and feeling the unpastor-like desire to grab Tilly and shake her and ask her why she'd had to tear his home apart, he slowly walked back downstairs, breathing deeply and counting to ten. He stood scratching his head, debating his next step: to figure out if anything was missing, or call the police?

The flashing message light caught his eye. The phone had been knocked to the floor but not before someone had left a message. It was the landline that demanded attention first. He picked the phone up, set it back where it belonged, and played the message. His anger fled, replaced by naked fear, and his legs turned to water. The personal attack on him lost all importance.

He had to sit down and play it again and then sit and think about the significance of the call before he realized what he had to do.

He phoned the police station, surprised when the chief herself answered.

"Ah, Chief . . . O'Rourke, I . . . uh, I guess

I expected someone else to answer."

"I'm here working, might as well answer the phone. What's the matter, Pa— Oliver?"

"I got . . . I . . . well, I received a disturbing phone message. I think you need to hear it."

"At your home or at the church?"

"Home."

"I'll be right there."

Tess hesitated for a second at her cruiser and then kept going. Pastor Mac's residence was on church grounds, right across the street from the police station. There was no reason to take the car. In Long Beach she would have taken the patrol car in case she got a priority one call and had to leave in a hurry. That was common in the big city, but here in Rogue's Hollow, just about everything was within walking distance.

Besides, she'd not been keeping up on her workouts, the excuse being she needed to spend time familiarizing herself with the new job. The walk through town this morning had reminded her that she better start running again. Workouts usually helped clear her mind, helped her to think logically, but recently Tess didn't want to stop and think logically. She was afraid her thoughts would revolt and dwell on the shooting that brought her here to this small town.

Tess crossed the street and started off at a brisk pace and reached the pastor's house in a few minutes. She knocked on the door, taking a deep breath and putting on her game face. This was a police matter now and she knew how to handle police matters.

"Come in," Pastor Mac's deep voice bellowed from inside.

Tess opened the door but stopped short when she saw the devastation. She looked around the entire room, saw broken glass, ripped papers, and fabric and blankets. The mess was extensive, and Tess surveyed all the disorder until her gaze came to rest on the pastor, seated on the bottom stair, phone in his lap, glazed expression on his face.

"What in the world?" Tess asked.

He shook his head. "This happened while I was at the men's breakfast."

Tess continued inside, stepping over debris to get to where Macpherson sat. His chin looked bruised, she thought but didn't mention.

"They were looking for the money," she said.

He nodded, his brow furrowed in worry, maybe a hint of fear. "I can deal with the mess, but this message . . ."

"What is the message?"

"First, I want to show you the text I just received." He held up his phone and showed Tess the brief message.

I'm fine. I'll call you later.

Tess looked up, an optimistic comment dying on her lips when she saw Macpherson's face.

"I was relieved as well, until I heard this." He punched the button on a landline answering machine.

"Hi, Anna, it's Cora. Where are you, my dear? We were planning to work on the bedspread today. We wanted to finish it before fall. If we're going to do that, we have to get moving. Call me."

"The call came while I was at the men's breakfast this morning. That's Anna's best friend, Cora. She lives up the road in Prospect. Anna never would have missed that engagement. Never." The pain in his eyes radiated to Tess and took her breath away.

But why the text message? Tess thought but didn't say. If she went down that road, it would lead to speculation that the text message was fake, and if the text message were fake, then Anna was in serious trouble.

She realized then that though she'd dealt

with many crime victims in her career, delivered some awful news, more than she cared to remember, and always protected herself with a steel wall of professionalism, it was different now. She'd been here only two months, and wasn't even sure she'd stay, but this small town, the place she wasn't certain she could handle, had become more than a job. Pastor Mac was a big part of a larger family. She felt his pain maybe because she'd developed a certain amount of respect for him and not a little affection for Anna. And now the odds were high that Anna was most likely not coming home, and it broke Tess's heart.

Retreating behind her uniform, Tess pulled out her notebook. "I'm going to need some information."

Oliver nodded and Tess asked him all the questions she needed to have answered in order to complete a missing person report.

23

Tess went straight back to the station to enter the information on Anna Macpherson into NCIC, the national crime database. She was missing/endangered in NCIC lingo. Even her license plate was noted. If an officer came across her vehicle and ran the plate for any reason, the missing/endangered label would pop up. Any officer who came into contact with her and had reason to enter her information into the computer would see the flag and at least contact Rogue's Hollow and let them know.

Unless, of course, Anna wanted to be missing.

There was no crime in an adult running away. If Anna was fine and in her right mind and told the officer she didn't want to go home, there would be nothing anyone could do to bring her back against her will. But Tess's instincts were telling her that Anna was not missing voluntarily.

And the text messages were a sinister wrinkle.

That twisted Tess's gut with dread. Nice people like Anna Macpherson didn't flake out like this or taunt their husbands with vague messages.

Even if they were despondent about a cancer diagnosis.

Tess had pondered that wrinkle for a long moment. She barely knew Anna but felt that she understood the woman's pain. Yeah, it was a tough pill to swallow, but at least she had a faithful husband to lean on. Oliver was adamant that Anna was not suicidal.

"Yes, she was angry, but suicide would go against everything Anna believed."

But then that question nagged: *Was Oliver Macpherson all he seemed to be?*

Tess had not heard anyone speak badly of the pastor. She knew his church was usually packed on Sundays; she could see the lot from her hotel room. He ran three full services. And another service on Wednesday nights was likewise well attended.

But then O. J. was popular before Nicole.

Tess wondered if it would be better to turn this case over to the sheriff. She certainly felt personally involved. Anna was a friend. But after reflection, she decided not to delegate the case to another department.

She e-mailed a be-on-the-lookout to all of her personnel, then sent out a county- and statewide BOLO. After that, she wrote out a list of those people she needed to talk to about Pastor Mac and his wife. Her own landlords would be a good start. Klaus and Addie were close to the pastor. The quilt group as well; she'd heard a couple of them were founding members of the church. And she'd have to talk to the mayor.

Tess tried to remember all she'd learned about tactful leadership.

After Chief O'Rourke left, Oliver made the call he'd been dreading, to Anna's parents, and wrestled with the fact that he'd not told the chief he recognized Tilly. He didn't know why he withheld that bit of information and was a little unsettled by the omission. But Tilly was a lost soul and he believed she needed some protection. She must have had a good reason for doing what she did. After all, Glen, her only advocate, was dead.

Anna's parents resided in an assisted-living home near Portland, about five hours away. Another aspect of collateral damage from the cancer was that because of Anna's iffy health, they'd not been able to bring her parents to live with them. It had been

Anna's fervent prayer that somehow they could do it, but her father was fading rapidly into dementia and her mother had two bad knees. Moving them into a two-story house was not wise without a full-time caregiver. Anna couldn't be that caregiver and had conceded as much, but Oliver knew that was a blow to his wife.

Oliver had spoken to his mother-in-law the first morning Anna hadn't come home. He'd only called to surreptitiously figure out if Anna was there. When Esther asked to speak to Anna, Oliver got his answer. Now, with this call, he did his best to tell Esther the truth gently, but he could tell the woman was completely unsettled by this news. After he hung up, he called the nurses' station at the home to let the head nurse know that Esther and Richard might need some extra care until Anna was located.

After speaking to the nurse, Oliver made a call to one of his assistant pastors, a rock of a man named Jethro Bishop who oversaw the prayer ministry. He was also the man Oliver had called to check out the cabin in Union Creek. He'd confirmed Anna was not there.

Five years a widower, Jethro volunteered in the prison ministry, working with hardened criminals. A onetime boxer, he reminded Oliver of an old football legend, Dick Butkus. He was as broad as the man had been in his playing days, and had a nose that had been broken so many times it lay flat on his face. But Jethro was the definition of a gentle giant and a formidable prayer warrior. Even though gossip was a no-no, Oliver knew that as soon as Anna's disappearance was on the prayer chain, word would spread through the whole town and probably the whole valley. Was he ready for the onslaught of questions?

He punched in Jethro's number and prayed that he was.

He'd just hung up after talking to Jethro when Travis May, the church youth pastor, knocked on the doorframe. Oliver hadn't yet closed the front door, for no particular reason other than he just hadn't thought about it.

"Wow." Travis's eyes went wide when he saw the destruction to Oliver's home. "What happened?"

"Long story," Oliver said, putting the phone down and facing the young man. Travis wouldn't be knocking at his door without calling unless it was important.

"Maybe you're not up for this, but Frank Devaroux is dead. His wife found him unresponsive in his recliner a little while ago. She called the church office. She's a mess."

Oliver closed his eyes and rubbed his forehead. This was a blow. Frank was a founding member of the church, a stalwart deacon and a man Oliver considered a good friend. He could only imagine how Sonya, his wife, was doing.

Opening his eyes, he looked at Travis. "This just happened?"

"Yeah, Sonya panicked and ran to a neighbor, who phoned 911, and then she called the church."

Oliver didn't hesitate. "I'll head out there." He searched around for his car keys.

Travis grabbed his arm, concern in his eyes. "You sure? It looks like something is going on here."

"Travis, I think someone was looking for that money from last week, remember? Anyway, Frank and Sonya are good friends. I need to be there for her."

"Can I at least call some folks to help clean this up?"

"Sure. I'd appreciate that, actually." He found his keys and his phone and started to leave.

"Where's Anna?" Travis asked. "Is she feeling okay?"

Oliver turned and faced Travis. "I'm not sure where Anna is at the moment. I've spoken to Chief O'Rourke about it. I'd appreciate your prayers. I explained a lot to Jethro. Call him."

He turned away and hurried for his car, leaving Travis with a shocked expression on his face and feeling bad about that. But Oliver's thinking was churned up like the water at the bottom of a waterfall. He couldn't grip on to anything except the fact that Sonya needed some support immediately. That was a lifeline — doing his job, providing her with a little bit of comfort, and leaving Anna in the arms of God because Oliver had no idea where to put his arms around that problem.

Tess finished all the details with Anna Macpherson's missing person report and the report about the Macpherson house being burglarized and ransacked. She wished Oliver could give her a better description of his attacker but was very glad the burglar just wanted to get away and Oliver was not hurt badly in the attack. She notified Mayor Dixon.

"Missing? Anna Macpherson? My heavens. Do you have any leads?"

Tess told him what they had, which was

nothing. He surprised her by being helpful and not trying to micromanage.

"A sweeter person never walked the earth!" He seemed genuinely shocked and dismayed by the news. Tess heard his voice break.

"I think so too," she said, "but I need to look at this as a law enforcement officer."

"Of course, of course. How can I help?"

"Have you ever seen any problems between the Macphersons?"

"No, they are what they seem, what they advertise. And that church — well, it's the real deal. I'm an atheist and yet they welcome me to the men's breakfast. I think no one knows the Macphersons better than Klaus and Addie."

"Thank you for the information."

"Certainly. If I can help, let me know."

Tess hung up, glad that went well, and made a note to talk to the pair when she went home. She then called the Jackson County sheriff.

"I was about to call you," the sheriff said. "When I saw that BOLO, I prayed it was a mistake. Do you want me to gear up for a full-scale search?"

"We need to be prepared, but further than that, currently I don't know where to start. Anna and her car are in NCIC, but no one is certain about where she might have gone. I'm not sure where to stage a search."

"Gotcha. I'll make sure all my guys have this information and I'll personally contact Josephine, Douglas, and Siskiyou Counties if you like."

"Thank you, Sheriff. I appreciate that."

"No problem. Anna Macpherson is a gem. I pray to God she's okay."

Tess already knew that Oliver Macpherson was a big name, not only in the Upper Rogue, but in the whole Rogue Valley. But it was hitting home now how big. His church was the third largest in the area. As soon as the local newspaper got wind of his wife being missing, they'd be all over it. That could help, but she needed to be certain Oliver knew about the possibility. She called to let him know.

"Yes," he sighed. Tess heard weariness in his voice. "I knew this would be a newsworthy story. Is that a bad thing?"

"Not for me," Tess said. "If Anna is news, that puts more eyes out looking for her. But I wanted you to be prepared."

"I have a lot of people praying and looking. All I want is Anna home."

"Me too. Where are you now, Oliver?"

"On my way to a parishioner's home. Her husband died suddenly this morning. She needs me."

Tess didn't know what to say. "But if I need to contact you —"

"I'll leave my phone on. I need to do this. It's more than my job. This is family."

Tess hung up and wondered about this man of faith. He had his own personal crisis going on, yet he was seeing to someone else in their time of need. Crazy, dedicated, or guilty? She wasn't sure of the answer to that question.

She didn't believe in God per se — she wouldn't call herself an atheist, but this all-knowing, all-seeing God didn't make sense to her. She'd gone to church for years with her dad when she was a kid, but stopped when she was sixteen and he was murdered. The idea of a good God and a murdered father did not mix in Tess's mind, so she never tried to force it.

After doing all she could for Oliver Macpherson, Tess went back to pondering Glen's case. But even after time percolating, she could find no new insight. A knock on her doorframe interrupted her musing. She lifted her gaze and saw a welcome familiar face.

Steve Logan.

She'd been thinking about him, wondering if he'd pop up to help with the Elders homicide, and had even considered calling him if he didn't show. He was the type of guy she was used to. Military-style haircut, squared-away tan uniform, and a steely gaze that had cop written all over it.

"Chief O'Rourke." He flashed a bright smile and Tess had to fight the jump in her heart rate.

"Now there's a hunk of man," she could hear Jeannie say. Thinking of the leer that would follow almost made her smile.

Clearing her throat, Tess said, "Sergeant Logan, after reading your last text, I was afraid you'd not step foot in Rogue's Hollow ever again." She flashed her own smile, thinking about the text he'd sent, detailing how Bubba Magee had barfed in the back of his patrol car twice before he could get the man to jail. The mess and cleanup kept him from being able to help with the homicide yesterday. She felt not a little pleasure at seeing him now, in spite of that unfortunate event.

He stepped into the room and Tess stood.

"You know, stuff happens. I was able to clean the car out, and after about a hundred dollars' worth of air freshener, it smells okay. I'm concluding that Rogue's Hollow is going to be a tough place to stay away from. And now you have a murder. When it rains, it pours. I'd like to help. And I'm cleared to."

Tess held her breath for a minute. With blond hair, blue eyes, classically chiseled features, and a build that said he worked out, the man was devastatingly handsome, but so was Paul, her ex-husband. Underneath Paul's beautiful exterior had lurked a shallow, selfish heart. Tess needed to be on guard. But the crush of loneliness that had stalked her for two months was going to be a difficult bear to combat.

"I think things are handled so far, Sergeant."

"You know, I think I'd rather you call me Steve. I mean, we handled a few scrapes together, and I have a feeling we're going to be working together a lot. No need to be formal." He smiled warmly and extended his hand.

Tess took his hand and relaxed. She liked Logan as a cop and could be a little less formal, but was she opening a door she wasn't ready to step through?

"Come, have a seat. You have something for me?"

"I do." He held up a folder and stepped past the chair to drop it on her desk. "Coroner's report." Logan sat in the offered chair.

Nonplussed, Tess picked it up and then sat back in her chair. "So soon?" She was used to waiting a week or more in Long Beach.

"Except for the tox screen. That'll be a couple of weeks."

She opened the folder and pulled out the report. Time of death interested her right off the bat. Coroner estimated that was between 5 and 5:45 a.m., while it was still dark but getting light. He then stated what had been obvious from the scene: death was a homicide, caused by a 9mm bullet to the head. As Tess feared, there was no usable bullet or fragments found. The head shot was too badly deformed, and in the body the fast-moving projectiles had gone through and through. She made a mental note to go back out to the scene and search again for a bullet. But for the slug taken from the dog, it might be the only piece of evidence tying the killer to the murder. She wasn't holding out hope they'd find prints on the casing.

"He put up a fight. There were scratches on his face and a defensive wound in his hand; the round went through and through." Logan held his hand up. "He was trying to stop a bullet. Elders was shot at least four times."

Tess considered this, visualizing the scene in her mind. "I wish I had a better picture of what happened that morning. Because he held his hand up, do you think there's a possibility the bullet was aimed at someone else? Maybe he was trying to shield a friend. Or his dog." Even as she asked the question, she thought of Tilly. Had she been with Glen?

He gave a head tilt. "You think someone else was there with Glen?"

"Let me show you the pictures, see what you think." Tess turned to her computer and pulled up the crime scene photos. Logan got up and walked around to look over her shoulder. The familiar squeak of leather gear and the light pleasant scent of his aftershave very nearly went to Tess's head. She worked to concentrate on showing him the scene photos.

"This is not a local fishing spot. Look at the smashed grass. It just looks like more than two people were there."

"Hmm, maybe. But maybe there were two killers?"

His nearness caused a jolt of attraction to flare. She pushed back a bit.

"At this point I guess anything is possible. Are you familiar with Tilly Dover?"

He grunted and rolled his eyes. Straightening up, he moved around to the front of her desk but stayed standing. "Everyone knows Tilly. I went to school with her and her brother, Bart. She was relatively normal then — I mean, on medication and stuff. She's bipolar. But she hasn't always been on the streets. After high school she took some junior college classes, wanted to be a paramedic. If I remember right, she might have even become an EMT-1. She also taught Sunday school in church and was functioning for a while. But then her dad died. That sent her around the bend and she's been on the streets ever since. I think Bart washed his hands of her."

He made a fist with his left hand and tapped it with his right palm, pensive expression on his face. "Yep, she and Glen were close. I see where you're going. You think she was with him? That's why you gave us the information about a possible body in the creek."

Tess nodded. "I'm guessing if someone did go into the creek right there, their body would have been seen or located by now."

"Most likely. The creek calms when it reaches the Rogue. Lots of people swim there and fish; a body making it that far would attract attention. It's not cold right now or deep enough to keep a body from decomposing and floating to the surface."

"I thought so. I also recovered a piece of fabric." She frowned. "I'd have wagered money someone went into the creek there."

"And you think it's Tilly?"

"You said yourself that they were close." Tess told him what Pete had said about the tab Glen started for Tilly.

"So if she was there, and she hasn't washed up because she's alive somewhere, she'd be a witness?" Logan shook his head. "Don't bet on it. Girl's brain is scrambled. You'd have better luck with the dog as a witness. Why do you think Glen was there anyway?"

"I can only guess he was meeting someone for some reason. I'm trying to get phone records."

"You find a phone?"

"No, but I have his number. He'd dropped his ride off for repairs, called someone; then a few days later he's dead."

"Well —" Logan hiked a shoulder — "Glen Elders was a dirtbag. He ran with a rough crowd. He probably owed someone money." He held his hand up like a gun. "Pow — said person got tired of waiting."

Tess thought about the bag of money Elders had handed Anna. That certainly was enough money to kill for. She closed the autopsy file and told Logan about the money.

His eyes widened. "Fifty grand? No lie?"

"A notice is due to print in the paper next week. Other than his staff, Pastor Macpherson decided to keep quiet about it until the notice comes out."

He didn't hide his shock. "Well, that's a lot of motive."

Tess agreed. "You dealt with Elders a lot?"

"It's a small valley. He normally bounced between Shady Cove and White City. They don't have their own PDs, so they contract with us — you know that. Elders was a frequent flier. The only thing I'm sure of is that the money wasn't his."

"Money is always a strong motive for murder."

"You just have to find the guy short fifty grand." His smile was brilliant, warm, and Tess bit back a sigh.

She held up the coroner's report. "Thanks for dropping this by."

"Not a problem." He checked his watch. "How about I buy you lunch, get to know the new chief better."

This time Tess thought carefully. He'd been a great help for two months, and she did like him, wanted to get to know him better, but where she came from, too many cops were players. She doubted it was any different here. But she was hungry. She'd done everything she could do for Anna and Glen to this point. Rule #10 applied: "Good cops never get wet or go hungry." And it was better to be on Logan's good side than not.

"I have an investigation to get back to, but it is lunchtime." She smiled back, deciding she'd play friendly for the time being. "You have any place in mind?"

"Sure do. Max's Grill makes the best bacon burger in the Upper Rogue." He stood. "Shall we walk or drive?"

24

Sonya was in shock, crying one minute, composed the next, when Oliver arrived. As a pastor he'd been present at many death-beds, presided over many funeral and memorial services, saw a lot of raw grief, and he never got used to it. It was a painful, broken world they lived in. He never pretended to have all the answers and had learned a long time ago that a simple hug coupled with a quiet presence went a long way. He met Sonya on the porch and just held her for a long while, feeling her pain mingle with his own. After she'd calmed a bit, gained some composure, they sat together on the glider rocker on the front porch. Oliver held her hand and waited to see what she needed most from him.

"Hey, Pastor Mac." Her oldest son shook his hand. The other two Devaroux children lived out of state. "Thanks for coming."

"Of course. Your father was a good man."

After a minute Sonya sniffled. "He said he wasn't feeling good . . . you know, a little under the weather. I thought he was going to take a nap . . ." She squeezed Oliver's hand. "I wasn't expecting this — I wasn't. He was healthy."

She leaned into him and sighed. Oliver rubbed her shoulder and prayed for comfort. He thought of Anna. Typically, she never went with him to situations like this, didn't feel offering immediate comfort was her calling. She would cook for the family, pray for the family, but didn't reach out until the grief was less raw.

Oliver never minded her absence. This was a difficult calling — he knew that — but he also knew it was his place to be here at this time. Now, though, as the mystery of Anna's disappearance was shredding his heart, Oliver wished she were here with him or, at the very least, home waiting for him when he finished.

Anna wasn't home like he'd hoped when he arrived, but his house was clean and full of people. The prayer team was there, along with his pastoral staff. Like Sonya had welcomed his presence, Oliver welcomed theirs. His tank was empty and it wasn't beneath him to admit that he needed support.

Everyone in his living room was worried, not accusatory, but wondering why he'd waited so long to make a report.

"I wasn't certain," he told them. "Maybe she did need time away to pray. We've told you how disheartening the last doctor's appointment was. Anna was angry about the prognosis and she has in the past needed time to herself in order to work things out."

Nods all around. He and Anna had been before the board many times, asking for prayer about the cancer situation.

Casey Reno burst into the house breathless. "Pastor Mac! I just heard. Anna is missing?"

The words sliced Oliver with a reality he could deny if it wasn't voiced, and he had to take a breath before answering. "Casey, I just don't have any idea where she could be."

"I saw her just before she left town the day before yesterday. I . . . I can't believe this."

"You saw her?"

"Yes, she came into the bookstore and asked me to order the books for the women's Bible study. She was on her way to Butte Falls to talk to Octavio."

Oliver frowned. Anna hadn't mentioned planning to take such a trip. Octavio was a pastor in the small town of Butte Falls, southeast of Rogue's Hollow. He had a tiny congregation but a way with the most difficult of people.

"Why was she going there?"

"She didn't say. She just told me in an offhand way as she was leaving the shop."

"I didn't know she'd gone to see Octavio. Will you tell Chief O'Rourke what you just told me?" He pulled out his phone.

"Sure."

"I'm calling Octavio. You call the chief."

Tess's phone began ringing before she finished lunch. Steve Logan turned out to be charming lunch company and she was sorry for the interruption. The first couple of calls were from local news, the paper and all the area TV stations. She'd expected coverage but soon realized that Glen's murder and Anna's disappearance would be the lead stories. Murder and missing cases were sometimes ho-hum in Long Beach, but not here. She'd already sent the media press releases, but they wanted on-air interviews. She was trying to think of a way to hand that off to Mayor Dixon when Casey Reno called.

"Chief O'Rourke, I'm here with Pastor Mac, and I need to tell you that I saw Anna on Wednesday as she was getting ready to leave town."

Reno was talking very fast and Tess caught only a bit of what she was saying.

"Slow down. I'm not getting everything. You saw Anna?"

"Yes, she came into the bookstore. She told me that she was headed out to Butte Falls to talk to a pastor there, Octavio Donner. Pastor Mac is trying to get ahold of him now. It looks like the last place Anna was, was the Butte Falls church."

Butte Falls. An old logging town, small and still somewhat rural. Was this a place they could start searching?

"Good news?" Logan asked when she disconnected.

"Maybe. A possible lead in the Anna Macpherson case."

"Ah, good news for Pastor Mac. She turn up?"

"No, but she was last seen on her way to Butte Falls. Maybe there's a clue there. Thanks for lunch." She got up and he stood with her.

"My pleasure. I enjoyed the conversation." His eyes sparkled with warmth.

Tess felt her face redden slightly. It had

264

been too long since she enjoyed this kind of attention from a man. "Likewise, Steve."

"You heading out to Butte Falls?"

"I am."

"Want some company?"

Tess wanted to say yes immediately. Before lunch she was cool concerning the sergeant, but now she found herself wavering back and forth from enchantment to disenchantment, stronger on the enchantment, when it came to Steve Logan. And she had to admit, she liked his company. He was a bright, entertaining guy. They'd even talked about getting together off duty. He promised to take her rafting down the Rogue, something that appealed to her a great deal. It sounded good to Tess, but was it too good to be true?

"I was going to ask for the sheriff's department's help since Butte Falls is outside of my jurisdiction . . . ," she said, hoping she sounded professional and not as lonely as she felt. When it came to romance, a part of her thought that everything in her mind was covered with the black gunk her divorce had thrown over her life. Was that still too dark and gooey? The other part of her liked Logan and longed for some closeness, a closeness she'd not had with Paul since well before the marriage officially ended.

"I'll check in and let them know that I'm

with you."

"I have to stop by the church. Pastor Macpherson wants to come with me when I talk to this pastor in Butte Falls."

"You want him tagging along?"

"I do. He knows his wife's habits." She caught her breath when she realized there was a different meaning to his question. "Do you think he had something to do with his wife's disappearance?"

Logan shrugged, cop face securely in place. "Pastor Mac has a good reputation in the valley. I don't go to his church, but I know a lot who do. But you know as well as I do, appearances can be deceiving."

Tess nodded. She did know that — boy, did she know that. But her cop instincts told her Macpherson was innocent here. He'd have a better idea of his wife's route, habits, whatever, than she would.

"I think he'll be helpful. I'll pick him up and follow you to Butte Falls."

"You're the chief." He smiled and squeezed her upper arm in a casual way, but it nonetheless sent a pleasant shiver down Tess's spine. It might be quite uplifting to maintain friendly relations with the county sheriff's department liaison.

The church parking lot was packed when Tess pulled in. It looked as if the whole town and then some were at the pastor's home. She was happy to see someone had helped the pastor clean up the mess the burglar made. Logan didn't get out of his car when Tess went to get Pastor Macpherson. She could see that the pastor's head was down, and he was listening to an older man who was speaking into his ear. The crowd of people looked her way expectantly, and Tess did her best to project command presence and confidence.

"Chief, I wish I'd known at breakfast you were looking for Anna." Casey stepped forward, a familiar face in the crowd. But there was worry etched in her face.

"Me too, but we weren't certain then. Did she say anything about why she was going to Butte Falls? Did she have an appointment?"

"No." Casey bit her bottom lip. "I should have asked more questions, but it was so routine, so normal . . ." She wiped an eye.

"Chief O'Rourke, are the break-in at the pastor's house and Anna being missing related?" The question came from Damien Gangly, the man who compiled the crime section of the local paper. The area was small enough that weekly arrests were noted in the independent newspaper. Tess had dealt with Damien often and considered him a fair, thoughtful man. He had his signature camera slung around his neck and recorder in his hand.

"Everything is preliminary, Damien."

"But you must have a theory."

"Sure, I could speculate, but that won't get us anywhere at the moment. The pressing issue is the location of Anna Macpherson. As far as that goes, I want facts and good leads, not speculation. Now, excuse me. I need Pastor Macpherson."

She searched the sea of semi-familiar faces, and without her asking, they parted for the pastor to walk toward her. She noticed the man who'd been speaking to him was by his side, a man Tess vaguely recognized. She'd met a lot of people in two months; names were sometimes difficult to put to faces. This guy obviously had the pastor's ear. He had an interesting scarred face with a flattened nose, and Tess wondered if he'd been a boxer.

"I'm here, Chief, ready to go," Pastor Macpherson said.

"Are you going to Butte Falls?" Damien asked. "Do you need volunteers? Searchers?"

Tess held a hand up, cognizant that everyone was watching and listening to her. "We're going to talk to the person who possibly was the last to see Anna Macpherson and try and retrace her steps. It's important that we have a chance to evaluate this situation before we ask for volunteers or organize a large-scale search."

"Haven't you wasted enough time already?" That came from Mayor Dixon and it surprised Tess. He'd been supportive earlier.

The man with the flat nose cut off her answer. In a rough, deep voice he said, "Now, Douglas, stop being a wannabe cop and let the chief do her job. She needs to know all the facts before letting people like you muck it up." That got some chuckles from the crowd and Dixon shot the man a glare.

"Mayor Dixon —" Tess worked on her best conciliatory tone — "channel 10 and channel 12 are sending film crews to Rogue's Hollow. They'd like an on-air interview. It would be a great help if you could handle that."

Dixon's whole demeanor changed. "TV news? 10 and 12?"

"Yes. I e-mailed you the press release. There's really nothing else to add, but if you could do the interview, I'd appreciate it."

All eyes were on the mayor.

He nodded. "Yes, well, I believe I can handle that."

"Great."

She turned to Macpherson, who looked around at the crowd.

"Thank you, Jethro. Thank you for your help today. I ask that you keep Anna in your prayers until we have something else for you to do or we bring her home."

Nods and murmurs of approval rippled through the crowd. And Tess couldn't help but notice the effect Macpherson had on people. As tired as he looked, and as stressed as she bet he was, he could give a class on command presence and leadership, she thought. Part of her wondered what it would be like to listen to one of his sermons. She shook off the thought and directed the pastor to her patrol car.

Butte Falls was roughly forty minutes away, a left turn off of Highway 62. After they left Rogue's Hollow, they drove through Trail, then Shady Cove. The ride was quiet for the first ten or fifteen minutes. Finally Macpherson spoke up.

"That Steve Logan in the sheriff's car?" he asked.

"Yeah, you know him?"

"I've spoken to him once or twice."

"We're going to his jurisdiction, so it's

good to have his help." She cast a glance at the pastor. He was looking out the window and she couldn't read him.

"Your wife didn't mention going out here to speak to this other pastor, this Octavio fellow?"

"No, but I'd left just after breakfast, had a meeting to attend. She might have gotten a call from Octavio and didn't want to disturb me. I'm guessing. I called him but he was out cutting wood. By the time we get to the church, he'll be available."

"Is it out of the ordinary for her to head off to Butte Falls?"

"Not really. We work closely with Octavio, and Anna is good friends with his wife, Esperanza. She's learning to speak Spanish and likes to practice with Esperanza."

Tess made the turn for Butte Falls behind Logan and the car again fell silent. She realized then that she felt certain now the pastor was not guilty here. Anna needed to be found, but anxiety welled up inside. Tess's gut told her Anna was not missing voluntarily. And that left only the other alternative: she was missing because she couldn't come home, because someone was holding her against her will or she was dead.

The second possibility pained Tess more than she would have thought possible.

25

The Butte Falls church was on Crowfoot Road. Technically not in Butte Falls proper, it was in Eagle Point but served Butte Falls. It was small and reminded Tess of an old-fashioned one-room schoolhouse, with a peaked roof sporting a cross where a school bell might have been. They'd climbed some in elevation. There was forest all around and the smell of pine trees and fresh air hit as soon as she got out of the car. A slight man who looked Mexican met them as they approached the building.

"Pastor Mac." He smiled, looking hesitant as his eyes took in Tess and Logan. "What's up? Esperanza say you called for me." His speech was heavily accented.

"Octavio." Macpherson held his hand out and the two men shook. "I don't think you've met our new chief." He gestured to Tess. "This is Chief O'Rourke. And you know Sergeant Logan."

Octavio nodded and Tess shook his offered hand. "Nice to meet you, Chief O'Rourke, but I think something must be wrong, you here."

"We don't know that yet. We just wanted to ask you some questions."

"Yes," Macpherson jumped in. "Octavio, did Anna come to see you the day before yesterday?"

Octavio nodded slowly and set Tess on edge. There was something off about this guy.

"*Sí*. She come to talk about Glen."

"Glen?" Macpherson looked surprised. Tess and Logan exchanged glances.

"What about Glen?" Tess asked.

Octavio grinned. "He's a believer now. He came to Christ, got clean from the drugs. Anna, she want to make sure that Glen, he tell the truth." He paused. Then held his hands up. "Well, it's true. Glen, he Christian now."

Obviously the Rogue telegraph and news of Glen's murder had not reached here for some reason. However, Octavio's information brightened Macpherson. Tess remembered enough of church to know that this was important to believing individuals. For a brief second it brought back the memory of how happy her dad had been when she

273

was baptized. Shaking the memory from her thoughts, she concentrated on the task at hand and couldn't help but notice that Octavio would not look her in the eye. He concentrated on Macpherson. He didn't even glance at Logan.

"Glen's more than that, Octavio. He was murdered yesterday."

Octavio's eyes got wide. "Murdered? What, uh . . . how this happen?"

Macpherson filled him in.

"Oh, *Dios mío,*" he said, shaking his head. "Who would do this? What does it have to do with Anna?"

"We're trying to figure that out. How long was she here with you?" Tess asked.

Octavio hiked a shoulder. "We had lunch, my wife with us; then she go home. One, maybe one thirty."

"Did she tell you she was going home when she left?"

"*Sí,* she say she want to tell Pastor Mac about Glen. She was very happy." Again he muttered something in Spanish. Tess caught shock in his tone and his words, something about the devil's work. Murder was that.

Tess saw Macpherson frown. Octavio saw it too because he asked, "What's wrong? Something happen to Anna?"

"We don't know," Macpherson said.

"She . . . well, she hasn't called or anything and she's not been home since Wednesday morning. Glen told you that he changed his life, or you see that he did?"

"I see with my own eyes. He's a new person. And now he's with Jesus."

Tess folded her arms and stared at Octavio, wondering if this information about Glen could possibly have any bearing on Anna's whereabouts. "Anna didn't mention a side trip, another stop, anything?"

Octavio shrugged. "No, nothing." He looked down at his feet.

After a beat to get the man's reaction, she asked, "Is your wife here now?"

Octavio looked toward the church. "Yes, she's with the baby."

"I'd like to talk to her." Tess started for the door.

But Octavio stopped her. "Not here. My house. It's over there." He pointed to the other side of the lot to a single-wide trailer. "But she don't know where Anna is."

"I'd still like to ask her myself." Tess nodded to Logan. "I'll be right back."

He said nothing and Tess couldn't read his expression. Could Logan see there was something wrong here or was it just her?

As she walked away, she could hear the three men begin talking about Anna, Octavio's dismay sounding insincere as far as Tess was concerned.

A woman peered through the curtains as Tess approached the trailer. Her face was visible above a sticker with the PSS security logo. As she stepped up on a small wooden porch, the curtain dropped abruptly.

Tess rapped on the door. "Esperanza, it's the police. I just want to ask you a few questions."

She heard shuffling and the sound of a baby cooing. It was a long moment before the door opened.

"Sí?" A dark-haired woman with beautiful eyes and a fearful expression stood in the doorway, holding a baby on her hip. "I no speak English," she said, smiling tentatively.

"No importa. Hablo español." Tess was fluent in Spanish and she could tell Esperanza was surprised by that.

Tess asked about Anna, and Esperanza looked anxiously over Tess's shoulder at her husband before she answered. She basically said the same thing her husband did, except for the time Anna left. Esperanza said Anna left sometime after two and that she had a long, private talk with Octavio before she did go.

Tess mulled this over as she walked back across the parking lot to the church. Octavio was hiding something — she could feel it — but it didn't track with her that it was murder. Still, she couldn't assume. She glanced around the church grounds and knew there could be a car hidden somewhere. She and Logan would have to take a look.

"What specifically did you and Anna talk about?" she asked Octavio when she returned to the men.

"Glen. I told you."

Before Tess could follow up, Macpherson spoke up. "Octavio specializes in reaching hard-to-reach men. He's a prison chaplain. This is big that Glen turned away from his old life and wanted a new one."

"I get that," Tess said, keeping eyes on Octavio. "But your wife said you had a long, private conversation with Anna. What did you talk about?"

He seemed prepared and answered quickly. "A job. We try to think of where we can find Glen a good job."

If Octavio was surprised by their visit at first, he clearly had recovered. He looked Tess in the eye and smiled, but for the life of her, she couldn't shake the feeling that there was something off about the guy.

"Do you mind if Sergeant Logan and I

take a look around the grounds?"
He shook his head. "No, go ahead."

26

"There are two ways to get home from here," Oliver said after the chief asked him which way Anna would have gone home from the Butte Falls church. Logan had already left to return to White City, but not before he and the chief had a lengthy private conversation while they searched the church grounds. Oliver worked hard to stay calm, but it was clear the chief had a problem with Octavio.

She was way off base, he was sure. Oliver had known Octavio for five years and seen only a man dedicated to helping those who could not seem to break away from drugs or a life of criminality.

"What is the most likely route for her to take?"

"The way we came. The other way is to head up Crowfoot to Highway 62. It takes longer because it's winding and more scenic."

She started the car and pulled out of the church lot, heading in the direction of the scenic route. "Since we didn't see any indication that her car broke down coming here, we'll check out this route," she said.

He agreed with her by nodding but said nothing. The gravity of the search was striking home; what if they found Anna's car on this road after all this time?

He noticed that she drove less than the speed limit. Normally Oliver liked this route. Crowfoot climbed up into the mountains bordering Butte Falls. It was rural here. A lot of houses were set on large pieces of forested land. He'd lived here as a child, and while he didn't remember much of that time in his life, the pictures his parents cherished, the trees and the forests of southern Oregon, had cemented his desire to return to the area. God had since blessed him with a thriving church, and he soaked in the culture of the area, recognizing that the rich history of logging gave Oregonians an affinity with the land many people from out of state couldn't understand. The forested scenery often gave him peace. But today he felt ready to jump out of his skin.

"You're wrong, you know," he said to Chief O'Rourke.

"About what?"

"About Octavio. He would never hurt Anna."

"Do you think she's hurt?"

That question hit Oliver like a right cross to the jaw. "I, uh . . ." He sucked in a breath. Grabbing hold of the handle above the door, he squeezed and braced himself to say what he'd been thinking but didn't want to be true.

It was out there now. The implication hung over Oliver like a noose.

"I can't imagine any other reason why she hasn't called or come home."

Anna was not coming home.

He felt Chief O'Rourke glance his way but he wouldn't meet her eyes.

"I just have a bad feeling about your friend. A gut instinct he's hiding something. It might not be about Glen's murder, but it's something. I trust my instincts; they've always served me well. Rule #4: 'Always trust your gut.' "

"Maybe, but I trust Octavio."

"Trust him because he's a fellow pastor?"

Now Oliver did meet her gaze. "No, because he's a friend."

"Fair enough," she said and returned her attention to the road.

She slowed a couple of times. Oliver noticed her checking out side roads, driveways, anything that looked traveled, he thought. They were losing daylight. It was when they began to travel downhill that she pulled over and stopped at an overgrown logging road.

"Ever been on that road?"

He eyeballed the side road. "No. Doesn't look passable."

"Someone has driven it lately." She shifted the car into park and got out.

Oliver followed after a few seconds. The chief made her way down the road as it jogged right into a copse of trees. He wasn't certain who saw it first, but there in the brush, he saw the rear end of a sedan.

Anna's car.

Oliver lurched forward, but Chief O'Rourke grabbed his arm, the strength of her grip surprising him and stopping him cold.

"Let me look first. I don't want you destroying any evidence."

A protest died on Oliver's lips, the impulse to scream for Anna almost overpowering. He knew the chief was right, but the urge to leap forward and look inside the car was all-consuming.

She stepped toward the vehicle carefully, pulling gloves out of her pocket as she did so. He saw her touch the trunk and lean down and sniff before continuing to the driver's door. After an inspection she turned back toward Oliver.

"No one is inside the car."

He didn't know whether to be happy or sad at that pronouncement. Then the chief opened the driver's door and leaned down to pop the trunk. Oliver felt some relief when he saw the trunk was empty as well. But dread settled in like a cold, heavy, wet fog.

Where was Anna?

27

There was nothing wrong with Anna's car. There were no keys, and when Oliver produced his keys, the car started easily. If she'd parked the car here herself, she could have easily walked back to the road to flag someone down. But why leave a perfectly running car?

Tess immediately called Sergeant Logan back to the scene.

He did his own once-over of the car. Wearing a stoic cop face, he stood next to Tess and Oliver. "It will take some time to call in all the personnel in the area's search and rescue team. If you want, I'll go get us some coffee or water for while we wait."

"Thanks, Steve. That'd be nice." Tess wasn't hungry or thirsty but worried for Oliver. While they waited for Steve to return, Victor Camus showed up.

"Can I help with anything?" he asked. "I heard the call for search and rescue on my scanner."

Since Tess didn't know the man too well, she wasn't sure, but Oliver was happy to see him.

"He's the best tracker in the area," the pastor explained.

Tess outlined the situation.

Victor shook his head. "I'll wait for the dogs. If I go traipsing about the brush now, I'll mess up any scent trail."

Tess saw the disappointment in Oliver's face that Victor couldn't charge in and search; she felt his impatience. Waiting was the most difficult task in the world. But Camus had a steadying effect on the pastor, and she was glad that he'd shown up.

Steve returned a few minutes later, but it was an hour before the first Jackson County search and rescue vehicles began arriving, and another half hour before the sheriff arrived and organized everyone so he could brief them. Tess was certain the fear that the woman was dead was dancing on the fringes of everyone's thoughts, if not completely settled in.

But the first dogs on scene showed no indication Anna was in the area. In fact, there was no sign of Anna Macpherson anywhere within a large radius of the car, and the investigation took an ominous turn.

The text messages were obvious fakes. Tess believed Anna had not sent the ones Oliver received.

The disappearance was now deemed "foul play suspected." A somber Victor took Oliver home while Tess stayed to talk to the Jackson County sheriff as the search and rescue teams packed up to leave and a tow truck arrived for Anna's car.

Tess had a long conversation with the sheriff. He had the resources to conduct a wide-ranging search and was moving forward, and for that, Tess was grateful.

"It's obvious her car didn't break down. But if she was kidnapped, why?" Sheriff Gray wondered. "Did she pick up a hitchhiker and get into trouble? Yet her absence would seem to indicate she was taken somewhere in another car. We've got more questions than answers."

"I agree," Tess said. "If she was kidnapped for ransom, no one has contacted Pastor Mac."

"You hear anything at all, let me know."

"I will." Tess thanked him, grateful that Gray was thorough, easy to talk to, and not a game player.

By Saturday morning the case was front page and helicopters were scouring the forest from the air. Search and rescue sent teams into the area where the car was found to check out some old logging roads, but there was no sign or scent of Anna. The consensus was someone in another car took her from the scene. The million-dollar question was why.

Mayor Dixon had taped a poignant and classy interview for TV while Tess was in Butte Falls, Tess had to admit. She hoped it would bring calls, because it was taped before they'd found the car. The only downside to the interview was that second-guessers were questioning her reticence to start a large-scale search and call for helicopters the minute the missing report had been filed. She resisted the urge to be snarky and say, "Until we knew where the car was, we had no idea where to search." To mobilize man and machine they needed a starting place.

As for the search, Anna Macpherson could be anywhere in an area as big as Long Beach and covered in trees. Tess was up late studying a topographical map of the area between her town and Octavio's church.

At breakfast Saturday morning, yawning, she was still looking at the map, and that caught Addie's attention.

"You think Anna's in there somewhere?" She filled Tess's coffee cup.

Anna had displaced Glen as the topic of conversation, though Tess couldn't shake the feeling that the two cases were one.

Tess hiked a shoulder. "No, I don't. It's looking as if someone took Anna somewhere. She could be anywhere. This is so frustrating. I'd rather do just about anything other than *wait*. But there's almost nothing to do right now except wait." She held out her hands, palms up.

"Kidnapped? By who and why?" Addie was aghast. She set her coffeepot down and leaned over the table to look Tess in the eye. "Please find her."

The concern and fear in her eyes radiated across the table and hit Tess hard. She swallowed, put her hand over Addie's. "I will. . . . I will."

She wasn't hungry, but Tess ordered an omelet for breakfast anyway, knowing she'd need the energy. Addie gave a satisfied nod and moved on to another table.

Through her sleep-deprived fog, Tess felt the full import of finding Anna's car all over again and it took her breath away. Oliver had prayed last night for his wife, and while Tess listened, she had too much experience under her belt to believe there would be a positive result to Anna's situation. It hurt. Anna was a victim in this mess; Tess had to believe that. Oliver obviously believed in God and that his God had some modicum of control over this life. If that were true, why did innocents like Anna suffer, even die, at the hands of evil men?

It brought back the memory of that day, years ago, her sixteenth birthday. She'd been so excited. She and her dad were going to celebrate with a b-day Dodgers game. They were both true-blue Dodgers fans. He worked days and was planning an early out so they'd make the game. She was waiting for his shift to end, his car to pull into the driveway.

But it wasn't her dad's car that pulled into the driveway. It was the chief of police bringing the news that Daniel O'Rourke was never going to come home. He'd stepped in front of a battered woman to protect her from her crazed husband and taken a bullet in the forehead. He died instantly on the ground in front of a beat-up Long Beach duplex. His partner, Ronnie Riggs, returned fire and killed the husband, but it was little consolation to sixteen-year-old Tess.

Emotions from that day came flooding back. Tess choked them down, gulping coffee and wondering how anyone could believe God was good when innocent, even heroic people died too soon due to the actions of evil men.

Tess cast a glance around the dining room, struggling to keep her composure. She wiped her eyes, hoping no one noticed, and forced her thoughts back to the present.

She'd been up late with Pastor Macpherson and Officer Bender, hashing over any possible scenario for why someone would kidnap Anna. Macpherson was shell-shocked but he was still helpful. He pulled up a file he kept of all the threatening e-mails he'd received over the years — there weren't many — hoping maybe they held a clue, maybe this was personal, not related to Glen. But the threats were all directed at Oliver. Anna was never mentioned.

None of it made sense. The Macphersons were not wealthy, and if the bag of money were the issue, no demands had been made. Tess submitted requests for Anna's phone records, and Macpherson had logged into their bank account. There had been no activity on the debit card for a week. As for the phone, it was an older model with GPS, but there was no ping, so the device was obviously off.

This morning Tess had noticed all the activity over at the church. She could see cars filling up the lot as if it were Sunday before she left her room to come to breakfast.

Help and support or folks looking to stare at tragedy? Tess wondered. Then she chastised herself for being so cynical. Anna was a nice person. Even though Tess herself had only known the woman for a couple of months, she felt her absence keenly. These people who'd known and loved her for years must be hurting.

She ate half of her omelet, then asked Addie for a thermos of coffee to go.

Before Addie handed Tess the coffee, she said, "Don't wear yourself out. Call the sheriff if you need to."

"I've talked to the sheriff at length, Addie. Don't worry. I'm not afraid to ask for help if I think I need it." Even after she made the comment to Addie, she felt a twinge of guilt. Glen's murder investigation had taken a backseat to Anna's disappearance. Both deserved a thorough look. Should she hand one off to an agency with more resources?

But a thought nagged: if they were related, one and the same case, then logically, Anna was most likely dead. It pained Tess to consider that thought.

Tess left the restaurant and headed for her office. Yeah, she'd spoken to the sheriff and he was already helping her by doing the house-to-house knock-and-talk on Crow-foot. He'd also gotten a helicopter in the air. But no matter how much help she had, she needed a motive, a starting point, and didn't have one. That was driving her crazy.

A group of people was waiting for her outside the police station when she arrived. She didn't recognize any of them, but that didn't mean they weren't from Rogue's Hollow. Tess doubted she'd met everyone.

"Can I help you all?"

"Are you the chief?" a woman asked.

"Yes."

"We're here to help find Anna Macpherson."

"What are you doing to find her?" another asked.

"I'm doing all I can to find her —"

"Looks like you're going to sit in your office and drink coffee."

"Yeah, you got donuts in there?"

An ugly laughter rippled through the group.

"Are you only good at shooting children and not at helping adults?"

That comment struck like a baton blow and Tess blinked. Had she failed Anna? She took a deep breath and moved up to the top step and faced the crowd. "Search and rescue found no indication Anna was anywhere near her car."

"Send out a helicopter or search dogs. Do something — we pay you for that."

"Helicopters are up, but the dogs didn't key on anything —"

"Is that just an excuse?"

Tess tensed, felt perspiration form on her forehead, and worked to keep a cop face. She'd faced hostile crowds before, but this unexpected group was hitting like a thousand bee stings, ripping the scab off the wound from the Cullen Hoover shooting. That battle had rocked her self-confidence, and she suddenly felt so completely inadequate.

The group started to get uglier, angry, but someone approaching caught Tess's eye. It was Oliver Macpherson.

A person in the crowd saw him also, and like a wave they turned toward him.

"We're trying to get the police to do something to find your wife," the first woman said.

"All she knows how to do is shoot kids."

For a second, for Tess, it was Long Beach all over again. If Oliver hadn't been there, if his quiet presence hadn't bolstered her, Tess wasn't certain she would have been able to stand calmly.

Macpherson stepped toward Tess and the crowd parted.

"The chief is doing everything in her power to find Anna," he said. "I heard some very unhelpful suggestions coming from this group. Chief O'Rourke hasn't taken any time off since Anna went missing; she's doing everything possible. I appreciate your help, but casting aspersions on the chief won't help."

There were murmurs, a little contrition.

"It just doesn't seem like anything is happening," someone called out.

"Well, as soon as we have a better handle on what we have, you can bet a lot will be happening," the pastor said. "Please, you'll help Anna and me by praying for this situation and supporting the chief." He pointed across the street. "At the church a group is forming to search, knock on doors. If you want to help, Travis and Jethro are the people to talk to."

Slowly the crowd broke up, several people shaking Macpherson's hand as they left the station. He turned to Tess. "Sorry about that."

She swallowed, some strength returning. "Not your fault. People watch too many cop shows on TV that they think adequately represent reality." She shrugged with fake nonchalance, wanting to open the door, step inside, and shut it tightly behind her. "Makes them expect us to be miracle workers. I'm just a cop, not clairvoyant."

He nodded. "I came to see if I could help you with anything."

She pushed into the station, empty today. Civilian personnel were off on the weekends. The officer on duty was Del. Tess had heard him respond to a vehicle versus deer near the trailer park. Bender wanted to come in on his own time, but Tess had advised him to get some sleep, said she would call if she needed him. Right now her thin wall of composure was about to crack.

"Give me a second," she said, handing Macpherson the thermos of coffee. "I'll be back in a jiff. Take a seat in my office."

Without waiting for an acknowledgment, she hurried to the ladies' room. Tess closed the door to the small room behind her and leaned against it, wiping the perspiration from her forehead with the back of her trembling hand.

I should have known, sooner or later, something like this would happen, she thought to herself. The shooting was never going to let her go. Wiping her sweaty palms on her thighs, Tess took a deep breath, fighting panic. It wouldn't have hit so hard if some part of her didn't feel that she'd let Anna and Oliver Macpherson down in some way. Maybe she should have left law enforcement completely, given up the vain hope she'd be able to salvage her career. Were people dead because she couldn't let go? Was that honoring her father?

Pop. Always in the back of her mind was her father. He'd died a hero, and Tess was never going to reach his stature. She was tainted, frozen, ineffectual.

Stepping to the sink, she cupped her hand, filled it with water, and splashed some on her face. The cold water was bracing, but it didn't stop the tears. She let them fall, feeling as if her only way out was to give everything to the sheriff and leave, go home to Long Beach, find a place to hide and not ever be in a place where she'd let people down like this.

Let her father down.

Sucking it up, hating the weakness of tears, Tess grabbed a couple of paper towels and patted her face dry, wishing harder than she had in weeks that her father were there for her to talk to.

Staring at her red-faced reflection in the mirror, she said, "Was there something else I should have done? Pop, I tried, but just when it feels as if my feet are under me, I get tripped up. What would you do? What would you say?"

Her voice echoed in the empty restroom. She knew there would be no audible answer. She leaned over the sink, warm forehead pressed against the cool mirror, breath fogging the glass. Something did come to mind.

"When you don't know, go back to what you do know."

It was one of her father's rules, another one that hadn't made her list. She couldn't remember why it wasn't on her list because it hit her like he'd tossed her a lifeline.

Standing straight and taking a deep breath, she said, "I don't know a lot; that's for sure. But I do know there's a killer out there who needs catching. And there are good people like Oliver and Anna who have faith in me."

She felt control return slowly.

"And I do know I'm not a quitter. I won't quit, Pop. I can't. And I won't quit on Anna or Glen."

Tess blew her nose and rinsed her face again, working to make herself presentable and hoping Oliver wouldn't recognize her breakdown. She straightened her uniform and remembered how her father always fussed to make sure his uniform was squared away and spotless, shoes sporting a deep shine, when he hit the streets.

"Want respect? Earn it with spit and polish and hard work."

Confidence snapped her straight. *I'm the chief of police. I know my job.*

There would be doubts and doubters until they found Anna, but she wasn't going to let that tie her up in knots. Anna and Oliver deserved her best, and that's what they'd get.

Inhaling deeply, Tess wadded the paper towel up and made a two-pointer into the trash basket.

"Thanks, Pop," she said before she turned away from the mirror and left the restroom to get back to work.

Oliver was standing when she stepped into her office. He was looking at her father's folded flag. It was the one personal decoration she had hanging on the wall.

"Did you pour yourself some coffee?" she asked as she grabbed a cup for herself.

He faced her and shook his head. "Thought I'd wait for you." He pointed to the flag. "I've noticed this before but never read the plaque. That's your father's?"

"Yes," she said, concentrating on pouring coffee. "He was killed in the line of duty. I had to fight my brother for it, but he eventually conceded that it would go better in my

298

office than his." She handed him a cup of coffee and then changed the subject. "I saw a lot of traffic at church this morning."

"People want to help." He took the coffee.

Tess considered this for a minute. "So those people are searchers?"

"And prayer warriors. Travis is a great organizer. I'm too distracted."

She could see he was tired; he'd probably gotten less sleep than she had. "Have a seat, Oliver. I'll check my e-mail and see if there's anything there to help us."

She and Macpherson settled in her office. Tess turned on her computer. There were a couple of e-mails waiting, and she knew immediately they were the phone records she'd been waiting for. Both for Glen and Anna. Could this finally be a lead?

28

"One of the last calls Glen made was to your wife's cell phone." Tess noted the cell towers used. She knew the basics of cell phone triangulation because of the system cell phone companies developed for 911 dispatchers. Multiple towers are used to track the phone's location by measuring the time delay that a signal takes to return back to the towers. The delay is calculated into distance and gives a fairly accurate location of the phone. There wasn't a tower in Rogue's Hollow. Calls made in this town generally pinged off a tower on Crowfoot or one in Shady Cove. There was also a tower in Butte Falls, and that was where Anna's phone was identified as being. It looked like Anna was in Butte Falls when she talked to Glen, and Glen was here in Rogue's Hollow.

Oliver looked thoughtful. She saw his throat work as he swallowed.

"Can you tell if she answered or not?"

Tess nodded. "The call lasted fifteen minutes. It's the last call showing on your wife's phone record, but there are three more on Glen's phone." She highlighted the calls and showed them to the pastor. "Do you recognize any of the numbers?"

Oliver took the sheet from her and studied the numbers. "One is to Octavio — at least that's the number for the Butte Falls church. The others I don't recognize." He handed it back.

Tess dialed the unknown numbers and got a "number not in service" recording for one. When she dialed the other, she got the recording for the PSS business office.

"What?" She stared at the phone and saw Oliver staring at her.

"He called PSS. What on earth would a homeless man need with a security system?" Tess left a message for Beto Acosta, asking for a call back.

She checked the time and date on the phone calls. Based on what Casey had said about Anna being in her shop, and the time Octavio had given for Anna's arrival at the church, Anna probably talked to Glen while she drove to Butte Falls. Tess wished she could know what the conversation was about. One missing, one dead — that phone

301

call might just tell a tale.

She studied Oliver. He seemed defeated and deflated but determined to soldier on. Tess felt a twinge in her own gut as his pain radiated to her. The odds that his wife was still alive were not good. But she would not say that to him.

Bringing her hands together, she tapped her fingertips and asked, "What do you think they talked about?"

"Glen's salvation. I'm sure of it." He seemed to get a second wind and stood to pace. "Glen probably told her he was ready to change his life."

"Why wouldn't he have told her that when he gave her the money? And maybe where the money came from?"

"I can't know for certain, but at that point Anna might not have believed him and instead called the police."

"Why?"

"One time a few years ago, Glen told us he'd changed. We believed him and let him come stay with us." He shook his head.

"It was a mistake?"

"A big one. Turned out he only needed money. We don't have much of value now, and we didn't then, but Anna had a ring her mother had given her and an expensive guitar. Glen stole them both and pawned them. We never got either back and learned our lesson. Trust but verify." He flashed a wry, sad smile.

"A good rule."

Oliver continued. "Anna probably wanted to talk to Octavio, see what he thought, determine if the conversion was real this time."

"When we talked to him yesterday, he seemed to think Glen was telling the truth. And I suppose him giving you all that money . . ."

Since Tess was just about certain Glen was killed because of the money, it followed that he'd obviously gotten ahold of it illegally and wanted to come clean, which was why he gave it to his cousin. Did that gesture seal her fate?

Tess fought a shudder. If Glen was dead because of the money, it's possible Anna was also dead because of the money. She wasn't ready to voice that thought to Oliver.

"We'll give him the benefit of the doubt," she said. "He was trying to turn over a new leaf. But it had to be other people's money he gave you, and they could not have been happy about it. Glen should have known something bad would happen because of what he did."

"I've wondered about that. Do you think that if we'd found him sooner, maybe . . . ? Well, I mean we could have . . ."

"Prevented what happened?" She frowned and shook her head. "If it was the money that got Glen killed, he made the choice to take it. That's on him, not you."

Oliver was quiet for a moment. "Are you certain the money is what got Glen killed?" he finally asked.

"Not 100 percent. But right now, it's a logical supposition. I'm thinking he was confronted by the man he stole from. Glen no longer had the money, couldn't give it back, and that got him killed. Next, your home was broken into and ransacked. Someone wanted their money back." *Maybe that's what happened to Anna. She also ran afoul of the person who wanted his money back,* she thought but didn't say.

Oliver looked at her, an odd expression on his face. "I doubt that my house being broken into had anything to do with money. I can't say why I think that, but . . ."

"But what? Is there something you're not telling me?"

He nodded and pinched the bridge of his nose. "Chief, I know who ransacked my house. I didn't tell you earlier because, well, I really had to think about it."

"What?" Tess tensed. "You know who ransacked your house?"

"I recognized her face. It was Tilly Dover. She's —"

"Tilly? I've been looking for her. She's Glen's friend. Why would you keep this from me?" Tess felt her pulse pound. She thought she could trust this man, and here he was withholding evidence.

"Because she needs help, not jail. I was hoping to find her, ask her why she did what she did. Yes, she was often with Glen. But she's not his killer and she would never hurt Anna." He held her gaze and Tess saw hopeful naiveté there.

Was this a sinister omission or just because the man was a pastor and he saw good in people where none existed?

LTS. Listen. Think. Speak. Tess waited and let her pulse calm. She knew she'd need to reevaluate this.

"She's a drug addict, unpredictable. Why wouldn't she be after the money? She must have known he gave it to you —" Tess stopped midsentence.

"What?" Oliver asked. "Did you remember something?"

"No, it's just pieces falling into place. She knew Glen was dead. She's not in any information stream that I know of. She was

305

there when he was shot."

She saw realization spread across Oliver's face. "And she survived?"

"Someone else was there — I'm sure of it. We thought someone went into the creek, but a body hasn't surfaced. It must have been Tilly who was there; that's the only thing that makes sense."

Oliver arched an eyebrow. "A witness to the murder."

"Hopefully someone we can talk to eventually."

He nodded and said nothing.

Tess thought for a minute, energized. "This is something to do. I need to find Tilly."

"I want to help."

"Pastor Macpherson —"

"Oliver."

"Oliver, there is really nothing for you to do. This is a police matter."

"It's my wife."

"Yes, I realize that. But you need to be at home in case someone does call and demand a ransom. And you still have a church to run."

"The church is second to Anna, no matter what. I'm just not a good bench sitter."

"Neither am I. I'll do everything I can to find her, I promise."

Again he held her gaze and Tess saw the pain in his eyes, the questioning, the fear. But there was also strength and resolve there. The more she knew Oliver Macpherson, the more she doubted that his wife would ever walk away voluntarily.

Tess vowed to herself that she'd turn over every rock. Trouble was, was it already too late?

29

"How well do you know Bart Dover?" Tess asked Oliver.

"Pretty well. He's a regular church attender and I've dedicated all of his children." He paused and looked away.

"What is it?"

"He tried to help Tilly. It was just too much. She is so often not in her right mind that he feared for his children. We thought tough love would have an impact, wake her up, but . . . well, that hasn't been the case."

Tess shook her head. "Not your fault, not his fault. I dealt with so many homeless people in Long Beach with mental issues. No one has the best answer for how to help them. They fall through the cracks too easily. And drug abuse issues exacerbate the problem. If I were a parent, I'd think my first priority would be my children. I don't blame Bart for giving up."

"Anna never gave up on her. She prayed

with her often and tried to direct her to programs that would help her beat the addiction. Tilly was never ready to take that step to sobriety."

"And they can't be forced. If they don't want the help, it will never stick." She got up. "I'm going to have a talk with Mr. Dover. With any luck, he might have an idea where I'm likely to find his sister."

Oliver stood. "I'm going with you." Before Tess could raise an objection, he said, "He might be more forthcoming with me there."

Tess thought about that for a moment and then agreed. The family might be more inclined to talk if it meant helping Pastor Macpherson.

The Dovers had several acres on the western boundary of Rogue's Hollow. They grew pears and peaches and touted that everything was organic. Tess drove west past Wild Automotive on River Drive. She passed residential streets on her left — Broken Wheel, Baldwin, Deerfield, and Anglers Lane, streets that wound back into the hills, the area of Rogue's Hollow where larger homes and property were.

The Dover farm was at the end of River Drive, and Tess drove slowly down the gravel driveway, noting that there were several pickers tending to the pear trees.

She hadn't seen Bart Dover since her swearing in. She guessed he was in his early thirties, but he looked older. He worked hard; she could still remember the rough, hard feel of his hand when he'd shaken hers. He was wiping his face with a rag when they pulled up to the house. In front of his house was his truck, *Dover's Pears and Peaches* written on the side.

He frowned when they parked and got out of the cruiser. There were four kids of various ages playing in the yard. They all stopped what they were doing to stare. A woman came out onto the porch. Tess recognized Jessica Dover. She'd brought a blackberry pie to the swearing in. It was the first fresh berry pie Tess had ever eaten and it was heavenly.

Bart stepped toward them. "Pastor Mac, you coming here with the police — well, that can't be good."

Tess realized he probably thought the worst about his sister.

"No tragedy, Bart. We're trying to find Tilly and wondering if you have any idea where she might be. You know Chief O'Rourke."

He nodded and sighed heavily. "Well, for a minute there I thought you were going to tell me she was dead. She might as well be.

Chief, I told her in no uncertain terms to stay away from me and my family the last time she was here. I felt sorry for her, but she left her drug stuff out, and I found my youngest playing with a coke pipe. You can understand I don't need that stuff around here."

"I do understand, Mr. Dover. But it's important that I find Tilly as soon as possible. Anything you can tell me might help."

He played with the rag in his hands for a few seconds. "The only person I know who could help you is Glen. And I heard what happened to him."

Weariness seemed to settle over him, and he leaned against his truck. "It's sad, really. Tilly was always the smart one. I was the one who struggled in school while she sailed through. Mom died when we were little. Dad raised us. He expected great things from her. But something isn't right in her head, and when he died —" His voice caught, and for a second Tess felt the pain he'd been dealing with for probably too long resonate within her.

He cleared his throat. "Well, she lost all touch with reality. She stopped taking her legal medicine and started up with the illegal stuff, and you know the rest. Just glad he's not around to see it."

He shoved the rag in his pocket. "I'm sorry, Chief, but I don't know where she is. I doubt she'll come to me, but if I do see her, I'll call you right away."

They left the Dover farm and drove back to the station in silence. Tess could understand the man wanting to protect his family from what Tilly had become. Too often people with mental issues ended up self-medicating and becoming a faceless smudge in the homeless world. They became a police problem when the police had no resources to deal with them. Whose problem were they really?

She was considering the situation when a 911 dispatcher came over the radio with a call for Rogue's Hollow, a call to aid an injured woman. Tess turned it up, and she and Oliver listened as Del answered and requested clarification.

"Anonymous 911 call, requested assistance, stating there is an injured female on the east side of Midas Creek, below the Stairsteps. Paramedics are asking for more information, a better location, and what type of injuries. The caller disconnected. NFD."

No further details.

Tess was all ears. Del indicated he was en route and would advise. He must have cleared the accident he was on earlier.

"Do you think that could be Tilly?" Oliver asked.

"I'm not sure, but I'm very interested in what Del has to say."

After a few minutes, Del asked the dispatcher to raise Tess on the air.

"I copy, Boy-1," she said into the radio mike.

"Chief, we got a body, a woman."

Tess looked at Macpherson, saw him pale as they waited for Del to continue.

"I'm below the Stairsteps. In some brush. She's a few feet from the creek and barely breathing, but you better get down here."

30

"I'm going with you." Macpherson was adamant. Tess didn't have the heart to refuse him. Del was solo today, but just after Tess acknowledged she was en route, Gabe Bender called.

"I was listening to my scanner. I heard Del call in. I know where he's at. I can help you get down there quick."

Tess accepted his help and passed the station to continue to the viewing platform parking lot. She and Oliver met Gabe there. She saw the surprise in his face at the sight of Macpherson, but he didn't question the man's presence.

This was the first spot Tess had visited after her swearing in. Just about everyone who came to town came to see the Stairstep Falls and visited the viewing platform. A bridge spanned the creek here, with the viewing platform in the middle. The viewing platform and the trails on the west side of the creek were maintained by the city of Rogue's Hollow. Hiking trails on both sides of the creek were also accessed here. The east side of the creek and trail was not as maintained, nor did it go as far because it was technically BLM land.

"This way." Gabe motioned to them, and they followed him across the bridge, where several tourists stood watching the water. Tess couldn't see Del from here and she decided that was a good thing. Looky-loos couldn't see either. She saw the hiking path running parallel to the creek once they crossed the bridge. Bender started on the path and then cut off trail to continue down to the fence line. Sirens sounded close. At least Mercy Flights, the local ambulance/medic service, would be quick getting here. In Long Beach there were any number of ambulance companies; here in the Rogue Valley there was only Mercy Flights.

They held on to the fence to steady themselves, and she could feel the spray from the falls. When they got to where the fence ended, Bender pointed.

Tess could see Del standing next to a prone form covered in a blanket.

"Keep going this way," he said. "It levels off. I'll guide the medics in."

Tess nodded and she and Oliver continued

315

down. Here there was no trail. They were making their way through brush, but it was obvious Del had come this way as well. As the path leveled and they got closer, Macpherson pushed past.

"Anna," he called and rushed to her, stumbling as he went, barely keeping from falling.

Del moved and Tess saw Anna's pale face. Oliver fell on his knees beside his wife. He cradled her head and Tess heard him begin to pray. Anna's face was scratched and bruised. Her breathing was shallow, labored.

Del grabbed Tess's arm, face scrunched in distress. "I searched here the other night. She wasn't here — I know it." Tess wrenched her eyes away from Anna to pay attention to him. "You can see drag marks. She's on a tarp. Someone put her on the tarp and dragged her here."

Tess saw what he was indicating. Del anticipated her question. "Followed it a bit, but it ends. I don't know where she came from."

Tess took a deep breath, gathered her thoughts. Anna needed her best and she would give nothing less. "Find out if dispatch has any more information on the caller — a location, anything."

"Will do."

"Did she say anything?"

"Not making sense." He stepped away and carried on a conversation with dispatch.

Tess couldn't see what Anna was wearing, if she had on a shirt that matched the fabric she'd found in the bushes. But oddly, she looked all wrapped up, as if someone had laid her here carefully, bundled and dry.

She heard voices and turned to see the medics making the hike toward them, carrying a litter. Tess tried to be hopeful, wanted to say something encouraging to Oliver. The medics stepped in and Oliver moved to the side.

As they began to assess Anna, Tess couldn't believe what she was seeing. There were bruises and scratches, but there were also Band-Aids, and the clothing was clean and dry.

It didn't make sense. Had Anna been with Glen and did she go over the falls, or was something else going on? And now where did Tilly fit in? Would the crazy druggie she'd heard described have the wherewithal to pull Anna from the creek and patch her up?

In a few seconds, she had her answer.

Del finished with the dispatcher. "The call came from the Hollow Grind; they have one of the few pay phones left in the valley. I called Pete. He says the last person he saw on the phone was Tilly Dover."

"She still there?"

"No. She ran out as soon as she hung up."

"We need to find her."

"You want me to look or to stay with Mrs. Macpherson?"

Tess sighed. "Find Tilly. Odds are she can tell us much more than Anna can."

He nodded. "If she's lucid," he muttered.

Tess watched as he started back up the hill they'd come down. The view from here was beautiful as rushing water spilled out and over the two falls. A crowd was gathering on the other side of the creek, watching the activity. But they were still shielded by brush and trees. Tess felt confident that no clear, sad picture would make its way onto social media. The hiking path ran parallel to the creek but farther up and Tess turned to look that way. She couldn't see the path from here, but there were some obvious drag marks coming down the hill and ending where Anna lay.

Did someone drag Anna along the path and then down here creekside?

Frowning, she considered the area where she stood. Things had leveled off, but it was very rocky and rough. Did Tilly save Anna and hide her somewhere up there? Then for some reason drag her back to the creek today? That had to be the only explanation.

A headache started, and Tess realized how unlikely it was that she'd ever figure out what went on in the tortured, drugged-out brain of Tilly Dover. But she had to find the girl and give it a chance.

As she turned back to Macpherson, she found herself hoping his prayers were getting to someone or something that had the power to help her friend. If Anna had gone in on Thursday and it was now Saturday, that she was breathing at all astounded Tess.

But the medics were so serious, so concentrated, wearing faces that said things were not good, she doubted the outcome would be a good one.

31

Tilly hunkered down to hide, knowing too many people had seen her. But she'd had to make the call. Her thoughts cleared enough, she knew Anna needed way more help than she could ever give her. But her head clearing was not without its issues; it came with a pounding headache.

Boom. Boom. Boom. She brought her hands to her temples, just certain her brains would burst from her skull any minute.

The excruciating memory of Glen's death came roaring back. She couldn't get the sound of the gunfire out of her head, of seeing Glen fall, of seeing the man stand over her best friend and shoot him again. She'd have died herself that moment if the spark to help Anna hadn't kept her briefly lucid.

So much of that morning was a blur. Fear had gripped her like a boa constrictor then, squeezing what little courage she had right out of her, and it was all she could do to try to help Anna, take her to the shelter. She only partially remembered dragging Anna from the bowl underneath the Stairsteps. Someone had helped, but who?

Once she had Anna safe in the shelter, it wasn't until she was certain no one had seen her that she'd been brave enough to leave and look for help. And then she'd wanted to tell Pastor Mac, but fear won again and she ran, taking only what might help her friend.

The need for more drugs had started as an itch, but it was now a searing demand. She clenched her fists so tight that her fingernails cut into her palms. She wanted to stay clean, wanted to tell the police what she knew, what she'd seen, but she knew she'd fail.

A whimper escaped. It was so hard to try to remember. She'd been hiding. Glen and Anna were arguing with the man; he had a gun. He shot Killer, then Glen; then Anna and the dog went into the creek. Did Anna fall trying to help the dog? Or did the man with the gun shove her? It all happened so fast.

Tilly had raced down to help Anna. She couldn't help Glen or Killer. She remembered falling into the icy water herself and being pulled out even as she grabbed for Anna. She helped, fearing the man with the gun would come after them. But eventually she realized Anna was not getting better, and at least she'd thought clearly enough long enough to get her some help.

All of it had been too much for Tilly to process, even before the boom of the gun. She was lost and confused without Glen. And she felt guilty because she'd waited so long where Anna was concerned. But fear of the man with the gun had outweighed any reason. She wished things had happened differently that morning, wished she hadn't been loaded, that she'd been able to warn Glen. He didn't know she'd shadowed him, that she'd been on the other side of the creek and seen everything.

Now Anna was no longer her concern. She would be taken care of. But there was no one left to take care of Tilly, and she knew she couldn't stay hidden forever. As she opened her hands to see the cuts there, they began to shake. She needed a fix, a hit of something strong. But she also needed to stay clearheaded, to help Glen and Anna by telling the police what she knew.

She'd gotten Glen killed. Even the dog was her fault. Tears fell as Tilly stared at her shaking hands. She'd never last; she'd slip back into a drug-induced confusion. It was the only thing that would keep the pain and the fear away.

But Glen . . . she didn't want to fail him again. Thinking of him gave her energy, a small bit of strength to say no to the need . . . for a little while, anyway.

She changed her clothes and started down the hill. She could make her way to the police station and hope someone there would believe her.

32

By the time Tess got back to the station, she felt her headache turning into a nasty one. Anna Macpherson was in a coma in intensive care at a hospital in Medford. She was dehydrated, battered and bruised, and barely hanging on.

Tilly was nowhere to be found. How did that girl disappear so completely?

"She's used to staying off the radar," Bender said. He'd stayed on to help after the medics rushed away. Tess made a command decision. Instead of digging in the bushes and trying to figure out where Anna was dragged from, she asked Bender and Del to look for Tilly. That girl seemed to be the key to a lot.

That Anna had survived going over both falls boggled everyone's mind, but how had Tilly pulled her from the water and taken care of her? The drug addict apparently thought clearly enough to change Anna's clothes and dress her wounds.

Before leaving with the medics, Oliver had told Tess he recognized the blanket covering Anna.

"That's from Anna's sewing room. It was draped over the back of her chair. In the winter it's her favorite blanket to curl up under."

Was that what the burglary was about? Stealing things to help Anna?

Del was adamant he'd searched everywhere that Thursday when Glen was found, and Tess tried to console him.

"Tilly must have moved her. That's the only explanation. How and why are the questions we need to find answers to. Beating yourself up isn't going to help with that."

Late that afternoon, Tess revisited the scene of Glen's murder and had help when Steve Logan arrived.

"Think you missed something?" he asked.

She sighed, thinking before answering. His presence did a lot for Tess on many levels. Since he wasn't her employee, he was more a peer, an ear to bounce ideas and questions off. Tess wasn't responsible for him, so she felt freer to express her frustration. For better or worse, she was comfortable with Logan now, and she hoped he'd be around often.

"Not exactly," she said. "Well, maybe."

She pounded a fist into her palm. "I just wish I had a better picture in my mind of what happened that morning."

"Well, let's walk through it. I'll be the killer; you be Glen." He waved a hand toward where Glen had lain.

"Okay." She stepped toward the creek, faced Logan, back to the water.

Logan pointed at her with his index finger. "Now, we believe Anna was here also, and the dog . . ."

"But where was Tilly?" Tess held his gaze in the waning daylight. "If she was with Glen, she'd have been shot as well. I truly doubt she was with the killer."

Steve put his hands on hips and surveyed the area. "She could have been behind a tree or —" He looked over Tess's shoulder.

She turned. "She was on the other side of the creek."

Logan stepped to her side. "If she was in dark clothing, she might have seen everything without being seen."

"There's not enough light right now to do a thorough search. I'll get to it first thing in the morning." She turned toward him and smiled, thankful for his presence and for the new insight. His eyes were so intense, so blue, she almost lost her place. The crackle of the radio calling to tell her there was a news crew on scene broke the spell.

"I really hate TV cameras."

They started back to their cars.

Logan chuckled. "I don't mind them. I've got this."

When they reached the news crew, he was as good as his word. Logan had a charm about him and he knew all the newspeople. Tess had never liked being on air and had delegated that chore whenever possible. But Logan was a natural in front of the camera, and he, with the permission of the sheriff, gave a great interview.

Later, they joined Bender and Del in her office to go over all the information they had up to that point.

"I can't believe she's even barely alive," Logan said after he read Del's report.

"I stood there at the bottom of the Stairsteps and tried to imagine going over." Tess shook her head. "Did Anna pull herself out, or did Tilly do it? You guys have dealt with Tilly before; I haven't. We know now she probably viewed the murder from the other side of the creek. Is she capable of doing something like this, pulling Anna out of the creek and taking care of her for two days?"

"I'd have said no," Bender said, casting a glance at Logan. "But I don't have any other explanation."

"The only other option is that the guy responsible for killing Glen and putting Anna in the creek is the one who helped her," Logan said. "And that makes no sense."

Tess chewed on a knuckle and said nothing for a moment while she studied the board. Still more questions than answers.

Logan raised an eyebrow. "Penny for your thoughts."

"Well, if we're moving with the idea that the motive for Glen's murder was the money — whoever Glen stole the money from wanted it back — and they kidnapped Anna as leverage, maybe to force Glen into returning the money, only Glen couldn't give it back because he no longer has it . . ."

"Then the killer must still want it back," Logan finished for her. "He commits murder, attempts to get rid of the two people who know his connection to the money."

"He must know now that the money is here in the station."

"Maybe he figures he can break in here and get it back," Bender said. "This place would be a piece of cake to break into."

Tess nodded. "Acosta keeps trying to get me to push for a new PSS alarm here."

"Interesting," Logan said. "How come the

place isn't alarmed?"

Bender shrugged. "If you'd ever met Chief Bailey, you'd know." He hooked his thumbs in his belt and puffed his chest out. "Son," he said, adopting a pronounced drawl, "miscreants break out of the police station, not into it."

Tess and Logan laughed, and Tess was thankful for the break in tension.

"Chief Bailey was more Andy Griffith than Agent Gibbs," Bender said.

But the levity couldn't last; they had to get back to the murder.

"This guy has killed at least one person. It's a no-brainer he'd risk burglarizing the station," Logan observed.

"Maybe we can use that to our advantage." Tess stood and walked to the door of her office, where she could see the door to the evidence room. "Set a trap, put up cameras — something like that."

Logan nodded. "You'd have to make sure only —"

They heard voices in the outer office.

"Hello? Hello, is anyone here?"

Bender stepped out and a minute later stepped back in.

"Sorry to add this to the list, Chief, but Delia Peabody is here. She's demanding to talk to you."

Tess's protest died in her throat. Maybe she needed a distraction, something else to think about for a minute or two. A break might help.

"Do you want me to send her in?"

"No, I'll come out there." Tess walked to the outer office and saw a distraught Delia Peabody pacing.

"Mrs. Peabody, what's the problem?"

"Oh, please help. It's Duncan; he's run away. I can't find him anywhere."

33

"When it rains, it pours. I think I said that once already."

"Yeah, you did." Tess smiled, surprised that Steve's voice could be so soothing to hear so soon in their relationship.

She covered her mouth as a yawn forced itself on her. It was moving in on 1 a.m. Bender had gone home after they'd done all they could for Delia Peabody. Duncan was in the system as a runaway; the license plate of the car he was driving was flagged. The way he drove . . .

"I believe Duncan's situation will resolve itself quickly. As much of a pain as he is, Mom says he's never run away before. He'll be back."

Logan put a hand on her shoulder, and Tess felt the warmth and strength there. "You're right; he'll turn up. And I have to get home. I'll be back in the morning, after I file all the paper for what went on today.

Then maybe I can help you with the other case and set up a trap for the killer."

Tess looked into his clear blue eyes. "Thanks, Steve. For all of your help."

He squeezed her shoulder and stood to leave. "My pleasure. I'll help you anytime, with anything."

Tilly's strength and resolve faded and the push she'd felt to go to the police was in danger of dissipating. She needed some false courage. She had to find some meth. She'd left Rogue's Hollow as soon as she could after she'd made the 911 call. As luck would have it, some friends who were sad about Glen saw her and gave her a ride to Shady Cove. They shared their stash with her. It wasn't much, but after she smoked it, she felt the familiar rush.

Fear faded, a false courage developed, and she decided she was through hiding. Shaking gone, though not even certain what day it was, she once again resolved to tell the police what she knew, what she'd seen. For Glen, for Anna. She didn't even care what happened to her anymore.

It took a while to get a ride back to Rogue's Hollow, though, and by then, all her friends were warning her that the police were looking for her.

"They've been rousting everyone trying to find you," Dustin told her. She'd never liked him, but he'd been a good friend to Glen. After processing everything he'd said to her, her courage was gone, the high was over, and Tilly's mind fogged. But then she saw him.

The man who shot Glen.

At least she thought it was him. Her head pulsed, and her thought process worked in jumps and skips. He locked the door to his business, then climbed into a work truck and drove away. Tilly looked after him for a long moment. Then she glanced around and saw a rock. She picked it up and crossed the street. When she reached his business, she peered into the window. Empty.

He killed Glen.

He killed Anna.

Her breathing sped up. She raised her arm and threw the rock as hard as she could. The glass shattered and the alarm shrieked. She turned and ran.

34

First thing Sunday morning Tess planned to search the area she and Steve had observed across the creek, the spot where they decided Tilly was hiding when Glen got shot. Mind burdened with worry for Anna, she made it to the station early in the morning to enlist Del to go with her, only to find it already open and active. As she stepped inside, she saw Beto Acosta, animated and angry, while Del Jeffers nodded soothingly and wrote on a notepad.

"What's going on?"

"Ah, Chief." Acosta's voice rang with frustration. "It's unbelievable. I just left my office. I have an early meeting in Eugene, which I expect now I'll miss. Been here ten years and nothing like this has ever happened. I don't understand why anyone would attack me this way."

"Attack you?"

"Yeah, that crazy girl. She tossed a rock

through my front window. Shattered it. I had to hurry back to reset the alarm and I get cut by glass." He held his arm up to show her a streak of blood.

"What crazy girl?" Tess asked the question, already guessing who he referred to.

"Tilly Dover," Del said. "She showed up in town and for some reason she went a little nuts this morning."

"You have her in custody?" Hope flared.

"No," Del said. "Not yet."

Tess leaned against Sheila's desk and frowned. "We've been looking for her, haven't had any luck finding her. Did you see where she went?" she asked Acosta.

"No, she was gone by the time I got there. I was on 62, heading for the freeway, when I was notified that the alarm had popped."

"Nobody actually saw her throw the rock," Del added, and now Tess was confused.

"Pete at the coffee shop heard the crash and saw her run away," Acosta explained. "There was no one else on the street; it had to be her who broke the window." His manner bothered Tess. And he was inside the station and still had his sunglasses on, besides the fact that it was barely light outside. Was that a New York thing? If she were a suspicious person — and she would say she was — she'd think that he didn't want her to see his eyes.

"As soon as I finish this report, I'll go look for her," Del said.

Tess nodded. "I'll help. Might not be able to charge her with breaking your window if no one actually saw her do it. Do you have any security cameras?"

"Yes, but they are positioned on the door and sidewalk. She threw the rock from the middle of the street. Come on, I'd just left, Pete saw her running — that should fly in any court." He was fired up.

"Maybe. Are you willing to prosecute, Mr. Acosta?"

His expression changed, softened somewhat. "What do you mean?"

"Go to court, testify to what you know, add to what Pete saw."

It was as if the man were a balloon popped by a pin. "I, uh . . . That's time-consuming. You were looking for her anyway?"

"Yeah, I need to speak to her about another matter."

He blew out a breath and tossed his keys from one hand to the other.

A lot of nervous energy, Tess thought. Then she saw it. His key chain was busted. Only a portion of the *P* from the PSS was still there. She stiffened, alarms going off like crazy. What did she know about Beto Acosta?

"I'll need the report of the damage for my insurance," he said. "But that girl . . . she's a little off. I'm not sure prosecution is the way to go. She does need help; maybe you can get her some?"

Tess tore her eyes away from the keys and bit back a rude retort. She hated it when people thought cops were social workers. And the suggestion was coming from someone she now considered a murder suspect.

But how to proceed? Gabe had said the key chains were common. Maybe they were cheaply made as well. And she didn't want to spook him in any event. She wanted to get to her office and do some checking on Beto Acosta.

"We can take her to jail, Mr. Acosta. She broke your front window? That's a big window as I recall. You're the victim here."

"So much going on in town. A man murdered. Um, I don't think I have the heart to prosecute the girl." He calmed noticeably as he twirled the keys, and Tess considered his swift mood changes.

"Funny," Del said. He handed Acosta a card with a report number.

"What's that?" Tess asked, preoccupied with thoughts about Acosta and whether she should press him now about the key chain or work on a backdoor approach, finding more evidence that would point to him as a killer with motive, means, etc.

"Tilly's never been violent. I kinda wonder what made her so mad."

"Are you accusing me of something?" Suddenly Acosta bounced back to red-faced and angry.

Del started to say something, but by reflex Tess stepped up to his defense.

"Officer Jeffers simply made an observation. But your reaction troubles me. Did you do or say something that she took exception to?"

"I resent that!" He got all puffed up.

Tess decided to press. "I didn't mean it the way you took it. I've never met this Tilly, but I've heard a lot about her. I know she's unpredictable. Can you help me out here?"

Acosta settled down but kept jingling his keys. "Yeah. Yeah, I guess I can."

"Where were you Thursday morning?"

"What?" He frowned, defensiveness back. "Why do you need to know that?"

"I wondered if you'd seen Tilly then."

He huffed. "I'm between houses right now. I rent a room at Charlie's. I slept in until about eleven; then I hung out with Cole for a bit. We like to shoot the breeze when his wife is out of town."

"So you didn't see Tilly?"

"Didn't I just say that?" He moved toward the door, chest puffed out in indignation. "You two need to remember I'm a business owner who not only pays your salary, but who's just been the victim of a crime. I don't deserve to be accused of anything."

"And no one accused you of anything. You have your report for the insurance company, Mr. Acosta. If that's all, let Officer Jeffers get back to work."

He was already backing out the door. "You betcha, Chief." He glared at Tess and turned on his heel.

Tess shook her head after Acosta slammed the door. She turned to Del, who regarded her thoughtfully.

"He sure didn't like your line of questioning."

"Yeah, how about that. Did you notice his key chain? It was busted."

Del's eyebrows arched. "Broken key chain?"

"Yep. Would Acosta have a reason to kill Glen?"

"Ah, man." He brought a hand to his chin. "I've always liked the guy. He's pro law enforcement. I'm floored. It must be co-incidence." But then he frowned. "Yet he was acting awfully strange just now. I guess if he were anyone else, I might have suspected that —"

"He was under the influence?"

He held her gaze and nodded.

Tess hiked a shoulder. "Maybe we need to dig into Mr. Acosta. But first, we have to find Tilly."

"Agreed."

"And I'd like to search that area across the creek, see if anything there can help. I trust you know the quickest way to get there?"

"I do."

"I have to make a phone call. Once it's finished, let's head up there."

Tess walked past him to her office. Deciding to delay talking to Steve about Acosta, Tess knew there was another call she needed to make. She sat down and took a deep breath, trying to put Acosta on the back burner.

One call. A difficult call because she was pessimistic about Anna's condition. Familiar with loss herself, Tess knew this loss would bash Oliver Macpherson harder than he'd ever been hit. She had his contact info but couldn't punch the numbers. Instead, she phoned the church office.

Was Anna Macpherson still alive?

35

"It's obvious someone has been here," Del said as they reached the spot across from the murder scene. He'd taken Tess to a place above where Glen was killed, to a natural bridge formed by logs that made it possible to ford the creek. And crossing above made it easy for them to hike down to the spot they were looking for.

"This is where the kids who ride dirt bikes on BLM land cross," Del told Tess as they'd carefully made their way along the logs.

Once they reached their goal, it was clear the area had seen a lot of activity for a long time. There were rocks here that made good seats or hiding places, and there was also trash, cigarette butts, beer cans, food wrappers, and crude graffiti.

"Kids have been coming up here to smoke pot for as long as I can remember," Del said. "Technically not our jurisdiction; it's BLM's. We chase kids away when we can, but . . ." He shrugged and Tess knew what he meant. Rogue's Hollow had personnel for Rogue's Hollow, not to police outside their boundaries.

Finding the spot only confirmed what they'd deduced; it didn't move them any closer to finding the killer. And Tess was nursing some disappointment. Logan had called; he couldn't make it back to the Hollow today, but he'd be by on Monday.

They went back to town, and both concentrated on finding Tilly.

She eluded them all day Sunday. Tess teamed up with Del and he showed her some nooks and crannies in Rogue's Hollow that she'd not yet seen. She knew that there were issues in the one trailer park in town because whenever someone was arrested for possession, they seemed to come from the park.

Del introduced her to the park manager, who, he said, was trying to clean up the park.

"It's a family park," Henry Polk told her. He was probably in his seventies, but spry and wiry, with a head of thick white hair and smoking a pipe. Tess couldn't remember the last time she'd seen anyone smoking a pipe.

"I don't want it to be a senior park; I like

342

kids. It's the older kids who cause problems. Sometimes I wonder if that won't be the way to go to keep trouble away — make it a fifty-five and older park."

"I appreciate your efforts," Tess said.

"As for Tilly, she's not been here, but there are a couple of no-accounts who live in spaces 30 and 32 who are quick to give her rides. She's not allowed to stay here." He puffed on his pipe. "But I can't be everywhere all the time."

Tess and Del thanked him and checked out the two spaces, but no one was home. The spaces backed up to forest and were overflowing with junk and debris.

"Does Martha come here to cite people?" Tess asked Del, referring to the town's code enforcement officer.

"Not by herself. But I'll talk to Gabe and we'll make it a point to come over here with her."

When they returned to the station, Delia and Ellis Peabody were there with a pile of flyers for Duncan.

"Have you heard anything at all, Chief?" Ellis asked.

She could tell neither of them had gotten any sleep. "No, I haven't. Have you given any thought as to where he might run to?"

They looked at one another.

"Klamath Falls, maybe Portland."

"I've sent BOLOs to both those agencies. He'll turn up, I'm certain."

Delia was on the verge of tears. "This scares me, Chief, because of the murder. Suppose there's some crazed serial killer out and my —" She couldn't finish her sentence and dissolved into tears. Ellis grabbed his wife by the shoulders and held her tight.

"Mrs. Peabody, I can't see Duncan's disappearance being related to the murder of Glen Elders at all. I believe that murder was a personal matter, not the work of a crazed serial killer. Please, try not to let your mind wander; it will only make you crazy."

She blew her nose and they both nodded and then left to paper the town with their flyers.

Tess worked in the office for the remainder of the day, digging into Beto Acosta. She noted that the church was packed for services and even afterward. Casey Reno called and told her Oliver was staying at the hospital with Anna, but that there had been no change.

Reno was guarded in her comments, though still hoping for the best, Tess thought after hanging up with her. She had faith, like Oliver did, that some good God was in control and eventually things would work out.

But with no luck finding Tilly and only bad news coming from the hospital, Tess had a horrible feeling that things were not going to work out . . . and they were only going to get worse.

Monday morning Tess rubbed her tired eyes with one hand while she picked up the buzzing phone with the other. Her phone said *John Reno,* and for a second the name didn't register. It had been after midnight before Tess got back to her room to go to bed. Then she remembered Casey. Oh no, was Anna dead?

"Chief O'Rourke," she answered formally, sleep still fogging her brain.

"Hope you were . . . well, that I didn't wake you up."

Tess glanced at the time. "I should have been up twenty minutes ago."

"Guess today I'm your alarm clock. I called to tell you the dog is ready to be released."

The dog? For a second that confused Tess. She was immersed in Anna Macpherson and Tilly Dover and neither woman had a dog. Then she remembered Glen Elders and his pit bull.

"Oh, that dog. Released? Already? She had her leg amputated, didn't she?"

"Yeah, she did. But she's stitched up and healing well. The vet I took her to doesn't board animals and they need the space there for sick dogs."

Tess bit her tongue to keep from blurting out, "What am I going to do with a dog?" It had been her decision to save the dog, not euthanize her, and she had the charge on her credit card to prove it. It was a little too late to push the problem off to someone else. She realized she'd have to take precious time and go collect her.

"I'd help you out if I could," Casey said. "But I'm at the hospital with Pastor Mac."

"Any update on Anna?" She hadn't been good the night before.

"No, nothing new. She went through such a physical trauma, and cancer has so compromised her body . . ." She sniffled and Tess felt the pain radiate over the phone. A lump rose in her own throat; Anna was her closest friend here.

"Please catch whoever did this," Casey said with a sob in her voice.

"I'll do my best. With the dog as well. Glen might have family that wants her, though I haven't come across anyone yet. I'll work something out. Hopefully Addie doesn't mind dogs at the inn."

"I think you'll be fine. I'll touch base with you when I get home."

"Thanks. Tell Pastor Mac . . . well, tell him that he and Anna are in my thoughts."

Tess disconnected and got out of bed to stretch. Thinking of Anna and Oliver made her ready to start the day even though she could use more sleep. They needed her to find a killer. And now she had a suspect. She'd already built a thick file on Beto Acosta. Forty-five years old, he was actually an ex-cop. He'd lasted two years on the job in New York, but that was twenty years ago. Now, he'd been CEO of PSS for ten years. He was divorced, which she guessed was the reason he was "between houses" and renting a room at Charlie's.

He'd also hurt his back in a car accident two years ago, and that made Tess wonder if the guy was hooked on pain pills. His behavior in the office indicated something was up in that area.

She paused her search when the phone rang with a familiar number. Jeannie Haligan. It was good to hear her friend's voice. One of the many things Tess missed about Long Beach was the dispatch center. She'd been told by her first training officer to treat the dispatchers with respect because their job was a lot harder and more stressful than police work. At first Tess thought the man was teasing until he took her into the center one night and let her listen to what the dispatchers put up with. She'd sat with Jeannie for a shift and she understood what he meant. It wasn't just people who needed help who called 911; crazy people called, angry people called, and some downright scary people called. And people were more inclined to be nasty on the phone than face-to-face with someone carrying a gun.

After one particularly contentious call, Jeannie, angry and frustrated, turned to Tess. "And when you get there, in uniform, with your partner, both of you armed, that guy will be all sweetness and light."

Tess had left the communication center at end of watch, shaking her head. Dispatch was a job she could never do. Here in Jackson County, Oregon, there was one main dispatch center in Medford. All the 911 calls went there and the Rogue's Hollow cops were dispatched from there. While Tess had been given a tour when she was first hired, it was too far to go to drop in for a visit, and she missed being able to do that.

So she appreciated the chance to talk to Jeannie, who had a different take on the case. Jeannie had been hired about the same time as Tess, and as soon as they met, they became fast friends.

"It's the husband. It's always the husband," Jeannie said.

"He's a preacher. Why would he kill his wife's cousin and send his wife over the falls?"

"Must be a girlfriend somewhere. Maybe the cousin tried to stop him?"

"Well, the cousin is dead and the wife is alive — barely. And I don't think the pastor is a cold-blooded murderer."

"You do; you just don't want to admit it. Just because he's a pastor doesn't mean he's not a murderer. Does he have a gun?"

That gave Tess pause. She hadn't asked. Would she have asked if he wasn't a pastor?

"This is Oregon; everyone has a gun," she answered with a flippancy she didn't really feel. "This guy doesn't give me any negative vibes." Confidence returned quickly. Macpherson was genuinely concerned on Thursday morning. He didn't kill Glen and then try to kill his wife.

"He could have hired someone."

They went back and forth for nearly an hour, Jeannie being the devil's advocate. The more they threw out possibilities, the more a scenario formed in Tess's mind. It all came back to the money. She was sure

349

Glen was killed because of it. And there was the thought they'd had about setting a trap at the station for a burglar. But if Beto Acosta was their guy, and the money was his, why hadn't he reported the theft?

She showered and dressed quickly, remembering to call down and ask Addie to fix her a breakfast burrito to go.

Half an hour later, coffee and burrito in hand, Tess walked to the station only to find Mayor Dixon there already.

She'd rather have seen the angry crowd return.

"Good morning, Mayor. What can I do for you?" Tess asked as she pushed the door open with her hip. Dixon could see her hands were full, but he made no move to open the door for her.

"The city is falling apart. What are you doing about it?" He followed her in.

She worked hard to keep her face neutral as she nodded to Sheila and continued into her office.

"I'm doing my job, what you hired me to do." She put her things down on her desk, realizing the forlorn hope of eating her burrito warm had just evaporated. "I'd like to bring the day shift up on everything that went on over the weekend."

"The day shift is one officer."

She cocked her head. "He still needs to be informed."

Just then Gabe Bender poked his head into the office. "Anything up, Chief?"

Tess held Dixon's eyes. "Well, Mayor? Are you going to let me get back to work?"

"I think you're in over your head."

"Mayor, I'm —"

"I didn't come here to hear excuses. I want you to call in the sheriff, have him take over the murder investigation and whatever happened to Anna Macpherson."

Tess stared at him, blood boiling. True, the man standing before her was her boss, but there was nothing the sheriff could do with both investigations that she couldn't do.

"I and my people have things under control. Sergeant Logan is helping. There's no reason for us to turn the entire investigation over to another agency."

"I think there is. The sheriff has the resources to solve these crimes. You can work on the runaway case of Duncan Peabody."

"I disagree."

He folded his arms. "Then you give me no choice but to call an emergency meeting of the city council in order to discuss your continued employment with us."

Tess felt the blow of those words but kept herself calm, her face blank. She had been a cop for too long not to have perfected the cop face in the event of shocking or hurtful news. Even after being blindsided, rule #1 applied: "Listen. Think. Speak."

After a deep breath she said, "Mayor, I'm not sure why you're taking this line with me. But I'm confident in my and my officers' abilities to solve these crimes. Now, we have work to do. You do what you have to do."

"Count on it." The petulant little man turned and stormed out the door, hurling one last line at Tess. "I should have known you'd fail us like this."

Tess looked up. Until the mayor left, she hadn't realized Gabe Bender was still in the office, listening to the confrontation she'd just had with the man.

He regarded her, but not with his usual smirk. This morning he simply looked professional.

She forced the encounter with Dixon out of her mind. There was a homicide and attempted homicide on her plate to solve. She'd sent Bender an e-mail Sunday night about Tilly busting Acosta's window and the broken key chain.

"You read my e-mail?"

"I did. I'll admit, I have trouble seeing Beto as a drug dealer, much less a murderer."

"You guys friends?"

"Not like buddies, but Beto's always been a friend to cops, an upstanding guy. I think he was a cop at one time. He's even been invited to training sessions with us, on occasions, when we train with the SO or with Medford. He and the chief in Medford are tight."

Tess considered this. Del had said as much.

"I've always assumed this was about the money. I violated my own rule to never assume. We're missing something."

"I still think we need to follow the money, but maybe it's not drug money," Bender said.

"That's a thought. Still, that much cash . . . who keeps that at home in a paper bag? And who wouldn't scream bloody murder if it were stolen?"

"True. Beto lives at the B and B. But I think Markarov cuts him a deal because he has no money."

"Maybe Acosta just wants it to look that way. Let's say he was hiding the cash, and he can't report it stolen."

Bender frowned. "If I've learned anything

in this job, it's that anything is possible. I still wouldn't peg him for a murderer."

"I believe Tilly was across the creek and that she witnessed the murder. Why do you think she targeted Acosta and broke his window unless she was pointing a finger at him?"

"She's seldom thinking clearly. She could have broken his window at random. Elders always looked after her. Maybe she's acting out because he's gone, not necessarily targeting Beto."

"And the key chain? Are those things cheap?"

"Well, they're not solid gold. But they're not plastic either." Bender rubbed his chin. "Why on earth would Beto kill Glen Elders? I've racked my brain for any kind of connection between them."

Sitting, she motioned for him to do the same.

"There's something we're not seeing. Maybe he has another reason for hiding cash. Unless we were right in the first place and he is a drug dealer and hides it well. His name is coming up too often."

Bender considered this. "I don't believe in coincidences."

"Me either," Tess said. "Keep thinking about it. Job one is to find Tilly. How on earth does she disappear so completely and quickly?"

"There's a collection of lowlifes around who are quick to give her rides back and forth between here and Shady Cove or White City."

Tess nodded, thinking about her visit to the trailer park with Del. "You remember the break-in at the pastor's house? Well, Macpherson admitted to me it was Tilly who knocked him over running from his house."

"That's why Anna Macpherson had clean clothes on and was covered in a blanket."

"Yes. Find her."

"I will, but I may have to go to Shady Cove or even White City to do that."

Tess tapped a fist with her palm and thought for a minute. Dixon to the forefront again. One of his pet peeves was Rogue's Hollow officers going into other jurisdictions for just about any reason. He wanted them to utilize the sheriff's office if they had an out-of-area problem. Most of the other small communities in the area contracted with the sheriff's department anyway, so law enforcement problems were their responsibility outside of Rogue's Hollow.

But this was her investigation. And what

could he do, fire her? He was already threatening that.

"Okay, but after lunch. I need to run a quick errand. When I get back, if things in town are quiet, then you can head out of our jurisdiction. But let the SO know you'll be in their area and keep it on the down low if possible."

"Gotcha."

They both heard a call go out on the radio. Bender was needed at a dispute.

Tess nodded that he could go. After he left, she picked up her burrito, thoughts drifting back to Dixon and his threat. He was acting a little schizophrenically, she decided, supporting her one minute and threatening to fire her the next.

She took a bite of the now-cold meal and made a face. Shaking her head, she chewed and swallowed, then threw the rest away. It was time to pick up the dog and see if she'd created another crazy-making problem for herself.

36

Oliver barely slept while he kept watch at his wife's bedside. Jethro was at the hospital with him, intercepting parishioners who came to the hospital and letting them know how things were going. He and Travis had organized an around-the-clock prayer vigil and made out a schedule so there was someone in the church praying for Anna's recovery 24-7. There were plenty of volunteers, and it touched Oliver's heart.

Anna had not regained consciousness. Besides being scratched and bruised from her tumble over the falls, she was dehydrated and her right leg was broken. If Tilly had tended to her injuries, that had helped, but Anna should have been taken to a hospital immediately.

The doctors were not giving him much hope. While it was no small miracle that she survived going over the falls, it would take a bigger miracle for her cancer-ravaged body to rebound from all the insults it had endured over the past few days.

In spite of the pain, and because of the fear of losing her that he couldn't stamp out, Oliver sat holding her hand and praying, feeling the presence of his Lord like he'd not felt in a long time. He spoke to Anna from time to time, sometimes to recite a passage of Scripture, sometimes just to talk to her about things that were going on. He thought she'd like to hear about Chief O'Rourke.

"I trust our new chief. You were right about her, you know. She's good people, smart. She'll figure this all out — I know it. I also know that your first thought in all of this would be forgiveness. You'd be worried about the state of your attacker's soul."

Oliver couldn't say he was there yet, at forgiveness. He tried not to think about the attack and the fact that Tilly hid his wife when she needed medical attention. But he knew his wife would have arrived at forgiveness quickly.

After a visit from the doctor and another glum face, Oliver whispered to Anna, "God's not deaf, Anna. He's not turned a deaf ear — he hears all of our prayers. I want to tell you so with your eyes open, restore your faith in the promise of Scripture. He is an ever-present help in our times of trouble. He's here, with us now, baby."

"Oliver."

He looked up and saw Jethro in the doorway.

"You look like you need a break. How about a short walk to the coffee machine?"

Oliver's first impulse was to say no. But he was stiff and groggy, and coffee sounded good. He nodded and stood. Bending down, he kissed Anna's forehead. "Be right back."

As they walked down the hallway to the coffee machine, Jethro asked, "Is your phone on you?"

"Yeah, I turned it off. They don't like cell phones in ICU."

"Check your messages. Octavio has been trying to get ahold of you."

"Do you know why?"

"He won't tell me, says it's just for your ears."

They reached the machine. Jethro stopped Oliver when he reached into his pocket. "I've got this. Black?"

Oliver nodded, fatigue hitting him in a wave.

"Maybe you need to go home and get some sleep," Jethro suggested as he handed Oliver the coffee.

"I can't, Jethro. I have to be here for Anna,

whatever happens." He took a sip of the brew, ignoring the taste and waiting for the caffeine to kick in. He and Jethro sat in the waiting room. Oliver turned on his phone and called Octavio.

"Pastor Mac, I'm so sorry. I hear about Anna. We're praying for her."

"Thank you, Octavio. What did you want to tell me?"

"Ah, something I didn't tell you before, when the police were here, something maybe important. When Anna came here to ask about Glen, a man was here. He follow her when she leave."

Oliver felt his hands go numb and he nearly dropped his coffee. "What man? Who?"

"He was here about the alarm. He listen to our conversation, and when Anna leave, so did he."

"Who?"

"Beto Acosta."

"Beto?" Oliver frowned, exhausted mind trying to understand how or why this would be important.

"*Sí.* You know I do drugs, long time ago."

"Yes. But you're clean now."

"*Sí.* I know when people do drugs. I can tell. Beto, he try to hide it, he deny it, but he do drugs. Maybe nothing, but it bothers me. Maybe he just go home, but he was listening so hard to Anna talk, and now Anna, and Glen . . . well, I need tell you."

"Thank you, Octavio, thank you." Oliver said good-bye and disconnected.

"What was that about?" Jethro asked.

Oliver told him.

"Beto?" Jethro looked at him askance. "That man is solid; you think he had something to do with what happened to Anna?"

Oliver shook his head, then drained his coffee. "I can't think right now. Maybe this is important, maybe not. Do you think you can tell Chief O'Rourke, or maybe get Octavio to call her?"

"Sure, Oliver."

"I'm going back to sit with Anna."

37

As Tess made the short drive to the vet, besides wondering what she was going to do with a three-legged dog, she wondered about Anna Macpherson. She wanted to go to the hospital, not only to check on Anna, but to see how Oliver was holding up.

She understood his pain. In a way, he was lucky. The fact that Anna was still hanging on, that had to be a good sign. And if she didn't survive, at least he'd have the chance to say good-bye. Tess never got to say good-bye to her dad.

Thinking about her father's death and Anna's predicament made her consider God a capricious deity. She wondered if Oliver's faith would survive if Anna died.

Shaking away the negative thought, Tess decided that positive thinking was the key here. Anna would survive. And hopefully, when she came around, she could point them to her attacker and Glen's killer.

Will that get Dixon off my back? she wondered.

She also pondered her decision to save the dog. Did she do that because she was a woman and soft, like Cole Markarov thought? One of her dad's rules was "Never show weakness." In the back of her mind she could hear Terry Guff warn her about being soft, emotional.

"People will eat you alive if you show weakness," he'd said. *"Job is easier when they fear you just a bit."*

He himself was tough as nails; Gruff wasn't just a nickname. Her dad was always no-nonsense, but he never had the same hard-edged reputation as Gruff. But he wasn't emotional or soft; no, that would never be said about her dad. Was she being emotional?

Tess sighed. Gruff was from a different time. She'd never conducted herself on the job to be feared. Respected, but not feared. When it came to Killer . . . well, she just didn't want to see the loyal dog put down.

Loyalty clicked inside her brain and a light went on. That's what had done it for her that day at the creekside. The dog had sat bleeding and in pain for who knew how long at the side of her dead owner. Obviously, whoever killed her master had tried to kill her, but that didn't matter. She stayed with Elders, and Tess marveled at how a supposedly dumb animal could be so loyal in such dire circumstances when a smart human male could betray his marriage vows without a second thought.

Shaking her head, she realized that when she thought about Paul now, even the betrayal she'd felt in Long Beach didn't hurt as much as it used to. But she'd have to remind Jeannie, who liked to say, "All men are dogs," that nothing could be further from the truth. Dogs were more loyal than men could ever be.

The vet's parking lot was packed, and Tess ended up double-parking, hoping she'd be in and out quickly. Inside, the waiting room was as crowded as the parking lot but surprisingly quiet. An assortment of dogs wagged their tails and pranced nervously on one side, and on the other a couple of cat carriers sat at the feet of watchful owners. Tess could hear some meows from the waiting room and a lot of barks from the back.

Eyes followed her as she stepped up to the counter. Before she could say anything, the woman behind the counter said, "You're here for Killer, aren't you?"

Tess nodded. "Is she ready to go?"

"Yes, but the doctor wanted to talk to you.

I'll be right back."

Tess hooked her thumbs in her gun belt to wait, hoping it wouldn't be long but also feeling a bit guilty. She hated jumping in front of everyone, but too much was on her plate to waste time. She needed to get back to Rogue's Hollow.

"Chief O'Rourke?" A tall, long-armed man with a sinewy, muscular frame followed the receptionist to the front desk. Dr. Fox, according to his name badge.

"Yes, that's me." She shook his extended hand.

He motioned with his hand as he picked up a file. "Come back to the office and I'll explain about Killer." His speech had a distinct Midwestern bite.

Tess followed him into an office just behind the reception desk. He sat behind his desk and she took a seat in front.

"Thank you for preserving the bullet like you did. That was a big help."

"No problem. I worked in Chicago before moving here, dealt with a couple of police dogs that were shot, so I knew the drill. I just hope you catch the reprobate who shot her. She's a sweetheart, wouldn't hurt anyone. Everyone here loves her. We've never had any trouble treating her whenever she's been here."

"I'm amazed she's ready to go home so soon," Tess said.

"She's in good health but for the amputation," Dr. Fox said. "She needs to continue to heal in peace and quiet, and that's not going to happen here." He opened the file in front of him. "I was sorry to hear about Glen. He had his problems but he was an animal lover. He treated Killer well and trained her too. She's a good dog. Do you know what will happen to her now? I mean, you paid a lot to get her fixed up, so I can't see you sending her to the shelter or having her put down."

"I need to make certain no family wants her."

"And if no one does? I know several people who would happily adopt her. Like I said, everyone here loves her. Even with three legs she'll make someone a great pet."

"Thanks for telling me. I'll contact you if I need to find her a home."

He nodded. "Good. I'll explain her aftercare and then go get her and let you take her."

Tess was given antibiotics and painkillers and directions for their use. Killer would have to come back in two weeks to have her staples taken out. Then Tess realized she had nothing in her hotel room to take care

366

of a dog: no food, no bed — she didn't even have a leash.

"No problem," Dr. Fox said. "My receptionist can set you up with what you need. Glen bought her food here. We have a low-cost dog food pantry in back. The Grange and other businesses donate dog food so low-income people can afford to feed their dogs, so we can even help you with that."

Another hundred dollars later, her backseat holding dog food, a dog bed, and a couple of impulse dog toys, Tess walked back into the office to get Killer. Her heart caught in her throat when the red pit bull came limping out into the waiting room. The wagging tail almost brought Tess to tears. Stepping forward on her one good front leg, propelled by the two back ones, the swath of a pink bandage covering the spot where her leg used to be and encircling her powerful chest, Killer stuck her nose toward Tess, seemingly happy to see her and maybe sensing Tess would take her out of this place that smelled of fear and antiseptic.

"Hey, Killer." Tess got down on one knee, grasping the leash the vet technician had used to bring her out. She'd had dogs as a child; her father had loved dogs. At that moment Tess realized she hadn't had a dog since her father died. Tobey had pined for her father and then, after a time, became attached to Tess. He was her shadow until a vet visit discovered cancer and he had to be put down.

Tears threatened and she cleared her throat and swallowed, willing herself to keep her composure. Killer sniffed her hand. Tess held it out flat, let the dog sniff, and then patted her broad head. All the while the dog's tail never stopped wagging.

Sucking in a breath, composure back, she stood. "I'm going to have to find this dog a different name than Killer."

She'd just gotten back to her car and helped Killer into the backseat when her phone rang. It was an unknown number, but a local area code. She answered.

"Chief O'Rourke, Jethro Bishop here. I'm with Oliver at the hospital."

"Yes, I remember you. We met the other day at the pastor's home," Tess said, leaning against her SUV and bracing herself for bad news from the hospital.

"Oliver asked me to call you with some news that maybe you can use."

She listened, shaking her head, as he relayed what Octavio Donner had told the pastor. Tess had known Octavio was hiding something. Now, a little late, she learned that Beto Acosta had been the last person

368

to see Anna when she left the church and he had followed her onto Crowfoot.

Beto Acosta. *Again.* Tess could see in her mind's eye a mountain of circumstantial evidence piling up against the guy. But did it make sense? If he wanted the money back, Anna could have told him where it was and that Glen no longer had it. Why snatch her and kill Glen? It seemed the more information she gathered, the less things made sense. And in all of it, when she looked at Acosta, there had to be a strong motive to kill two people. What was it?

As she wrapped up the call and chewed on what Jethro had told her, a sheriff's car pulled into the lot.

Steve Logan. The pleasure she felt at seeing him surprised her.

"Well, hey, Steve, what brings you here?"

"I saw your unit; then I saw you. I was on my way to Rogue's Hollow." He smiled and Tess felt her stomach flutter.

"I just picked up Glen's dog." She nodded toward the car and Logan stepped forward and leaned in to say hello to Killer.

"Wow, she lost a leg." He frowned and shook his head.

Tess stifled an "aw," moved to see that he was as disturbed by the dog's fate as she was.

"You keeping her?" he asked.

"No, I don't even have a house yet. Not certain yet what I will do with her."

He nodded and hooked his thumbs in his belt.

Tess gave herself a mental head shake, pushing the strong attraction she felt for Logan to the back burner. "I thought you'd be by earlier."

"Yes, sorry about that, but I got tied up with some stuff at the jail. And now, besides wanting to help you, I need to give you a warning."

"Warning?"

"Yep. Mayor Dixon is making noises. Wants my boss to take over your cases." His expression touched her heart, supportive and helpful.

"Yeah, he told me as much. What did your boss say?"

"That you were the chief; he'd only do that if you asked."

"Remind me to thank your boss."

"Well, it might be a temporary stay. Dixon told me he was considering calling an emergency city council meeting to discuss your position. Thought you should know."

She took a deep breath and looked away from those warm blue eyes. "He told me as much. He's working on that meeting." She looked back. "But I have too much on my plate to worry about Mayor Dixon. Question: what can you tell me about Beto Acosta?"

"Smooth change of subject." He smiled and it gave his face a boyish look. "He's a successful businessman. My own home is protected by PSS. Why do you ask?"

She told him what Jethro had told her.

"I know Octavio too; he was a serious meth head at one time. Why does he think Beto followed Anna?"

"My information is secondhand. I'd like to talk directly with Octavio, but —" she pointed to the dog — "hands are tied right now. As for Acosta, I've only had a few discussions with him. For what it's worth, he always struck me on the up-and-up, until yesterday." She told him about the key chain and the window. "He never took off his sunglasses. He could have been trying to hide his eyes from me. And it rubbed me the wrong way because he wanted the report but didn't want us to prosecute."

"The glasses . . . I have to say I've been afraid he's a little too dependent on pain pills. Last training session he showed up for, let's just say he raised some eyebrows. But that doesn't make him a killer. And the window? I'd cut him some slack there. Trust me, you don't want to arrest Tilly unless you have to. Anything minor like that broken window, they'll kick her right back out. She's difficult to deal with. People with mental issues and drug problems . . ." He arched an eyebrow.

"I know what you mean. But when people want us to jump through hoops for them, but they don't want to help us solve the problem, sometimes that rubs me the wrong way."

"Preaching to the choir. Do you want me to go talk to Octavio? Get more out of him if I can?"

"Thank you." Tess smiled. "That would be awesome."

"Hey, I'm here to serve. And it's worth it to see that beautiful smile."

38

After Logan left, Tess sat in her car and hesitated to leave, unable to ignore the feeling she'd left something unfinished. Oliver. Casey had sounded dour, unhopeful about Anna. Tess wanted to talk to Oliver, since she couldn't be at the hospital just yet. She redialed Jethro and asked for the pastor.

"Any chance I can talk to him?"

"I'll see."

She waited, starting the car and turning on the AC.

"Chief."

Taking a deep breath, "Oliver, how is Anna?"

"There's been no change; she's still in a coma." He sounded tired, worried, and defeated.

"I'd be there if I could."

"You have your job to do. And I do believe God is in control, no matter what."

"I'm amazed you feel that way, Oliver. If

your God's in control, why did this happen to Anna? She was a good person." The words were out of her mouth before she thought them through, violating her own rule #1, and she winced. His wife was at death's door. Was she piling on?

She heard him sigh. "Chief, that's a valid question. The only way I can answer it is by saying that I trust God. I won't deny I'm worried and a little frightened." His voice broke. "But I have to trust God, or nothing in this life would make sense."

"I have to trust God, or nothing in this life would make sense."

Oliver's words reverberated in Tess's thoughts as she drove back to the station. How did you trust someone — or something, for that matter — you couldn't really be certain was there? It was a conversation she wanted to have with him someday. Hopefully with Anna by his side.

As soon as she got back to town, Tess released Officer Bender to travel to Shady Cove. She gave him a brief outline of what she'd heard from Octavio and that Logan was checking it out. Bender had been nothing if not extremely professional, and Tess wondered at the change in the man. But she wasn't going to look a gift horse in the mouth. And when she got a call from Medford PD, where Bender had applied to lateral, she told the background investigator the truth: he was a good cop and she'd hate to lose him.

She let Killer out of the car to go to the bathroom and then brought the dog and her bed into the station. Gwen and Sheila cooed over the dog, and for her part, Killer seemed to love the attention. But she was tired. As soon as Tess set the dog bed down in her office, Killer curled up on it and went to sleep.

Bender reported that everything had been quiet in town, and Tess hoped it stayed that way. She needed to study her murder board and make certain she'd not forgotten anything. It was time to look for connections missed and to reexamine everything related to the murder of Glen Elders and the injury to Anna. It was a crowded board, but would anything she put up there be a clue that would lead her somewhere?

Her dad's rule again came to mind: *"When you don't know, go back to what you do know."*

She worked on it for about an hour and a half, going over what she knew.

Glen gave Anna Macpherson a bag of money a week before he was shot. No one had yet claimed the money as theirs. Anna

Macpherson disappeared on Wednesday; Glen was murdered on Thursday. Besides their familial relation, the only other connection was the money: Glen gave Anna the money. The way Glen was killed strongly indicated he knew his killer. Did Anna know the person as well?

It was a small town; odds were good that the killer knew both Anna and Glen. She remembered the odd conversation she'd had with Cole Markarov and noted it on the board. Casey had told her Cole was a close friend to Glen, but Cole denied that when she talked to him. How did that fit in here? Cole was known to be temperamental, but not criminal. Everyone said Acosta was solid as well. Was the money Acosta's? Was assuming it was drug money a big mistake? It most certainly was a violation of rule #8: "Never assume."

But how did Anna fit in? Was she with Glen for no other reason than that they were cousins? And why would the killer push her into the creek instead of shooting her? Her being there by accident didn't jibe with the discovery of her abandoned car. Someone took her from the car.

That thought gave her pause. As Tess chewed on her lip and considered the board, she recognized that this small town, this place where everyone knew your name, wasn't all it was cracked up to be. Someone in Rogue's Hollow was a murderer; someone wasn't who they pretended to be. And it was looking like that person was Beto Acosta.

Further research on the man showed some cracks. He'd declared personal bankruptcy after his divorce. A search of public records showed the divorce was particularly acrimonious. He paid an enormous sum of alimony to his ex. At one point he'd even had his wages garnished.

This was a whole new angle. Maybe the money never was drug money but simply cash Acosta was hiding from his wife. Guys at work in LB used to joke darkly, "It's cheaper to keep her." Cash squirreled away somewhere, without records, something Acosta could never report as stolen, because if he did, sooner or later his wife would find out.

Tess was just about to close her office door when Bender got back.

"Any breakthrough?" he asked, nodding toward the board.

"More questions. You have any luck?"

"No one in Shady Cove or White City has seen her lately. I need to find someone here in town who might have information."

"Who are you looking for?"

"Guy named Dustin. He was close with Elders. I'm sure you've seen him around. He's a handyman of sorts. Does yard cleanup and the like. Skinny like a crackhead, but he's clean that way, just dirty as far as hygiene goes. Nickname is Pig-Pen."

Tess remembered the skinny guy she'd seen at Charlie's Place. "I think I saw him the other day at Charlie's."

"Makes sense. He often does yard work there. I'll go see if I can round him up."

"Wait. I have a question about Cole Markarov." She pointed to her entry on the board. "Was he a close friend of Glen's? He says no."

"Close? I don't know that I'd say that. They were friends, at least in high school," Bender said. "Cole has helped him out a couple of times. I don't see anything sinister in what he said to you. The guy is pompous and arrogant. He probably doesn't want you to see him as a man who helps others out. Plus, he's all bark and no bite. Cole pretends to be tough, but . . ." He gave a dismissive wave of his hand.

"Thanks for that perspective."

Bender nodded and left to find Dustin.

Tess resisted the urge to tag along for two reasons: Killer being one, and the other that she didn't want to be a micromanager like Dixon. Bender seemed to be on her side now and she didn't want to ruin that. She busied herself with paperwork until he raised her on the radio.

"Can you meet me up on the walking bridge over Midas Creek?"

"Did you get something?"

"Dustin pointed me in a direction we need to check out."

"I'll be right there." Hope infused, Tess quickly cleared her desk. If Bender continued to do good work, this situation could allow them to find common ground.

She noticed that Killer had gotten up when she did. "So you only pretend to be asleep, huh. You're ever vigilant, aren't you?"

Killer's tail wagged and she hobbled over to lean against Tess's leg.

Hands on hips, she wondered if she should ask Sheila or Martha to watch the dog while she was gone. There was no way to know how long she'd be gone, and the dog was her responsibility right now.

"You want to come with me?" she asked, half-expecting the dog to answer. Killer did look at her adoringly and kept wagging her tail. Tess decided she'd take the dog. Killer could sleep in the car; she'd seemed comfortable enough there earlier.

As she considered the dog, she also remembered that she couldn't leave the murder board facing her desk so that anyone who came into the office could see it. She moved some furniture out of the way and turned the board to the wall.

Tess hooked up Killer's leash and walked her out to the car. A few minutes later she parked behind Bender's patrol car.

"Did Dustin give up Glen's hiding place?" she asked when he walked up to her window.

"He did. We had a nice chat. According to him, a few months ago Glen started showing up around town more often than usual. When Dustin asked him about it, Glen told him he'd set up a camp nearby."

Tess frowned. "At the campground?"

"No, he stayed off grid. He wouldn't have money for a hotel and he'd never stay with the Macphersons."

"But what changed? Why did someone who lived out of his car in Shady Cove suddenly set up a camp in Rogue's Hollow?"

"Dustin didn't know. Might have to do with Tilly. Apparently Tilly lived in this hidey-hole as well. Dustin saw him head to his hole with Tilly often."

"Tilly."

"Yep. And Dustin heard where we found Anna, at the bottom of the falls. He says the hideout is above that."

That sentence gave Tess pause. "But we searched, Del especially. I saw drag marks, but we couldn't figure out where they originated." She admitted to herself that they didn't spend a lot of time looking; they wanted to find Tilly.

Bender nodded. "Dustin says you have to know what you're looking for. And a hideout certainly would explain how Tilly appeared and disappeared so quickly and why Del didn't see any sign of her by the creek."

"Okay, hopefully luck will be on our side today and Tilly will be there now and we'll finally be on the way to some answers."

"Agreed. I thought I knew this area better than anyone, but I've never come across his camp," Bender said with a head shake. "Let's see what we can find."

"You think it's close?"

"Dustin drew me a map." He showed her a crude drawing on a page in his small notebook. "I understand where he's directing us. Dustin is working, so I didn't want to interrupt gainful employment to bring him here. Glen would have wanted a place close to town but not too close." Bender looked up the hillside. "And Tilly hid Anna; she couldn't have dragged her far. I'm guessing, but I think it's an educated guess.

His camp has to be around here some-where."

Tess followed his gaze, certain he was on the right track but hesitant for some reason. She was a city girl through and through. The only time she'd had to search in a natural setting for anyone was when a five-year-old got lost in El Dorado Park, a city park in Long Beach. But she'd been in this forest several times over the past few days. That wasn't what was spooking her now; it was Gabe. Gabe was testing her, probably so he could regale his buddies with stories about the clueless chief from California.

But if she refused to help or sloughed the job off to someone else, she'd be a wimp, a coward. Just then Killer shifted in the backseat and caught Gabe's attention.

"What's that? You get a dog?"

"Uh, it's Elder's dog. I just picked it up from the vet."

"That's right; you didn't kill it." His eyes widened with admiration. "It took a close-range 9mm slug and lived. Tough dog."

"She lost her leg, but she's perky." Tess had a thought and blurted it out. "You think she'd be able to find the camp?" As soon as the words were out of her mouth, she winced. He was going to think she was an idiot, that she got her police work training from the TV. But he surprised her.

"She might," he said. "I have hunting dogs. If we get separated, they always make it back to camp. Dogs are smart. I have more faith in them than I do in most humans."

Tess swallowed, hoping she was making headway with this guy. She climbed out of her SUV. "Let's see if she's up to it."

She opened the back door and Killer looked up, tail thumping. Grabbing the leash, Tess coaxed the dog out of the car. When she hit the ground, she looked at Bender.

Bender cursed and got down on his knees, holding his hand out for Killer to sniff.

"I can't believe he shot the dog. You poor thing." He ran a hand over her head and leaned forward to kiss the dog's nose. Tess was flabbergasted. This was the hard-as-nails cop who'd been a thorn in her side for two months?

He stood. "Is she okay to walk around?"

"The vet said to take it easy, that she was likely to be self-limiting."

Killer looked from Tess to Bender and then toward the bridge.

"I'm not sure what to do," Tess said. "Is there a command?"

Bender shrugged. "Unhook her leash and

let's see what happens."

Tess hesitated a moment. But how fast could a three-legged dog travel? She unhooked the leash, and Killer turned and hopped toward the bridge. She looked back once and then took off across the bridge, moving at a good clip. She went across and then down to the well-worn trail that ran along the creek, taking almost the identical path they'd taken to get to Anna.

Tess and Bender scrambled after her. But the dog didn't turn down the hillside like they had on Saturday; she turned up. When she was above where Anna had been, she veered off the trail.

"She's moving pretty good for a three-legged dog," Bender commented.

"On a mission," Tess said. They kept after the dog in silence, first climbing and then turning to parallel the river. There was barely a trail. They were up and away from the Stairsteps, and the roar of the water diminished somewhat. Then Killer disappeared.

Tess, a bit ahead of Bender, stopped, hands on hips, breath somewhat labored.

"Where?"

"To the right, behind that rock." Bender pointed. He was sweating and breathing hard.

Tess headed for the rock and made a left around it, then stopped short as what she saw surprised her. Killer lay panting on a plain red dog bed. It wasn't a cave, exactly, that she was in, but it was close. Elders had set up a camouflage shelter, virtually invisible unless you were right on it. Killer was under a tarp. Farther into the indentation in the hillside she saw a sleeping bag and other indications that someone had been living here.

"Well, I'll be," Bender said. "He was smarter than I gave him credit for. This hidey-hole is handy and well hidden."

They approached the shelter, Tess's hopes high they'd find something that would break her case wide-open.

39

Anna passed away silently early Monday afternoon without ever regaining consciousness. Oliver held her hand and stroked her forehead as nurses silenced beeping machines.

One of the doctors stood next to him. "We did everything we could, Pastor. Her body had just been through too much."

Oliver couldn't speak, so he just nodded. Not seeing a battered and bruised shell in front of him, instead seeing the woman he married eighteen years ago, smiling and full of life. His chest felt as if it would explode from the pain. The only thing keeping him together was the recognition that all of Anna's days had been numbered by the Lord, and for some reason, today was the end of Anna's journey. Part of him wished to return to the time she was missing because there was still a hope then that she was fine, praying alone somewhere.

But then Oliver felt a wave of thankfulness that she had been found. At least he'd been given the opportunity to say good-bye. It would have been excruciating if he'd never known her exact fate.

He kissed his wife one last time, then wiped his eyes with his palms before leaving her for the comfort of the church family standing by in the waiting room.

By the time Oliver headed home to Rogue's Hollow, he felt hollowed out with fatigue and grief. So many emotions swirled inside: anger, hurt, sorrow. Jethro was at the wheel, and he was glad for the man's silence so he could examine his personal thoughts quietly. It was difficult not to acknowledge that mixed with all the emotions swirling through him, there was anger toward God. The question he'd heard so often after tragedy, the one hurting members in his congregation asked, echoed in his head: *Why?*

Did God ever answer that question?

He remembered what he'd said to Chief O'Rourke: *"I have to trust God, or nothing in this life would make sense."* He gripped that thought as tightly as he could.

He also considered the widow Devaroux and how he'd held her and tried to provide comfort at the loss of her husband. How could he know he'd be going through the same painful loss three days later?

Round and round, musings running through his brain tied him up in knots. He lost track of time until Jethro slammed on the brakes and screeched to a stop. Oliver put his hand out on the dashboard as he was thrown forward, but the seat belt kept him tight in place.

"What? Was it a deer?"

"No, it's Tilly." He gave a wave of his hand toward the left, and Oliver saw Tilly Dover making her way across traffic lanes. They were in Shady Cove and Tilly was shuffling toward the 76 gas station mini-mart.

"She's such a sad child," Jethro said as he got the car moving again. "Glad I didn't hit her."

"Jethro, stop. Go back."

"What?"

"Go back to Tilly. She knew Glen, and she's the one who called about Anna, led us to where she was by the creek. Maybe she'll be able to tell me something about what happened to him and Anna."

"Useful information from Tilly? Oliver, she's crazy as a loon. She's a few clowns short of a circus."

"I know, I know. But something tells me she might know useful information about . . . about the situation, the crimes. Humor me."

"Okay." Jethro pulled over to make a U-turn as Oliver kept an eye on Tilly in the rearview mirror. He saw her go inside the mini market. He'd never told Jethro that Tilly had trashed his home and bowled him over in her attempt to escape. Watching her shuffle across the highway in her blue hoodie dulled his hope that she'd be helpful. Maybe Jethro was right. She was probably loaded. On an hourly basis, it was hit-or-miss as to whether or not Tilly would be lucid. Oliver prayed she'd be able to tell him something.

Jethro pulled into the gas station lot and found a place to park around back. Oliver got out, intending to walk around to the front door. But he nearly ran into Tilly as she came sprinting around the corner.

"Tilly."

Fear spread across the girl's dirt-smudged face like a wave. She skidded to a stop and looked to her right.

"I just want to talk to you." Oliver reached out a hand, but Tilly lurched away, breaking into a run back toward Highway 62.

Oliver started after her and then another person bolted out of the store, the mini-mart clerk.

"She just stole a beer!"

Both men scrambled to catch her but neither could reach her in time. Oliver saw the car and yelled for Tilly to stop, but it was too late.

The sound of a horn and squealing tires rent the air, punctuated by the dull thump of Tilly hitting the hood of the sedan, flying up, then rolling downward into the street. The beer can exploded when it slammed into the ground, and Oliver was showered in a stream of cold beer as he reached her side, kneeling down on the pavement, praying she wasn't hurt badly.

Tess asked Bender to wait while she jogged to her vehicle and retrieved her crime scene kit and an empty box. When she returned to the tent, she found him kneeling on the ground, petting Killer, who seemed perfectly content with the man.

"You've made a friend," Tess said as she opened her kit and pulled out her camera.

Bender stood and brushed himself off. "I've got a soft spot for dogs. What are you going to do with her?" He stepped back so she could photograph the area.

"Not sure," she said as she began snapping photos to document the scene. "I need to be certain no one in his family wants the dog before I make a decision."

He grunted and folded his arms, expression unreadable. Tess wondered if he was going to slip back into the jerk he'd been up until today.

"Chief, can I say something here? I need to get it off my chest."

Tess dropped the camera down to her side and faced Officer Bender. "About?"

"About the grief I gave you when you first came here." He hiked a shoulder. "I want you to know it had nothing to do with you being a woman. I don't have a problem with women. I was afraid you'd be a California cowboy and you'd run roughshod over all of us." He took a deep breath. "You haven't done that. Even with Dixon being, well, stifling. You've been . . . fair. And the fact that you cared enough to save this dog has helped change my mind-set. I just wanted you to know."

Tess gave him a nod, impressed that a guy who seemed like such a jerk a week ago would be big enough to make such an admission. "Thanks, Officer Bender. I appreciate that. Hope that means you won't be running off to Medford PD."

He chuckled and gave her a wry smile. "I'd much rather work here in the Hollow, if it's all the same to you."

"Glad to have you on board." She held out her hand and they shook. "Grab some gloves. As soon as I finish these pictures, let's tear this apart and hopefully find something that can help us."

"Yes, sir."

Buoyed by this turn of events, Tess resumed photographing and concentrating on uncovering something that would help her find a killer.

Photographing finished, together they began to pick through Glen's belongings. Tess found the flannel shirt matching the fabric she'd removed from the bushes where Glen was killed. It was wadded up in a ball in the corner of the tent, still damp.

There was mail in the shelter with Glen's name on it, addressed to a PO box in Shady Cove. There was also a brand-new Bible and a couple of books, a sleeping bag and some clothes, male and female, two hunting-type knives, dog food, and an assortment of canned food in a metal foot locker. She also came across a couple of brochures for Platinum Security Systems.

"Maybe he was looking for their tent package," Bender said.

Her cell phone rang and she stepped out to take the call. It was Klamath Falls PD. They'd found Duncan Peabody. He'd been stopped for speeding. Glad but irritated at the same time because she just didn't have a spare minute to deal with Duncan, Tess referred the officer to Duncan's parents.

"I'd like to, Chief, but the kid is adamant that he can't go home."

"What's he afraid of? He's not alleging abuse, is he?" she asked, reasonably certain the Peabodys were not abusive people, but stopping short of assuming.

"Won't say. Just insists he can't go home."

Tess went back and forth with the guy. Duncan was his problem. One of her father's old rules when dealing with other agencies: "You catch 'em, you clean 'em." The Klamath Falls officer had to deal with the parents.

"Bad news?" Bender asked.

She disconnected and hoped that Duncan's parents would handle their runaway on their own and not want her input.

"Klamath Falls PD found Duncan. He's giving them a hard time."

"Kid's a handful."

"And their problem right now. We're out of the loop now, I hope," she said. "Now let's get this cataloged."

The only oddity in the little shelter were some shin guards, the sort you'd wear on a dirt bike. She was pretty certain Glen didn't have a dirt bike. Tess photographed it all and collected a boxful to take back to the station.

"Nothing here to point to his killer," Bender noted.

"Unfortunately true." She sighed and wiped sweat from her brow. "Glen is an enigma to me."

"How so?"

She waved a hand over the tent. "He lives like this, uses food stamps, somehow scrapes together enough money to keep his Jeep running, but when he gets his hand on a bag full of money, he gives it to the Macphersons."

"He told Anna that only God could make the money clean. To me that means he thought the money was dirty."

"But what if instead of being drug money, it was just hidden money?"

"What do you mean?"

"Suppose Beto was stashing money to hide from his wife? Maybe taking money under the table?"

He arched an eyebrow. "That's a lot of under-the-table cash. I'm still having trouble with Beto as a bad guy. But I do remember that divorce: it was nasty. His wife hated it here. She lit out back to New York as if she were set on fire. Lives in a spendy condo, I hear, and Beto's complained about how she's sucking him dry."

"Beto might have been hiding money from his wife and somehow Glen found out. That could explain why he didn't report the money stolen."

They began to carry their stuff down the hillside. Killer followed when Tess called her name.

"Seems like a guy would find a better way to shelter that much cash."

"For you and me, maybe, thinking rationally. It hasn't been my experience that people going through painful divorces think rationally. Glen's own parents prove that."

"Oh yeah." Bender rolled his eyes. "I was a kid, but I do remember that. Their fights lit up the valley. Acosta and his wife were a close second. While I can't see Acosta as a drug dealer, I can see him hiding assets from his wife."

He frowned. "Maybe that's what happened: Glen found his stash, stole it, and gave it to Pastor Mac, but . . ."

"What?"

"I can see Beto being mad, furious, but I can't see him killing Glen and pushing Anna Macpherson into the creek. It doesn't track for me."

"Still, the scenario is something to think about," Tess said as they reached the cars.

40

Tess's phone rang again before she had a chance to climb into the car. She almost didn't answer because she didn't want to talk to the Klamath cops about Duncan again. But it was a different number, Casey Reno. Her heart sank as a somber premonition rolled through her. She answered the call and got the devastating news: Anna Macpherson had died.

She ended the call and leaned against the car, watching as Bender left the lot. It hurt. Anna was a good, if brief, friend. Why on earth did the woman end up dead? Her thoughts went to Oliver Macpherson. She knew firsthand the pain he was feeling. A fleeting thought crossed her mind. *Will he still believe the stuff he prayed, that God is a good and just God?* She doubted it.

I hope I can be there to help him walk through this, she thought.

Back at the station a subdued atmosphere

predominated as news of Anna Macpherson spread.

Tess helped Bender categorize the evidence they'd recovered from Glen's camp spot. They didn't break down the entire camp; they would have needed help to do that and bring everything down. Tess had opted for what she thought was most important. Everything except the shin guards was consistent with someone living off the grid.

When they finished, disappointed, Tess had to admit there was nothing in the box of items that gave a clue about who killed Glen and, now, Anna.

Tilly wasn't dead, but she was hurt badly. Oliver knew immediately she needed an ambulance. It was a good twenty minutes before one arrived, and she'd moaned and thrashed about the whole time. He guessed her hip or pelvis was broken from the way she writhed around.

"Jethro, I need to go with her to the hospital. I know she doesn't have anyone else."

"You need rest. There's nothing else on my plate today. I'll drop you off at home and then drive back to the hospital."

Too tired to argue, Oliver agreed.

They waited while the medics tended to

an agitated, obviously in pain Tilly. His phone rang and it was Mayor Dixon.

Hesitantly, Oliver answered. He had no idea why Doug would be calling him.

"Pastor, please accept my condolences for your loss."

"Thank you, Doug."

"I wanted to let you know that I'm trying to get the sheriff to take over the investigation. I've lost confidence in Chief O'Rourke's ability to get justice for you and Anna."

"What?" Through his grief and fatigue, Oliver was stunned Dixon would make such a statement. "I have all the confidence in the world Chief O'Rourke will solve this crime."

"I don't agree. I'm even calling for an emergency meeting of the town council. Hate to admit it, but Cole was right and I was wrong."

"You weren't wrong, Doug. I urge you to reconsider."

"It's already done. We meet first thing tomorrow morning. I have to go, Oliver. I have work to do."

Dixon disconnected and left Oliver standing there, stunned.

"What's the matter?" Jethro asked. "Who was that?"

Oliver sighed. "Just get me home. On second thought, drop me off at the PD."

Jethro nodded as the ambulance pulled away.

The Macpherson woman was dead. Finally. After learning she'd been found alive, he'd spent several panicked hours trying to piece together where she'd been all this time. How she'd managed to survive didn't matter to him as much as the fact that he knew she'd be a credible witness. She knew his secret; she could put him away. He relaxed for the first time in forty-eight hours when he heard the news of her death, but he had already put his plan to leave into place. He'd mollified the partners in Eugene who'd not received the shipment Acosta was supposed to deliver, and he'd shifted some money around for a safety net. He wanted to hop on a plane and flee, but he wasn't going alone.

After some wrangling, he was able to make two reservations at a small regional airport in central Oregon to fly to Denver. There, he had connections for IDs and travel paperwork. He'd need that to get him and his girlfriend out of the country. They'd have time to stop and change their appearances before boarding the plane. He'd hoped to deal with Acosta before he left but decided that would take too much time. Instead, he'd left some evidence in the man's place of business that would keep the police busy for some time on the wrong track, and far away from the right track.

He'd already gathered everything important to him. He'd put some real fear into his brother — threatening to expose his skeletons. And he was certain the mayor would keep the chief occupied while he fled. All he needed to do was deal with his wife, then wait until darkness fell to gather up his girlfriend and flee.

41

Tess and Bender were finishing up with the stuff they'd taken from the tent when Sheila knocked on the door.

"Chief?" Her eyes were red from crying. Tess had told her she could go home, but she'd opted to stay.

"Yes?"

"Pastor Mac is here to see you."

Tess stood as the pastor stepped in behind Sheila.

He looked old. Old and tired. And surprisingly, smelled of beer.

He must have noticed her expression. "A can of beer exploded on me." He pointed to his shirt. "I haven't been home to change yet, wanted to talk to you first."

Bender stepped up. "Pastor Mac, I'm so sorry. Anna was the best." He reached out his hand and Oliver shook it.

"Thanks, Gabe."

His tired eyes turned to Tess.

"Oliver, I don't know what to say. Anna didn't deserve this. You should probably be anywhere but here."

He nodded. "I actually came with news. I found Tilly. She's the one who dropped the beer."

"Where is she?"

He explained about the accident.

"How badly is she hurt?"

"I'm not certain; it looked as if her hip or pelvis was broken, but I'm only guessing. I do expect she'll be in the hospital for a while."

"But she'll live?"

"Paramedics had her stable when they left."

"Did she talk to you at all?"

"No. I'm afraid she was rather incoherent. Jethro thinks she was high on meth or coming down and soon to be in withdrawal. At least being stuck in the hospital, she won't be able to use anything illegal."

"That will be a good thing," Tess said, thinking out loud. If Tilly dried out, maybe she would be a witness. But if she was a witness, she could be in danger if the killer realized she was alive.

"I have to agree. She'll be confined to a bed for a while. Getting hit by a car might be the best thing that ever happened to her."

Tess sat behind her desk, thinking about Tilly and Anna.

"Oliver, I have to ask: did Anna . . . well, was she able to speak?"

He shook his head. "She never regained consciousness."

Tess acknowledged his answer with a sigh. The implication hung over the room like a haze.

"Tilly's possibly the only witness, isn't she?" he asked.

Tess nodded. "We found Glen's tent, and she appeared to be staying with him. I believe she saved Anna from the creek and that she witnessed his murder."

"Is she in danger?"

Tess exchanged glances with Bender.

"Not imminent. Most people probably think she's crazy and not credible. That being said, I think she's safer in the hospital than on the streets."

"Then thank God for the accident. The Lord was looking out for Tilly."

Tess didn't have a response for that. Why would God look after Tilly and not Anna?

42

Oliver walked home, feeling heavier than he'd ever felt in his life. The numbness and shock of Anna's death had worn off and left a harsh, deep ache, a slash across his heart. He saw the cars in the church parking lot and prayed no one saw him; he needed to be alone for a bit. For the first time as pastor of this church, he wished his home were somewhere else, that he lived far, far away. He made it inside without drawing any attention, closed the door, and let himself slide down till he was sitting on the floor with his back against the door.

He wanted to keep screaming, "Why?" To throw things and bellow out his pain. What kept him grounded was something Chief O'Rourke had said. She'd followed him out of the police station, grabbed his arm, to speak to him.

"I don't understand your faith, Oliver, but I understand your pain. I've been there. My

father was murdered when I was sixteen."
She'd looked at him, eyes filled with wisdom, understanding.

"How'd you get through the pain without faith?"

"I put one foot in front of the other and vowed to honor his memory every day. Life goes on."

I can do that, Oliver thought, *honor Anna's memory each and every day. But it's not a vow that will help. It's a lifetime of seeing God work in and with every circumstance, the good and the bad. I've walked this walk, a tightrope sometimes, when Anna's cancer was bad. I made it. We made it.*

Oliver held his head in his hands and knew that he had to concentrate on something other than Anna's absence right now. What would Anna want for him or from him? How could he best honor her?

She'd enjoyed Chief O'Rourke's company and believed with all of her heart the woman would be a great asset to the town. Oliver knew this was a place to start, a first step. As much as O'Rourke might help him by catching Anna's killer, he knew that it was important for him to help her. He'd warned her about Mayor Dixon and she'd not been surprised.

"I'll cross that bridge when I come to it. Just

because Dixon violates my rule #2, 'Be fair, not emotional,' doesn't mean that I will. And I'll catch the person responsible for two murders."

Oliver believed she would and found no small comfort in the fact that Anna would be pleased. Doug was misguided for some reason. Tess O'Rourke would solve the murder and bring him face-to-face with his wife's killer.

How would he react then? *I'll cross that bridge when I come to it.*

43

Monday night, Tess went by the PSS office. The broken window was boarded up and it was closed. Beto was nowhere in sight. The sign on the door said he'd be back at noon, but it was well past noon, so Tess wondered if he meant tomorrow. She still wasn't certain how she'd approach him. A messed-up financial record and a broken key chain were not slam-dunk pieces of evidence.

But she had also found that Acosta had a concealed carry permit and a gun registered in his name. A 9mm. She'd like to get ahold of that gun and send it to the lab for testing. But that would have to wait until she got ahold of Acosta.

Later, when she'd finally given up and gone home to go to bed, after clearing Killer with Addie, she found a note slipped under her door. It was from Mayor Dixon. She was being summoned to the council chambers tomorrow morning. They were voting on whether or not to keep her in the employ of Rogue's Hollow PD.

She tossed it in the trash with a sigh, not even able to muster up anger about the mayor's pettiness. Finding a killer was the number one thing on her agenda and she'd do it on her own dime if she had to.

She fed the dog and set up her dog bed in the corner of the room. Then, wanting nothing but a shower and sleep, she almost screamed when there was a knock on her door.

Looking up at the ceiling and counting to ten, Tess called out. "Who is it?"

"It's Delia and Ellis Peabody. We need to speak to you."

Groaning to herself, Tess walked to the door and opened it a crack. She saw the Peabodys with a sullen-looking Duncan in the hallway. She had no patience for an intervention right now.

"Can this wait until the morning? I'm really beat."

"It's important that you hear what my son has to say." Ellis leaned forward. "Really important."

Tess didn't have the energy to fight, so she let the family come in. Ellis was an older, balding version of his son, wearing stylish glasses and looking every bit the computer geek. He looked worried, not angry. Ditto Delia. She was tense, afraid of something. They noticed Killer and paused.

"She's okay," Tess told them. "As for Duncan, running away is technically not a crime." She closed the door. "If you two want to disci—"

Ellis interrupted. "This isn't about the runaway. Duncan —" he pointed at his son — "tell her what you told us — everything."

Tess looked at Duncan more closely and saw it wasn't sullenness he was projecting. It was fear; he was as fearful as his mother. What was going on?

She folded her arms. "What happened, Duncan?"

He wouldn't meet her eyes. "Uh . . . the other day . . . well, I rode my bike over to the other side of Midas Creek. I know I'm not supposed to, but —"

"You're not in trouble for that; you're not in trouble for anything," Delia said, urgency in her voice. "Just tell the chief."

"Yeah, well, I went up the trail, just above the Stairsteps to smoke a joint. I like to do that early, you know. It's neat to watch the sunrise loaded. My friend Micah was supposed to come too, but he got caught sneaking out of the house." He swallowed and

Tess saw the Adam's apple work in his throat.

Tension built inside Tess. "What morning was this?"

"Thursday. . . . I was there, on the other side of the creek. I saw him . . . I saw him shoot the dog, then Glen, and push Mrs. Macpherson into the creek."

44

"Did you know Glen Elders?"

He nodded, casting a sideways glance at his mom. "He used to sell us weed."

"Who did you see shoot Glen?"

"It was Mr. Acosta, I think."

"You think? You're not certain?"

He looked down and shook his head. "I couldn't see clearly. It was still kinda dark. But she said it was Acosta."

"She? Tilly?"

"Yeah, she said she and Glen had stolen his money and Acosta wanted it back."

Tess was back at the station twenty minutes after speaking with Duncan Peabody, Killer in tow. She'd had Duncan repeat his story into her digital recorder.

"I saw her slide down the hillside — it was barely light, but I realized she was trying to catch Mrs. Macpherson, so I went after her. That was when he shot at me, twice, maybe three times. The bullets went right over my head! I thought I was dead."

"Did he say anything, yell anything?"

"No, but by then I got to the bottom of the Stairsteps, next to the pool there, where Tilly was. I saw her stumble into the water. I thought she was trying to get to Mrs. Macpherson, and I ended up going in and pulling them both out. There was no more shooting, and I didn't know what happened to the dog." He pointed to Killer. "I was going to call for help, but Tilly stopped me."

He held up his right arm and Tess saw fingerprint marks, bruises on his forearm. "She squeezed my arm so hard I thought she'd break it. She said he'd kill us all, that he knew every alarm in the valley and could get into our house when we were sleeping."

"And she meant Beto Acosta?"

"Yeah, man. Had to. His security systems are everywhere. We even have one at our house. It freaked me out. I helped her carry Mrs. Macpherson up the hillside. Crazy Tilly, that's what we call her —"

"That's not nice," Delia interjected.

"Whatever. She had a tent up there and she just kept saying, 'Trust no one' over and over again like some old science fiction movie. It scared me. I told her Mrs. Macpherson needed help and she said she'd help her. And then I ran. I was just freaked out. I thought, Acosta, man, he was cold. He shot that guy point-blank and shoved Mrs. Macpherson into the creek like nothing. I thought he'd find me, kill me too, so I ran. I've never seen a real shooting before."

He also solved the mystery of the shin guards. He'd taken his off when he helped Tilly and forgotten them when he'd run off. In spite of being a thorn in her side for two months, Duncan was a very credible witness, but it was troubling he wasn't 100 percent certain that it was Acosta with the gun. But who else could it be? If Tilly was certain it was Acosta's money Glen had stolen, wouldn't Acosta be the logical person to try to get it back? Tess assured Duncan that Acosta was no threat, that he'd be in custody soon. She'd find hard evidence. Ellis said he'd change out his security system as soon as possible.

Duncan gave Killer a hug before they left. "I'm glad you saved the dog. She tried to help; that's why she got shot."

Tess called in Gabe Bender, Curtis Pounder, and Del Jeffers, signing authorization for overtime with a flourish. She knew she was being petty by not waking up Mayor Dixon, but he'd be up early anyway with his emergency city council meeting. If she was going to be fired, she was going out

414

with a bang. Pop would approve. She also sent Logan a text. He was on his days off but sent a text back saying he would come up and help if he could.

Tess woke up a judge who listened to everything she had on Beto Acosta.

"This juvenile is not 100 percent certain on his identification of this suspect?"

Reluctantly Tess said, "No, he's not." She explained the other evidence they had, which wasn't much.

"And no motive?"

"Possibly monetary." There was a pause and Tess was afraid she'd lose this battle, one that in California would have been difficult but doable, at least with the judges she knew.

"Your Honor, I have two bodies here, an eyewitness to the murders, and some physical evidence. I realize it's your name authorizing the search and arrest warrants, but we're on the right track here."

"Chief, I agree with you on many points. I just need a few minutes to think about what you've told me. I'll call you right back."

Logan stepped in as she slammed the phone down in frustration.

"Wrong number?"

She smiled; seeing him sucked the anger

out. "Ah, trying to secure warrants for Acosta, and the judge is dragging his feet."

"I think I know what judge." He took a seat in front of her desk. He was armed but wearing civvies — a dark T-shirt and tan cargo shorts showing off well-muscled legs. "Don't worry. He'll call you back; he's just a cautious man. Acosta doesn't know you're onto him, does he?" They both knew surprise was an advantage.

"He shouldn't. The Peabodys came to my room at the inn, and then they went straight home."

He nodded and started to speak when her phone rang. She grabbed for it; it was the judge, warrants approved. As she hung up, she gave Logan a thumbs-up.

"We're on. Warrant to search house, business, car, but not for his arrest."

"How can I help?"

"Your support will be awesome."

"You got it."

"We'll be in two teams. I'm sending Del and Curtis to the business. Bender and I will hit the residence and vehicle; he rents a room at Charlie's. You'll be with us."

While they were staging in the parking lot, as the day dawned, it was hard to miss the members of the city council filing into the council chamber, a room at the rear of the post office. Tess concentrated on the job at hand. Sheila arrived for her workday and agreed to look after Killer.

Jeffers and Pounder walked with the warrant to the PSS office on River Drive. Tess was about to start her car when another figure approached the station.

Oliver Macpherson.

He still looked devastated, but he'd obviously showered and trimmed his beard, maybe even gotten some sleep. Tess got out of the car to greet him.

"Pas— Oliver. How are you doing?"

"I'm okay, Chief. Where are you off to so early?"

"I'm serving search warrants."

"Beto?" He winced.

"Yes, but keep that quiet for now. What are you doing here?"

He raised an eyebrow. "I'm here to speak some sanity into Doug's council meeting. Anna thought a lot of you, and so do I."

That he would come here to do this the day after his wife died touched Tess more than she thought possible.

"Thank you." She held out her hand to shake his. "I won't let either of you down."

He gripped hers in both of his strong, rough, warm hands. "I know that, and I'm praying for you."

■ ■ ■ ■

There were several cars in Charlie's parking lot, one Tess recognized as belonging to Acosta. It was a utility truck with the PSS logo on both sides. Since Tess had seen Cole walk into the council chambers, she knew she'd be dealing with Charlotte.

"If I remember right," Logan said, "Beto's room has a separate entrance on the north side of the structure, close to the hollows tour building."

"Okay." Tess considered the logistics. She wanted to surprise Acosta, catch him off guard. "I want a key if possible. Gabe, you stay with the car. Steve, if you get eyes on the north side of the building, I'll see if Charlotte will give me a key."

Everyone moved into position and Tess went inside the business. Charlotte Markarov was behind the counter. She reminded Tess of a photo of a woman at the turn of the century. Her hair was swept up into a bun on the back of her head, she had a full figure, and she was wearing a long-sleeved, high-necked blouse. She was also wearing a lot of makeup. Tess wondered how long it took her to put all that goop on and be ready to work so early.

Her smile was tentative. "Chief O'Rourke, this is a surprise. What brings you here this early?"

"I have a search warrant to serve on one of your residents." Tess handed her the paperwork. "I'd like a key in the event that Mr. Acosta is not at home or he is home and doesn't want to open the door."

"Oh, my. I — I just don't know."

"Mrs. Markarov, I'm asking for a key as a courtesy. If I must use a battering ram, it will do damage."

"What is it you think Beto has done?"

"He's a suspect in two murders."

Charlotte paled. "Well, uh . . . okay then." She reached behind her and fumbled around for a moment. She handed Tess the key. "Is it okay if I come with you?"

Tess nodded. "But please don't try to interfere."

She joined Steve Logan on the north side of the inn. The door to Acosta's room was down five stairs and it faced the concession building for the tour through the hollows.

Tess knocked and announced their presence and heard nothing. She repeated herself two more times and still no response.

Nodding to Steve, who took a backup position, she opened the door and they went inside. But there was no sign of Beto Acosta.

Acosta was not at home nor in his office. But Tess got a call from Del informing her that the search of the office hit pay dirt. Anna Macpherson's purse and ID were recovered from a drawer in the office. Acosta was their man. They'd have to find him to figure out the why.

45

After watching Chief O'Rourke and the other officers leave, and praying they found success, Oliver walked into the council chambers, determined to do everything in his power to keep them from firing Tess O'Rourke. Doug Dixon was already there, as were Cole and Addie. Missing were Forest and Casey.

"Oliver!" Addie exclaimed. "What are you doing here?" She rushed over and gave him a hug.

He appreciated her warmth and support. "Felt I should be here."

"There's no need," Dixon said. "We know you're grieving."

"Hey, Pastor Mac."

He turned to see Forest walk in and he accepted a tight hug from him as well.

"So sorry, Pastor."

Oliver nodded thanks and everyone took their seats.

"I'll give Casey a few more minutes before I call this meeting to order," Dixon said.

This earned him a snort of derision from Addie. "Waste of time for us to all be here. The chief is doing a fine job. She was your pick, and for once I'd say you made a great decision. Why aren't you giving her a chance at it?"

Dixon held up a yellow pad. "I've documented fifteen reasons why she's fallen short of expectations. I'm not afraid to admit I made a mistake."

"Hear, hear," Cole said.

"We could argue all day about this," Addie said, "but the woman has done a good job."

"Two unsolved murders, a runaway, a malicious mischief epidemic, and you say good job?"

Forest jumped in to defend Tess before Oliver could. Instead, Oliver watched Dixon. The man was acting a bit hysterical, but he couldn't figure out why. His behavior was odd even for Dixon. The mayor had pushed so hard for Tess to be hired, the man couldn't really believe the crimes he listed were the chief's fault.

The group sparred back and forth for a few minutes before Dixon checked his watch. Casey was fifteen minutes late. That was very unlike her.

"I'd better give her a call."

Before the mayor could punch in her number, Casey burst through the door. "Where's the chief?"

Oliver stood, recognizing immediately that something was wrong. "She's serving a warrant. What is it?"

"It's Kayla; she's gone. Someone disabled our alarm and took her from the house. My daughter has been kidnapped."

46

It looked as though Beto had left in a hurry. The bed was unmade, and in the kitchenette, some tea in the microwave was still warm. Tess was putting on gloves when her phone rang. She saw it was Oliver, so she answered.

"Chief, sorry to interrupt, but we've got a crisis here. Casey Reno's daughter, Kayla, has been kidnapped."

Tess thought that she didn't hear correctly and had Oliver repeat. She was cognizant that Logan was looking at her, perplexed, but this bombshell was hard to process. When it sank in, she told Oliver she would be right there and disconnected to explain to Logan what had happened.

"Disabled the alarm?"

"That's what he said. That would point to Acosta; alarms are his business. But what on earth would he want with Kayla Reno? And his car is still here. He must be close."

She took her gloves off. "Steve, I've got to go back to the station, deal with Casey. Can you stay here with Gabe until I figure out what is going on with Kayla?"

"Of course."

Tess turned to leave, but Charlotte stopped her.

"Did I just hear you say Kayla Reno was kidnapped?"

"I'm not sure that's what happened, but she's missing." She moved past her.

"Do you think Beto is involved?"

"I'm not certain. That's why I want to get all the facts as soon as possible."

"I need to tell you something about Beto, something my husband doesn't think I know."

Tess stopped and faced Charlotte. "What?"

"He's been hiding money, cash, from his wife. My husband has been helping him. They think I don't have a clue, but I listen to more than Cole gives me credit for." She started to walk toward the back of the B and B and motioned for Tess to follow.

"I'm in a hurry."

"You'll want to see this."

Tess sent Logan to retrieve Bender and meet them at the back of the house. The terrain sloped gently here, and through the trees you could see the Rogue River rolling by.

Charlotte strode up to an old and weathered tree trunk. She bent down as if reaching under the tree and something clicked. She straightened, moved a step away, and the stump snapped back as if spring-loaded. Tess stepped around and saw a door like the opening to a storm cellar.

"What is this?" Tess looked to Charlotte to explain.

"It was a hidden basement we found years after we renovated the house. Cole decided it would be a useful hiding place — for what, I don't know. I let him deal with it because it kept him out of my hair. I thought he was building a man cave."

"What was he building?" Logan asked.

"It's a man cave, all right, but it's also a survival shelter. It's full of guns, freeze-dried food. Cole was letting Beto use it as a safe. The man didn't want his wife to get any of his money. He stores a lot of cash here."

"Do you think he's down there now?"

"I really don't know. Cole is going to be angry I showed this to you, but if Beto had anything to do with kidnapping Kayla . . ."

Tess looked at Logan. Then back to Charlotte. She motioned to the shelter and asked Charlotte, "Is there any other entrance to this cave?"

Charlotte shook her head.

"But if Beto is in there, it's not safe to just open the door," Bender said.

"We have to get in there," Tess said.

Logan stepped forward. "I agree, but he could be waiting in there for us to open the door. He could be ready for suicide by cop, and if Kayla is with him, it will be ugly."

"Or if she is with him, he could kill her while we wait."

"Or he has nothing at all to do with Kayla."

The ball was in Tess's court.

She turned to Charlotte. "There's no other entrance or exit?"

"No. Cole hoped it led to the hollows, and it might have at one time. But a possible passage is all concrete now."

"You have a key?"

She nodded and pulled a ring of keys from her pocket and began to sift through them. "Cole doesn't know that I made a copy of his key, but I had to know what was in there." She handed it to Tess.

Tess turned to Logan. "I'm going in."

He gripped her arm and started to say something, but she guessed he must have seen the look in her eyes because he simply nodded. "Then I've got your back."

Tess walked down the stairs. She put the key in the lock, then drew her weapon. Turning the lock, she pushed the door open, then brought her gun up with both hands.

The room was well lit. She saw containers of freeze-dried food in rows across the back wall and a large gun safe. The safe was closed; the room appeared empty.

"Beto Acosta, police. Show yourself, hands empty."

No response.

Tess stepped inside and around a sofa and saw him. Beto was facedown on the floor, gun in hand, not moving.

47

"I'd bet overdose," Logan said when he checked Acosta's pupils. "But still breathing."

Tess nodded. They'd already called for medics. She'd secured his weapon, a 9mm, and a bottle of pills — looked like oxycodone, and it was three-quarters empty. There were also a couple boxes of the drug in the man cave and several more boxes in the PSS truck, boxes that never should have been in the possession of Beto Acosta.

"Steve, can you handle the medics? I'm going to ask Gabe to search the premises. I need to go help Casey."

He stood. "No problem. Find the girl."

Tess climbed out of the basement, hurried to her car, and jetted back to the police station, where everyone was waiting for her.

Tess met Casey's husband, John, and listened as he told her where he'd searched and what he'd done since he discovered his daughter missing.

"Did Kayla ever have anything to do with Beto Acosta?"

"What do you mean?" John asked, face scrunched in fear and confusion.

"Did they talk? Were they friends? Any connection at all?"

"No. He sold us the alarm, but he wasn't the installer. I'm sure she knows who he is, but she's only fourteen years old. What would she have to do with him?"

She folded her arms and considered this. What a strange coincidence that Kayla would be kidnapped the same time they were closing in on Acosta. Tess didn't believe in coincidences, but that was what this appeared to be: a huge, ugly co-incidence. She turned to Jeffers and the Re-nos; Pounder had gone to help Logan secure the man cave.

"Del, you go to the Reno house. Search everywhere and everything. I'm going to notify the sheriff. We may even need to call in the FBI." To Casey and John, "We'll figure this out as quickly as we can."

Tess did all she could for the Renos and was about to make the call to the FBI when Logan phoned.

"Hey, it might not mean anything, but Acosta came to after they shot him full of

Narcan. He wouldn't answer questions, but he said we needed to find Roger Dixon. For what it's worth, that's all I got out of him. He's on his way to the hospital, in custody, with Pounder. I'll stay here and help Bender search."

Tess thanked him and hung up, not sure if this was important. Oliver was with the Renos in the outer office. She logged in to her computer and punched in Roger Dixon's name. There was an Oregon driver's license, but no other record. Frowning, Tess found his number in her directory and dialed it.

"Hello?" a male voice answered, but it didn't sound like Roger.

"Mr. Dixon?"

"Who is this?"

"Sorry; it's Chief O'Rourke. I'm looking for Roger Dixon."

"Are you clairvoyant?"

"Excuse me?"

"Chief, this is Victor Camus. Helen Dixon is my sister. I just got to her house. Roger emptied their bank account, slapped her around, and drugged her, then packed his things and fled. I'm getting ready to take her to the hospital; my next call was going to be to you. You'd better find him before I do."

■ ■ ■ ■

Tess got to the Dixon house in three minutes. Helen Dixon's face was bruised and puffy, and it looked as if her wrist was broken. She insisted she didn't need to be fussed over. Victor was as animated as Tess had ever seen him. He was unshaven, dressed in camo gear, and angry. One thing was certain: Roger was a dead man if the hunter found him first.

"What happened, Mrs. Dixon?"

"Please, it's Helen. It was the activity at the bank earlier today that got my attention. The branch manager called and asked me about the withdrawal. When I confronted Roger . . . well, he just said he was tired of me. When I tried to get more of an explanation, he got angry and did this." She pointed to her face and held up her arm. "He must have also drugged me because the last thing I remember before Victor woke me up is Roger packing his suitcase."

Victor jumped in. "She'd left a message for me when she found out about the bank account. But I was on a hunt and didn't have service right away. As soon as I did get the message, I came straight here. Helen was out cold when I got here."

"How long has he been gone?"

Helen looked at Victor, who shrugged. "I'm not sure," she said. "It was after midnight when we quarreled; he'd been out all day. I didn't confront him until he got home."

"Do you have any idea where he went?"

"No. But I do have something you might find interesting." Helen started to get up and Victor stopped her.

"I'll get it. Just tell me what it is."

"Top drawer of my desk, a brown envelope."

Victor retrieved the envelope and pulled out a strip of paper. "Roger Marshall?"

Helen nodded. "I think that's his real name. I don't think he's really Doug's brother."

"What?" Victor stared at his sister. "How long have you figured that?"

"You know he's not who he says he is?" Tess tried to keep the astonishment from her face.

Helen sighed, a sheepish expression on her face. "Chief, I'm an old woman who was blinded by a younger man who claimed to be madly in love with me." Her voice broke and tears started. Victor hugged his sister's shoulders.

She composed herself. "We really had a

good couple of years. But things have been off the last few months. I've been poking through his belongings. I found the name Roger Marshall on an envelope and wrote it down. I never had the courage to confront him about it."

Tess nodded. People often believed what they wanted to when it came to love and relationships.

She told Victor she'd have someone file the report for his sister as soon as possible.

"As soon as we get back from the hospital, I'll be at the PD."

Tess retreated to her patrol car. She ran Roger Marshall through NCIC with the same vital statistics she had for Roger Dixon.

When his record came up, Tess felt all her blood rush to her face. She remembered the day she'd seen Dixon in the market. The young girls, he was flirting with them.

Roger Marshall/Dixon was a pedophile.

48

Oliver started when the chief squealed to a stop in front of the station. She burst into the station, obviously upset.

"Is Mayor Dixon still in the council chambers?"

"Uh, yeah, I think so. What's the matter?"

"I need to talk to him." She strode out of the station and Oliver felt the need to follow.

"I'll let you know what's going on as soon as I do," he said to the Renos, who cast questioning glances his way.

Oliver was on O'Rourke's heels as she stormed into the council chambers.

"What are you doing here?" Dixon demanded. "This is not the place for you right now."

"I think it is. Where's your brother?"

"What?"

"You heard me. Where is your brother?"

"Don't you take that tone —"

435

In shock, Oliver watched as Tess moved faster than he thought anyone could. She grabbed the mayor, spun him around, and had him in handcuffs while he sputtered.

"What is the meaning of this?"

She jerked on one arm and pulled him around to face her, bringing him up on his tiptoes.

"He's not your brother, is he? He's a monster, a sex offender. A pedophile. And you've been covering for him. Where is he? You'll go down as aiding and abetting if you don't talk. Now."

Oliver saw Doug pale and his bluster ended. But what the chief had just said about Roger was beyond belief. Not his brother? Who was he?

"I don't know where he is." Doug went limp in the chief's grasp.

"I don't believe you. He's got Kayla Reno, so you'd better give me something."

That statement rattled Oliver but not as much as the fact that Doug never denied a thing the chief said.

"Diamond Lake," came the whispered response. "He has a cabin there. Under a different name. Urban, I think. He doesn't know I know that. If you're right and he does have the girl, it's possible he'd take her there. That's all I have for you."

■ ■ ■ ■

Tess drove like the devil north on Highway 62 toward Diamond Lake. They figured, based on when the Reno alarm had been disabled, Dixon had at least a two-hour head start. Oliver was in the passenger seat; he wouldn't take no for an answer and she hadn't wanted to take the time to argue. He knew Diamond Lake well; his family also had a cabin there, though he didn't believe it was anywhere near Roger Dixon's, or whatever his name was. And Diamond Lake was in Douglas County, not Jackson County. Tess had never been. Steve promised to do what he could to persuade the Douglas County sheriff to help, but he wasn't sure how far his efforts would go.

"He's a good guy, a good cop, but old-school. He golfs with Mayor Dixon, and I know that he didn't like all the negative press you got in Long Beach. He's very politically correct."

Tess hated political correctness with a passion because she saw it as dishonest. She hoped this didn't mean that the Douglas County sheriff would stand in her way.

"Who is Roger, really?" Oliver asked.

"A wanted man named Roger Marshall.

He's got child molest and child rape charges pending in three states back East."

"Oh, my word," Oliver said.

Tess glanced his way and saw his horrified expression.

He went on. "The arcade. That's why he had it in the market. He always said it was Helen's wish."

"Afraid so. When I tried searching for Roger Dixon, I got no hit. Helen Dixon was having doubts about him. She found some paperwork with the Marshall name and hung on to it."

"She just held on to it?"

"I didn't get all of her reasoning or timing. I was in a hurry and she needed to get to the hospital. I hope to sit down with her sometime —" she turned to Oliver — "after I'm certain that Kayla is okay."

"Is he related at all to Doug?"

"I have no idea."

"He's been a good manager at the market for four years. How did he manage to get that job?"

"How long has Doug Dixon been the mayor?"

"One and a half terms, so six years."

"Maybe he put in a good word for the guy. From what I've heard, Dixon's been a good mayor." She shrugged and stepped on the accelerator to pass a slow-moving car. Bender should be not far behind her; she'd tasked him with sealing up the man cave for the time being and trying to get any more information out of the mayor if he could. He'd follow when he was able. Tess wanted a friendly face with her in Douglas County. Diamond Lake was a little over an hour away and Marshall had too big a lead for Tess to waste any time waiting. "So it's possible he used some juice to get this guy hired."

"But why?"

"Everyone has secrets. Doug Dixon must have a doozy he never wants out, and this guy knew it."

Tess sped past Union Creek and passed the turnoff to Crater Lake. Diamond Lake was off of Highway 230. Here, she had to slow. The road was winding and passing was inadvisable, but thankfully traffic was light.

When she finally made the turnoff for the lake, she was stopped by two Douglas County sheriff vehicles blocking inbound traffic.

Two men leaned against one cruiser. One had to be the sheriff. Tess eased to a stop, and the man she assumed was the sheriff ambled toward the driver's side while the other headed toward Oliver on the passenger side.

"You'd be Chief O'Rourke, I'm guessing." Sheriff Hardin looked down his nose at her. Tess had never met him and only knew what Logan had told her.

Stifling her impatience, Tess dusted off her most diplomatic tone. "Yes, sir, I am. And with your permission, I'd like to proceed to check out a lake cabin for a fugitive."

"So I heard." He put his hands on his hips and straightened to his full height. Tess resisted the urge to get out of her cruiser and go toe-to-toe with him.

Before she could say another word, Oliver leaned over. "Walter, we're in kind of a hurry. Can we count on your assistance?"

Hardin bent down. "Pastor Mac, is that you?"

"Yes, I'm assisting Chief O'Rourke. Will you give us a hand instead of slowing us down?"

Hardin went down on one knee, peering across the car at Oliver. "Pastor, I heard about Anna. I'm devastated. You know how she brought us meals when my Peggy had that stroke. I'll be forever in her debt."

"I know. And we might just be on the trail of the man responsible for her death. Please let us go by. He's possibly in a summer cabin."

Hardin brought a hand to his face. "I need a word with Chief O'Rourke first." He stood and stepped back and motioned for Tess to get out. She jammed the car into park and struggled with her temper.

Oliver put a hand on her arm. "He'll help. Just tell him what we need."

Tess climbed out of her SUV and followed Hardin to his vehicle.

He towered over her and she knew he believed that to be an intimidation advantage. But bigger, taller people never intimidated Tess. One of her pop's rules again crossed her mind: *"The bigger they are, the harder they fall."* But rule #4 also applied: "Don't step on anyone's macho." She would try.

"Chief, I listened to Sergeant Logan try to outline what you're after, and I got to say, I'm not convinced. Roger Dixon is an upstanding citizen from what I've seen."

"Sheriff, I really don't have the time to try and convince you. I believe I'm after a dangerous pedophile, wanted in three states, who has kidnapped a fourteen-year-old girl. You holding me up just gives him more time with her. Is that what you want?"

"I don't think you have the evidence you need to make that assertion. If — and that's a big *if* — Dixon is your man, he could be halfway to Portland by now."

"Are you willing to bet a fourteen-year-old's life on that?" Tess held his gaze and watched indecision cloud his eyes briefly.

"If I'm wrong," Tess continued, "you win. But if I'm right and you continue to hold me up, that little girl loses."

He waved to his deputy to move a car. "I'll go along, but just so you know, I don't like cowboys, cops who don't look before they leap. I hear you're already in trouble there in Rogue's Hollow. If you drag us on a wild-goose chase to disturb a law-abiding man, you can bet that city council will get my input. Follow me in." He turned on his heel, climbed into his patrol car, and slammed the door.

Tess hurried back behind the wheel and followed Hardin.

"I don't particularly believe in prayer, Oliver. But I know you do."

"Yes, of course I do."

"Please pray that this guy's ego doesn't cost Kayla her life."

49

Oliver felt the tension in Tess fill the car. He knew Walter Hardin could be a stubborn man but believed that he was ultimately fair.

They had a few miles to get to the Diamond Lake resort and another six past that to get to the road that would take them to the lake cabins. Oliver knew this area quite well. His parents had owned a cabin here when he was a boy. Twice while they were living in Scotland they'd returned here for summer vacations. Oliver loved this area; he'd brought Anna here many times.

Thinking of Anna pierced his heart. He still had arrangements to make. But he knew she'd want him here, now, to help Chief O'Rourke and Kayla in any way he could.

Tess followed the sheriff, chafing as he drove just the speed limit. She'd never been to this lake and was trying to imagine the scenario she would face at a secluded cabin. The trees were tall pines, she guessed. There was also some scrub brush, but would she have cover? Would the approach to the cabin signal to Roger, before they had any chance to save the girl, that they were coming?

Hardin slowed and pulled to the right. Tess pulled even with him and saw that they were in front of a directory of names and cabin numbers.

"What was the name on the cabin?" Hardin asked.

"Urban. Dixon was almost certain it was Urban." Tess scanned the directory and saw Urban next to the number 42.

"Cabin 42 sits off the same road as cabin 43, but it's high and to the right. What's your plan, Chief?" Hardin looked past Oliver at Tess, skepticism in his eyes.

"Will he be able to see us drive up?"

"You get a free hundred, hundred and fifty feet. Then the road rises and he will see you, if he's looking."

"Well, Sheriff, I plan on driving as far as I can, then sneaking in quietly to see exactly what he's up to. Do you have a problem with that?"

"Nope. We'll be right behind you, but this is your circus; you can hang yourself."

Tess pulled onto the road and continued

forward. She could see to the left small cabins dotting the area. The driveways to the cabins were marked with posts showing the cabin numbers; each post had at least two numbers on it.

When she got to 39, she slowed, watching the terrain ahead. There was a slight rise, tree lined, and a cabin barely visible. There were also piles of wood and wood debris everywhere, as if the whole area had been raked and cleaned and these piles were ready to be cleared out. They were big piles and could work to her advantage if she needed cover.

"See those piles of wood?" She pointed and turned to Oliver. "What's up with that?"

"Brush clearance for fire danger, I believe."

They reached the post that had 42 on it and Tess turned right onto the dirt road. It was narrow with tall, thin trees on either side. When she thought she'd gone as far as she could while remaining safe from Roger's eyes, she stopped the car and put it in park.

"There aren't a lot of people around here, huh?"

"It's a weekday. Most of the cabins are probably occupied on the weekends. The resort was more crowded than it is here."

"I guess I should have left you with Sheriff

Hardin. I'm going the rest of the way on my own."

"Chief, is that wise?"

"Oliver, I still can't figure you out." Tess kept her eyes on the rise, where she could just see the roof of cabin 42. "Your wife just died, yet you're concerned about me. And with almost anyone else I'd say it was because you wanted her murderer to pay." She turned, held his gaze, searched his eyes. "But that's not it with you, is it?"

He shook his head, eyes calm, steady. "No. I'm here because I want to make certain you're okay. Anna would have wanted to be sure you were treated fairly. I didn't want Douglas to force you out. You said one way you got through the loss of your dad was to put one foot in front of the other and honor his memory. That's what I'm doing here: putting one foot in front of the other and honoring Anna's memory."

"Fair enough. Stay in the car. I have a radio. I can call Hardin if I need to."

She opened the door and climbed out of the car, eyes still focused on the cabin. It was possible she'd get to a position where she could see the whole cabin and discover that Roger was not there with the girl. What would she do then?

50

The piles of wood were good cover. Tess was able to find a stack on the rise, and while using it for cover, she had a line of sight on cabin 42. She recognized Roger's SUV and her adrenaline surged. She keyed her mike and let Hardin know a vehicle was present.

All he said was "10-4." It was obvious he was going to let her sink or swim on her own.

Very carefully, Tess threaded her way through the trees and wood stacks to the vehicle.

Keeping the SUV between herself and the cabin, she peered around the rear of the vehicle and saw a figure pass in front of one of the cabin windows. Tall and thin, it had to be Roger. She turned down her radio, not wanting the crackle of radio traffic to tip her hand.

Hand on the butt of her gun, she went

down on one knee and considered her options. She could knock; he could deny knowing anything about Kayla and slam the door in her face. She could wait, hoping that Bender got something from the mayor that would help with a warrant. But that would take so much time. She could use exigent circumstances to burst into the cabin without a warrant, but her justification for exigency was thin — a strong hunch wouldn't cut it. She was stuck with a conundrum.

If Kayla wasn't here, they were back to square one and she was wasting precious time. If Kayla was here, they needed to get to her ASAP. Standing, she peered inside the SUV and saw a suitcase and a box of food, canned and boxed quick meals. Either he was planning on running or he had not yet unloaded the car.

Tess needed to get closer to the cabin, try to confirm. She was about to move from the SUV and peek into a cabin window when she heard a crash and a curse.

A male voice yelled, *"Ow! Why, you little . . . Come back here!"*

Things banging, another crash, breaking glass, a man howling in pain, then the back door burst open and out stumbled Kayla, barefoot, hands bound in front of her, clothes ripped, a look of pure terror on her face.

Tess leaped from behind the car toward Kayla at the same time Roger shoved the door open. There was a gun in his hand.

Drawing her own weapon, Tess knew that she'd have to get between Kayla and Roger before she could fire. Weapon in her right hand, she reached across her body with the left, extending a hand to the terrified girl.

"Here!" Tess yelled.

In her peripheral vision she saw Roger raise his weapon. Time seemed to slow. She thought of her dad, she thought of Cullen Hoover, and she knew that no matter what she had to save this girl.

Tess grasped Kayla's wrists and pulled her down and behind her as she shifted her attention to Roger. Off-balance, she raised her gun and pulled the trigger even as he did the same.

Oliver got out of the cruiser to stretch and to wait and hear from Tess. The woman's confidence and instincts continued to impress him. It also made him realize just how much he was going to miss Anna and her insight into people. Just then a wave hit — of loss, of pain, and even a little bit of fear. What was he going to do now with his life?

Put one foot in front of the other and honor her life.

He sighed as the pain settled in, tempered ever so slightly by the knowledge that he could, at least, put one foot in front of the other. Then movement on the road caught his eye. It was a blue-and-white Rogue's Hollow PD vehicle flying up the drive. It screeched to a stop by Sheriff Hardin's car, and Oliver recognized Gabe Bender getting out of the car. He was animated, but whatever he said affected Hardin and they both hopped back in their patrol cars and headed up the road toward Oliver.

He would have waited for them, but then he heard the gunshots. How many, he wasn't sure, but without thought for his own safety, he sprinted up the hill toward the sound.

The scene that was unfolding before him as he crested the rise took his breath away. Kayla knelt over the prone form of Chief O'Rourke, sobbing, while the man he knew as Roger Dixon writhed in pain near the cabin door.

Oliver sprinted to Tess, falling on his knees next to her and addressing Kayla. "What happened?"

"She saved me. She saved me."

Like a wave crashing over his head, Oliver

felt the fear that Tess was dead.

But she moved, then moaned and tried to rise, coughing as she did. She looked at Oliver and shifted, pointing her gun toward Roger. But he was no threat, seemingly oblivious to all of them, concerned only with his pain.

"He's down," Oliver said, at the same time as Bender came skidding to a stop beside her.

Hardin and his deputy descended on Roger. Oliver exhaled in relief and gathered Kayla in his arms to calm her as Bender saw to the chief.

"Chief?"

With a rough intake of breath, Tess said, "I'm okay. . . . Wind knocked out . . ."

Oliver looked where Tess was pointing and realized her vest had stopped a bullet.

"Take care of the girl," she said.

"I've got her," he said. He breathed a prayer of thanks, grateful beyond measure that Kayla was alive and safe. Grateful, too, for Tess, who was probably the only person who could have made the right connections and saved the day like she just had.

51

Her chest felt as if she'd been slammed by a hammer wielded by a giant. Tess inspected the area where the projectile had struck. It had glanced off the bottom of her badge — she could feel a dent — and hit her chest a bit off center. She figured it was because of the way her body was turned at the time. The deformed projectile stuck in her trauma plate. She doubted anything was broken, but she was certain there'd be a big bruise.

But Kayla was safe and a predator was in custody, and those facts acted like a natural painkiller.

Oliver had come running up the hill like a knight in shining armor — an unarmed knight. Tess instinctively raised her gun, but Marshall was incapacitated. The scene had settled down a bit. Hardin and his deputy were dealing with Marshall, who was screaming and moaning that his arm was broken. Bender took a look and then walked back over to Tess.

"Looks like you hit his collarbone." He winced and pointed to his. "Not a lot of blood, but it's all collapsed. Bet it stings."

"Are you sure that you're okay?" Oliver asked Tess.

"Oh yeah, I'm fine," Tess said. She nodded to Bender as she leaned against Marshall's SUV while they waited for medics. Hardin had secured the scene and called more deputies. Oliver stood next to Tess. Kayla had been walked back down the driveway to Tess's car, where Del sat with her. He'd arrived shortly after Bender.

"I want to know what else you found out about Marshall from brother Doug."

Bender arched a brow. "Dixon fell apart and told the whole story after you left."

"I'm listening," Tess said.

"In a way, Roger was the mayor's brother — his foster brother," Bender said. "When they were kids, they were adopted by the same foster parents.

"The mayor claimed he hadn't seen the guy in years when Roger found him on the Internet and began to correspond. Dixon said he had no interest in reconnecting, but when he was in Vegas a few years ago at a conference, Marshall showed up. He professed to have reformed his life and was trying to start over clean. It seems both have records."

"Doug Dixon is wanted too?" Tess shifted in surprise and winced as pain flashed through her body.

"Not wanted, but back in New Hampshire he did five years for federal embezzlement when he was in his twenties. The mayor says that after he was released, he'd learned his lesson. But he couldn't get a second chance when he disclosed the conviction. So he left it off, came west to start over, and built a life here. He tried to forget his foster brother, who he said always had problems and has been a sex offender since his teens."

"And Marshall held Dixon's past over his head? Help your dear old foster brother get a new lease on life and he would keep the secret about the old conviction?"

"Surely the mayor didn't think people would hold that old conviction against him?" Oliver said.

"Didn't want to take the chance."

"Even though he knew Marshall was a dirtbag?" Tess asked.

"Dixon says at first he thought his brother was on the up-and-up, that he really had changed. Marshall told him he'd legally changed his name to Dixon to get away from the stigma of being an ex-con. He played Dixon like a violin."

"He played a lot of people," Oliver said. "I've known him since he moved here. My associate pastor married him and Helen Camus."

"Right." Bender nodded. "The first couple of years, especially after he married Helen, who he seemed to make happy, Dixon says he breathed a sigh of relief, thinking that Marshall was a different man. It was only lately, in the last year and a half, that he realized there was something off. And now he had more to lose, what with his wife's condition and all, so he looked the other way where Marshall was concerned."

"Besides, he'd already covered for the guy for years," Tess said.

"Yep. He admits he almost —" Bender held his fingers up as if he were placing quotes around the word — "called the FBI. But he was too afraid of Marshall and too afraid he'd go to jail, and no one would be there to care for his wife."

That made sense in a twisted way to Tess. "As time went on, it would have been harder and harder to tell the truth."

The drone of sirens drowned out the rest of the conversation as medics arrived. Hardin directed them to Tess first, but she waved them off. She was sore but okay. And

Marshall's whining was getting on her nerves.

She and Oliver walked down the drive to where Del sat with Kayla.

"How are you holding up?" she asked, noting that the girl's tears were gone and Kayla seemed composed and calm.

"I'm okay." She gave a heavy sigh. "But can I ask you a question, Chief?"

"Sure."

"Mr. Dixon was the kind of man my dad is always warning me about. I never thought — I mean, he seemed so normal, but he isn't at all, is he?" Her voice broke, the first crack Tess had seen in the brave girl. She wiped her nose and continued. "How do we keep away from bad people if they don't seem bad?"

Tess sucked in a breath, ignoring the twinge of pain in her chest when she did. The girl had come face-to-face with evil and survived, but at what cost? Was there any way to prevent her from being scarred for life? Tess hoped so. "You did everything possible, Kayla. This wasn't your fault. Mr. Dixon fooled us all. Just keep listening to your parents. Now, I have a question for you. How'd you get away from him?"

She shrugged in a way only a fourteen-year-old girl could. "I started to wake up and got scared. My dad always says to try and think before you react. Mr. Dixon carried me out of the car into the cabin. Then he took a shower. I could hear the water running. I worked on the ropes the whole time. I got them loose enough so that when he bent down and got in my face, I was able to poke him in the eye. Then I kicked him in the shin and ran."

"That was a great self-defense move," she said to Kayla. She figured Marshall had drugged Kayla when he took her from her house.

"You were brave and strong," Oliver added.

"My dad taught me that."

"Good for your dad," Del said. He'd calmed Kayla and let her talk to her parents on the phone. Casey and John were on the way and Tess expected them any minute. Steve Logan was bringing them and she could admit to herself that she was looking forward to seeing him even more.

"How are you feeling now, Chief?" Oliver asked.

She started to sigh, but it hurt to inhale. "I'm okay. I'm gratified everything has worked out." She looked at the pastor. He'd been a great help, but she knew that when they were finished, he'd be going back to town to make funeral arrangements. "You know, Pastor, you've insisted I call you Oliver. I think it's time you call me Tess. Fair is fair."

He nodded and started to say something when they heard a car approaching. Tess turned and saw the green-and-white Jackson County sheriff car coming up the drive to park behind the line of cars already there.

Her heart gave a little flutter when Steve Logan got out of the driver's seat and looked her way. He then turned and opened the back door so that John and Casey Reno could get out. The anxious parents fairly ran up the drive to hug their daughter, and Tess felt the joy.

"Hey, good job, Chief." Logan gave her a high-wattage smile and gripped her hand in both of his. "You melted Hardin and everything. He thinks you earned a medal today."

"It was a team effort." She let her hand linger in his.

"I second that sentiment." Casey Reno wiped her eyes and looked at Tess, who reluctantly let Logan's hand go. "I'll never be able to thank you enough, Chief."

"Please, it's Tess."

Casey nodded. "I'm glad you're the chief. And if the mayor pressed the vote today, you have mine." She sniffled and went back

458

to hugging her daughter.

Just then, Tess's phone rang. She recognized the number. It was the station in Long Beach, homicide office.

Placing a hand on Logan's shoulder, she said, "I have to take this." He nodded and she stepped away to answer the call.

It was Jack O'Reilly.

"We got 'em, Tess."

"What?"

"The other actors in the shooting, the ones who ran away. We acted on a tip, got the first one. When we told his mom why we were there for her son, she commenced to put a whooping on the kid. He confessed, led us to the other two. It was a setup."

Tess cleared her throat, still not completely comprehending. "A setup?"

"Yep. It was Cullen's idea, but these knuckleheads went along. The other kids, they baited JT. When he ran into the alley, Cullen smacked him with the bat. Cullen wanted to kill a cop, Tess. He was trying to rack up gang creds and thought this would be the best way. The plan was to kill JT with his own gun. The truth is finally out there, and we have three in custody for attempted murder of a police officer. Consider your name cleared."

52

It was early morning before Tess got back to Rogue's Hollow. Since she'd shot someone in a different jurisdiction, she'd had to stay and be interviewed by their shooting team. She cooperated fully with Sheriff Hardin in his investigation and was pleased to see a thaw in the man. He was an old-school guy, a good cop, and cordial when he realized that the same was true of Tess. Her chest was still pretty sore, but she'd opted not to go to the hospital.

Who killed Glen and Anna became a mystery again. In spite of the evidence all pointing at Acosta, now that Tess knew who and what Roger Marshall was, she didn't see Beto as the killer. She tried to talk to Marshall before the medics left, but he wouldn't say much.

He denied shooting Glen and pushing Anna into the creek. He blamed Acosta and then clammed up, screaming for a lawyer. It didn't matter to Tess; the man would be in custody for the rest of his life anyway, for other things. They had time to prove their case while he was safely tucked away.

Tess wanted only to get to bed. She planned to interview Beto Acosta as soon as possible and needed some shut-eye. He'd recovered from his overdose and was being held in the Jackson County Jail. Pounder had sent her a text saying that Acosta wanted to talk to her.

River Drive was quiet when she turned off of Highway 62; no one was out. It was a cool early morning; temperatures had dipped into the forties when Tess got out of her car. Oliver had come back hours earlier with Bender, and Tess wondered if he was still awake. She'd wanted to talk to him about his capricious God. Tess believed it was sheer luck they'd caught Marshall before he'd had a chance to hurt Kayla.

Oliver disagreed. *"I believe in God's providence, not luck."*

Tess frowned. *"Why then does his providence apply only in some situations? Where was his providence where Anna was concerned?"*

"Tess, I don't have an answer you would accept for that question. I have to trust. Either he's God over everything or he's God over

461

nothing."

Those words had bothered her but not as much as what he said next.

"You did a selfless thing, Tess. You were ready to lay down your life for Kayla. That's a selfless act. 'Greater love —' "

" '. . . has no one than this, that someone lay down his life for his friends.' "

He'd seemed surprised when she finished the verse for him.

"You know the verse?"

"It's on my dad's headstone. At the time, when he was buried, I didn't want it there. My mom overruled me. I was angry. I hated that woman he saved, wished she was in the ground and not him."

"And now?"

Tess shrugged and grimaced as pain from the bullet bit. Weariness settled in. *"I'm proud of my father. He's a hero. I would consider myself a success to be half the cop he was."*

He'd smiled. Tess hadn't seen him really smile since the dinner she'd shared with him and Anna. Oliver had a nice smile. His stormy green-gray eyes twinkled and a dimple appeared on the right side of his face.

"You're a success, Tess, a heroic success. Don't ever think you're not."

When she'd left Diamond Lake, Oliver's

words had stuck in her mind and she'd wanted to call him, talk more about heroes and saviors. But now, as she climbed out of the car and trudged into the inn, there was only weariness. She was dead tired.

There was a note on the door to her room from Sheila. Klaus and Addie had Killer; they said they would care for her for as long as Tess needed.

Tess knew she'd have to find a permanent solution for Killer. Her lifestyle would not be fair to a dog. But she didn't have the energy to think about a solution at the moment; she didn't even have the energy to shower.

She shucked off her clothes and fell into bed. The last thought on her mind was that she was going to have to write commendations for all of her people. Everyone involved performed above and beyond the call of duty, and Tess was proud of them. But as she began to list the names, her mind shut off and she was instantly asleep.

53

Acosta looked horrible. He needed a shave, and the dark circles under his eyes reminded Tess of truck tires. She guessed he was beginning to come down from the oxycodone addiction. She'd heard that was a nasty withdrawal. He'd refused to talk to anyone except Tess yet had not invoked his right to counsel.

"I didn't kill Glen Elders or Anna Macpherson," he said before Tess even had a chance to read him his rights. It was around 1 p.m. and they were seated in an interview room, just Tess and Acosta. The jail deputy was outside the door.

"I have to advise you of your right to an attorney."

"I understand my rights and I waive them. They told me you found Anna's belongings in my office. Roger put them there; he must have."

She slid the form across the counter with

a pen and he signed.

"He's not talking. He lawyered up. But we guessed it was your money Glen took. Care to explain that?"

"Yeah, it was my cash. I admit to being an alimony weasel, but I'm no killer."

"Why would Roger want to kill Glen for taking your money?"

Acosta ground his palms into his forehead. "I know how it looks. But you have to believe me — I'm not a killer."

"Are you just a drug dealer?"

"No, I'm not that either. Look, you found me with my gun. I couldn't even shoot myself. I guess I took too many pills."

Tess set the digital recorder on the table and went through all the legal requirements. "Okay, then tell me what you are."

An hour and a half later, Tess left with the story that Beto Acosta was telling. Roger had come to him two years earlier with an opportunity to make some extra money.

"He knew I was hurting from the divorce. He said all of this would be under the table and untraceable. All I had to do was pick up boxes from him — sometimes it was prescription drugs; sometimes it was something else. He packed them in my truck and I took them to Eugene, where someone else took them off. I got money and a couple of bottles of oxy. All I did was transfer the stuff. I never sold it."

"Where'd you pick the stuff up and where did you drop it off in Eugene?"

"I always picked it up behind the market. Usually early in the morning. As for Eugene . . . well, it was always someplace different. The address would be written on the boxes."

"Glen found out about this operation?"

"He said he and his girlfriend watched me for a few weeks. I didn't even know. But somehow he did and he broke into my hiding place and stole my money. He thought it was all money from selling drugs. It wasn't. I often got paid under the table for alarm jobs. He wouldn't listen." He paused and rubbed his face with his hands.

"He tried to blackmail me, said he knew everything and would go to the police if I didn't stop selling drugs to kids." He frowned. "Kids? I didn't know what he was talking about. I heard Anna tell Octavio she knew where Glen was, that he had promised to tell her something important. I freaked out. I was afraid he was going to tell her about the operation. I called Roger while Anna was talking to Octavio. He said he'd handle it."

"When was that?"

"Wednesday. The Wednesday before Roger killed Glen."

"That was when Anna disappeared. You followed her from the church."

"Yeah, I admit that. But it was Roger who stopped her. I saw them by the side of the road. I swear I didn't know he was going to kill her."

"You just stood by and watched? She's dead now."

"Look, it's the drugs — they mess with my head. I had no idea Roger was a killer. I thought he'd just talk to her."

"Yet you're certain it was Roger who killed Glen?"

"He told me he did it. He said nothing about Anna Macpherson."

Tess wanted to reach across the table and slap him. Instead, she continued to question him. "Where did Roger get all these drugs you delivered?"

"All I know is that it was from some guy in California. That's it. We called him Shorty; there's no other name I know. I didn't want to know."

Tess gave a copy of the interview to the sheriff, who would forward to DEA. Federal marshals had already been notified about the fugitive, but he was out of Tess's control. Sheriff Hardin had Marshall in Douglas

467

County. And since he invoked his rights, she was certain he would not be talking.

She considered Acosta's statement. As angry as he made her, she believed the guy. Marshall was the cold-blooded killer, not Acosta.

On a lark, since she was in Medford, Tess decided to stop by the hospital and check on Tilly. She knew the hospital couldn't force the girl to stay and be treated if she insisted on leaving, but if Tilly's hip was broken as Oliver thought, she couldn't have walked out yet. And an idea was brewing in Tess's mind, a plan she hoped would tie up a couple of loose ends.

She asked for the girl's room at the information counter and was directed upstairs.

"Chief."

Tess turned when someone said her name as she waited for the elevator. Bart Dover stepped up. His forehead creased in a frown.

"Mr. Dover."

"Are you here to arrest Tilly?"

"No. I was nearby and thought I would see how she was doing. I'm hoping she can tell me what she saw the day Glen was killed."

The man relaxed. The elevator opened and they stepped inside.

"It's been rough. Her femur was broken

468

and they had to do surgery to insert a pin. At first she was screaming to leave, but she can't walk. They called me to get her to consent to the surgery." He shook his head. "It took some pleading, but they fixed her leg. Surgery went well, and she calmed down some last night, but it's hard for them to manage her pain with the addiction issues. I'm not sure what I'll find this morning."

They got off the elevator and he put a hand on her arm. "I think this is my sister's last chance to get clean. Her doctor came to assess her and hopefully get her back on her legal drugs. If she goes to jail, she'll be back on meth and I know we'll lose the fight." His eyes were filled with emotion. Tess remembered how a few days ago the man had been prepared to completely write his sister off.

She patted his hand. "I'm not here to arrest her," Tess repeated. "As far as I know, she's witnessed a murder and been a victim of a car crash. All I want to do is ask her what she remembers."

He relaxed and then led her to Tilly's room.

Tess looked toward the bed and saw a slight, pale girl, left leg casted with pins sticking out that looked like some sort of torture device. Tilly's eyes were closed, her straw-colored hair a wild mess, but it looked clean.

Bart stepped to her side. "Tills, it's Bart. You awake?"

Her eyes opened, and she gave a low moan and spoke in a harsh whisper. "I hurt."

"I know, I know. They're doing all they can. You have a visitor. She just came to talk — if you want to — that's all."

Tilly turned her head to look at Tess. Tess saw pain in her eyes, but a bit of clarity.

"Do you mind talking to the chief?" Bart asked.

She licked her lips and swallowed, and Bart grabbed her water and held it close so she could take a sip through the straw.

"I'll talk," she said in a barely audible voice.

Tess moved to the side of the bed. Tilly looked run over by a truck. The circles under her eyes would rival Beto Acosta's.

"Hi, Tilly. I'm Chief O'Rourke."

Tilly nodded.

"I need to ask you about Glen, what you saw that day. Do you remember?"

"He's dead."

"Yes, and Anna too."

Tilly sucked in a sob. "I killed Anna, didn't I?" A tear rolled down her face.

"I doubt Pastor Mac would place that blame on you. You tried to help her, and you saw who pushed her into the creek, didn't you?"

The head bobbed again. "I thought it was Beto Acosta. Glen and I took his money."

"How did you guys get to his money?"

She swallowed. Tess saw the muscles in her neck work. But she seemed to be getting stronger.

"I heard him one night, saw him with the drugs. Glen and I wanted to stop him. We followed him for a long time. Figured his routine, saw the cash, took it. He was out cold. I think he does drugs."

Yeah, Tess thought, he sure did.

"Beto called Glen, asked him to meet. I wasn't supposed to be there. I hid on the other side of the creek. I thought it was Beto. But it wasn't."

"It wasn't Beto?" Tess frowned. "You saw the man clearly?"

She gave a slight nod. "It was dark, but getting light. I assumed it would be Beto. There was yelling — the voice was wrong; it wasn't New York. Then, when he pushed Anna into the creek, I saw."

"What did you see?"

"It was Dixon, the store guy. Glen yelled his name. Glen said, 'No, Roger, no.' But he fired anyway."

She reached a hand out and Tess took it. The grip was weak. "Glen wanted me to get clean. He tried to help me. But that day I was so messed up, so loaded. Thought I remembered things wrong. I kept thinking Beto just wanted his money back, but the voice was wrong. Now I can think a little clearer. I'm sure of it. It was Dixon who killed Glen."

The girl began to sob softly. "I'm as worthless as people say, aren't I? Glen, Anna, Killer, they're all dead because of me."

Tess leaned close to the bed, inhaling antiseptic hospital smells, hoping what she had to say would make an impression. "Listen to me. The only person responsible for Glen's and Anna's deaths is the killer, the one who fired the gun. You are a victim here, not a murderer. And Killer is alive; she didn't die."

Tilly sniffled, opened her eyes, and looked at Tess. "But she got shot first."

"I can't explain it, but she lived. She lost her leg, but she's alive."

"Glen loved that dog."

"She got shot trying to protect him. Now she needs someone to take care of her."

"Who?"

"I was hoping you would. I know you're going to have a hard time walking. Killer has to learn to live on three legs. Do you think you'd be up to taking care of her when you're back on your feet?"

Tilly swallowed, face brightening. "You'd trust me to do that?"

"I think Glen would trust you."

Tess drove back to Rogue's Hollow deep in thought. Tilly seemed lucid and certain now, but she'd be shredded in court. They had a strong circumstantial case against Marshall, but she hoped something more solid would come up. Bender and Logan were both lobbying the state lab for results. They had two handguns, the one Beto'd had in his hand, which was the gun registered to him, and the one found in his office, which had the serial number filed off, plus the weapon recovered from Marshall at the cabin. They had the brass Tess had found and the slug from the dog, so they could determine which gun fired the bullet.

She checked her phone. No message from them yet.

As she approached the turnoff for Rogue's Hollow, she thought about Jack O'Reilly's news about the three missing subjects being located after all this time. That had rocked her world. But not as much as the news about Roger Marshall rocked the little town of Rogue's Hollow. Doug Dixon had resigned, effective immediately. Whether or not charges would be filed against him for harboring his foster brother remained to be seen. Because Marshall was a fugitive, it would be up to the Feds to file charges. She found herself feeling sorry for the little man. While there was no excuse for sheltering a monster like Marshall, if Dixon truly didn't know . . . well, Tess found that Oliver's phrase "have a little grace" resonated with her. He'd been able to say that about Dixon after discovering it was likely because of the mayor's actions that Anna was dead.

If Oliver could show mercy, then so could Tess.

She was waiting to hear when Anna's service would be. Oliver had said there would be a small private service and a larger public memorial. Though Tess hated funerals, there was no way she was going to miss Anna's.

Yawning as she parked her car, seemingly unable to shake the fatigue she'd felt since the long day yesterday, Tess made her way into the station. Bender was waiting for her, huge grin on his face.

Tess perked up. "You have news?"

"I do. Great news. The lab rushed ballistics through as soon as they got the slug the vet pulled from the dog. The gun we found in Acosta's office was the gun that shot the dog and Glen."

Tess leaned against the doorframe to her office. "I just spoke to Tilly. She said Marshall was the shooter."

"Well, I have more news." He rubbed his hands together. "The gun had been wiped clean; there were no prints on it. There was, however, a print lifted from the brass you found."

"Marshall."

"Yep. And the gun matches the one used in two of the crimes he committed back East. He's toast."

Tess smiled as fatigue fled. She gave her grinning officer a high five.

"Great. I'm buying dinner. Max's okay with everyone?"

54

Everybody has their own truth.

Tess considered truth and lies as she looked out the window of her hotel room. Hector Connor-Ruiz was still convinced she'd killed Cullen in cold blood and that there was a massive cover-up happening. Thankfully, he now had only a small following, but what about the next shooting? Soon enough another would come, and if it was at all questionable, what of that cop?

She knew that her father would say, "Worry about today, Tess. Tomorrow will come; deal with it then." So she tried to turn her thoughts elsewhere. She was staying in a downtown Long Beach hotel and she had a view of the harbor, the *Queen Mary.* It was a nostalgic view as the years she'd worked in and around the area flashed in her mind's eye.

The drunk driver.

The homicide.

Jeannie's wedding at the Queen Mary.

The biker riot at the Queen Mary.

Some good memories, some awful.

The boys Jack found were supposed to be arraigned in the morning, but she'd just been notified by him that it looked more like they were going to plead out.

"These aren't bad kids," he told her. "With Cullen gone, they all settled back into school. Two of them will be going to college. They got caught up in the moment, infected by Cullen."

I can afford a little grace. She didn't mind the boys getting lighter sentences because of the plea. She was glad they'd opened up and that now she knew the whole story. But it still horrified her that a fourteen-year-old could get so worked up he'd want to kill a police officer, and he'd almost been successful.

How do you prevent another Cullen Hoover?

The boys' story had meant nothing to Connor-Ruiz. Tess's homecoming had been met with a scathing blog post about killer cops evading justice because the system wasn't fair. Everybody had their own truth.

Tess had been able to meet and catch up with old friends — Jeannie, Ronnie, Gruff, and others — and she found the pain and loss she'd felt when she'd left LBPD those months ago had lessened, if not disappeared altogether. Paul wasn't around to taunt her. His new wife had just had a baby and he was on vacation. Even Connor-Ruiz's words hadn't scorched her like she knew he'd wanted. She wasn't frozen anymore.

The phone rang and she saw the Oregon area code. Steve Logan.

Tess answered. "Hey, it's late. What are you still doing up?"

"I was thinking about you," he said.

Tess felt a catch in her chest.

"How's it all going down there in the big city?"

"Better in some ways, worse in others." She told him about the pleas. "They'll get minimal jail time."

"You okay with that?"

"I am. I want this chapter closed and in the rearview mirror." She almost added, "So I can come home," but then realized Long Beach wasn't home anymore.

"I'm glad for you," Steve was saying. "Closure is a good thing."

"It is. And so is opening new doors. I can't wait to get back to the Hollow."

A NOTE FROM THE AUTHOR

Law enforcement is a tough job in any environment. Since 2001, when seventy-two officers died in the terrorist attacks on the Twin Towers (altogether 242 died in the line of duty that year), we've averaged 162 line of duty deaths annually (http://www.odmp.org/search/year). We die a lot of different ways: aircraft accidents, assaults, vehicle crashes, heart attacks, gunfire, etc. And no one sugarcoats the risk in pinning on a badge. We know going in that the job is dangerous.

When I was in the academy, we talked a lot about the number of officers dying in the line of duty, often dissecting the tragic incidents that led to the deaths, seriously contemplating, "What would I have done in that situation?" And we hoped that better training, safer tactics would cut into the number and lower it.

In some respects, better training has

helped, but 2016 will go down in my mind as one of the deadliest years for law enforcement not because of numbers, but because of the animosity I saw leveled at police officers. Animosity that led to ambushes like the one in Dallas that left five officers dead one July evening. There is really no training that can prepare you for a skilled gunman, set up in a secure location during an event requiring law enforcement protection, who is bent on killing as many officers in uniform as possible.

Ironically, the officers were protecting people who were protesting *them.*

In the aftermath of the tragedy in Dallas, there was so much commentary out there, some informed, some completely uninformed. The video that recorded the tragedy pretty much sums it up. All those people on the street protesting the cops, painting all officers with a broad brush — and when the shooting started, who did they look to for protection? To the very people they were protesting and vilifying, the people in blue. And the people in blue did not disappoint. They ran toward the danger, toward the shots, and some of them died protecting the very people who hate them.

Because that is what we do.

Even before social media, police work was

visible and minutely scrutinized. Police work is 24-7; police stations never close and officers contact people all the time. They encounter situations that seem out of place, that look dangerous, that *are* dangerous, and they don't look the other way. Police respond to emotional calls, to active criminal behavior; they don't exclusively drive through safe, quiet neighborhoods. By sheer volume, odds are that some contacts will not go well. Not every citizen interaction can be handled with a please and thank-you; after all, we take people to *jail.*

Police work is not always pretty, but that does not mean it's illegal, wrong, or racist. With the explosion of social media, there is more scrutiny than ever. This is good if bad cops are exposed, but horrible if there is a rush to judgment and good cops are tarnished by half the story or unfortunate situations.

When I was in uniform, we went through a tough period of anti-cop sentiment and rioting after the Rodney King verdict. It was scary and it was dangerous, but there was always the feeling that the majority of the people we served were behind us and that most people had our backs. With all this violence directed at law enforcement recently, with headline after headline proclaiming an officer shot, or an officer's death, I wonder if the men and women in law enforcement still feel that the majority of the people they serve have their backs.

I understand people protesting when they have a legitimate grievance or pain. But in some of the protests I saw, people actively called for officers to be murdered. (One sign read *All my heroes kill cops.*) To call for the murder of those who put their lives on the line protecting you is beyond reprehensible.

This craziness has to stop. The problem is, police officers, for the most part, cannot do their work in secret; neither can they be selective in the calls they handle. They head out to where they are dispatched in a clearly marked vehicle in a clearly noticeable uniform. If someone wants to take a shot, it's easy.

How can the average person help? You can pray for police; you can offer your support when you see them out in the community; and you can teach your children to respect the law and law enforcement. Our culture should be a culture that holds the law in high regard.

If you need a cop in an emergency, 911 will bring them to your aid. And cops will continue to do what they do, protecting and serving their communities. The men and women I proudly served with took their jobs seriously and rushed into dangerous situations time and time again, to help, to protect, *all* citizens.

Now more than ever, police officers put their lives on the line. They deserve the support of every law-abiding citizen. Let's start our own reverse 911 and pray and support those who protect us.

DISCUSSION QUESTIONS

1. In the opening scene of *Crisis Shot,* Tess O'Rourke is forced to make a split-second decision that results in major fallout. Are her actions justified? Consider the different stances members of the Rogue's Hollow council take. Which is closest to your view? Many Americans have seen similar shooting incidents play out in their own communities. Are the police taking appropriate steps to ensure public safety, or is there more that should be done?

2. Tess bemoans the idea that "the truth didn't seem to matter" to the media or the public. Are there things she could have done to fight harder for her job, or is it, as the LBPD deputy chief says, a waste of time in a battle she was bound to lose? How can you champion the truth when it seems like everyone makes up their own truth?

3. When Oliver Macpherson and his wife receive the devastating news that Anna's cancer has returned, Anna tells Oliver that God isn't listening to their prayers. How does Oliver respond to that? How would you respond to Anna?

4. Oliver struggles at times to lay his petitions before God and truly let go of the worry he has. What does Philippians 4:6-7 say about worry? What other verses come to mind when you struggle with fear or worry?

5. Tilly is a tortured soul . . . and an unlikely hero. In what ways does she show a desire to help? What happens when drugs cloud her mind or paranoia takes over?

6. Steve Logan reminds Tess a bit too much of her ex-husband, but he's also a desperately needed ally. What do you think will happen with their relationship in future stories?

7. Tess and her dad each have a list of rules — mostly pertaining to police work. Which of the rules do you imagine yourself referring to over and over? What other rules would you put on a list for your life?

8. Tess wrestles with the idea of a good God when innocent, and sometimes heroic, people die at the hands of evil men, or when one person is spared while another isn't. What does Oliver tell her about God's providence? What would you say to her? When have you seen God at work despite the intentions of a corrupt world?

9. When people in Rogue's Hollow begin questioning Tess's ability to find Anna, she wonders if she should have left policing altogether. What knocks her out of this attitude? What do you do when you have doubts about proceeding along the path set before you?

10. As Tess searches for Tilly, she notes that the police are often called on to intervene with the homeless, some of whom have mental issues. Do you agree with her assessment that "no one has the best answer for how to help them," or does that make it seem like they are beyond hope? Who should be responsible for caring for the least of these?

11. When Oliver calls Tess a hero, she seems reluctant to accept the title. What prevents her from embracing his praise? Few people

may actually have the opportunity to live out John 15:13, but are there other ways to show "greater love"?

12. Oliver's ability to "have a little grace" even after he learns the truth about Anna resonates with Tess. Do you think she'll be able to release some of the tension she's held since the Long Beach shooting? What steps can you take to extend a little grace toward the people in your life?

ABOUT THE AUTHOR

A former Long Beach, California, police officer of twenty-two years, **Janice Cantore** worked a variety of assignments, including patrol, administration, juvenile investigations, and training. She's always enjoyed writing and published two short articles on faith at work for *Cop and Christ* and *Today's Christian Woman* before tackling novels. She now lives in a small town in southern Oregon, where she enjoys exploring the forests, rivers, and lakes with her Labrador retrievers, Abbie and Tilly.

Janice writes suspense novels designed to keep readers engrossed and leave them inspired. *Crisis Shot* is the first title in her latest series. Janice also authored the Cold Case Justice series — *Drawing Fire, Burning Proof,* and *Catching Heat* — the Pacific Coast Justice series — *Accused, Abducted,* and *Avenged* — and the Brinna Caruso novels, *Critical Pursuit* and *Visible Threat.*

Visit Janice's website at www.janicecantore.com and connect with her on Facebook at www.facebook.com/JaniceCantore.